A DARKNESS BELOW

A WILLOW MARSH NOVEL
BOOK II

JO CASSIDY

MONSTER IVY
PUBLISHING

For those who have lost someone they love. May you feel peace in your hearts.

CONTENTS

CHAPTER 1

Deep inside, a darkness wormed its way through my veins, taunting me. It had been dormant the last couple of months, but every now and then I'd feel it squirm, begging to be let out. Lately, I'd been having a difficult time keeping it at bay.

The darkness pushed at my skin, each poke searing me from the inside. It made the warm, humid air of the summer practically unbearable. Shaking my arms to douse the fire, I hurried to catch up with the others on the trail.

"How are you slower than me?" Leya yelled from the top of the hill, her hands cupped over her mouth. She wore round sunglasses that took up half her face. With all the gold she wore, she sparkled like a goddess under the afternoon sun. "You're like a marathon runner."

I was so glad her parents had agreed to let her come stay with us in Willow Marsh for the summer. Being states away from my best friend was wearing on me, especially with my dark passenger. Leya and her bubbly attitude were always a good distraction.

I ran the rest of the way to catch up with her and the

others. My new Nike Pegasus' made it feel like I was strolling on a cloud. "I've never run a marathon."

"You should." Marcel grinned ear to ear. His eyeglasses had tinted in the sun. "That would be awesome."

Jade sulked in her hooded denim jacket, mad that we made her go on a hike with us. The fact that she could wear a jacket in this heat was beyond me. She set her arm on Marcel's shoulder and pointed at him. "He could whittle you a medal."

Marcel chuckled, his shoulders moving up and down with the movement, and Jade dropped her arm with a scowl. I could have been wrong, but she'd seemed to be more irritated with him lately. I'd always thought they were odd together, but I guess options were limited in this town.

Marcel rubbed his hands together. "I'd love that." The boy could whittle anything. I had no doubt it would be amazing.

Two arms wrapped around my neck, and Graham pulled me into him. "She's preparing for a 5k," he said, his cheek pressed against the side of my head. His volume went down when he'd said, "5k," trying to shut out his stutter.

I rested my chin on his arms in front of me. "I want to do a fundraiser for Willow Marsh High."

Out of the corner of my eye, I saw a raven land on a branch of a willow tree, reminding me of the vampire finch that used to follow me around. I so didn't miss that thing.

"Is it so we can get edible cafeteria food?" Jade tugged up the sleeves of her jacket, showing off the tattoo on the inside of her wrist of three birds flying to freedom.

Bringing it up would upset Jade, but I couldn't push it off much longer. There were only a few weeks left until school started. I wrapped my hands around Graham's arms that were still around me, trying to siphon some of his resident calm to put me at ease.

"So we can build a memorial for Corrine," I said, staring out at the small town below us.

Silence floated in the thick, muggy air. Leya already knew about the race. For his own safety, Marcel probably didn't want to say anything until Jade reacted and he could gauge her mood.

Losing Corrine hit all of us hard, but it almost destroyed Jade. They'd been best friends since they were in diapers. To be killed in cold blood by the creepiest man alive made it that much worse. At least that man was six feet under as well.

I'd only known Corrine a couple of months before she was murdered, but that was all the time a person needed to come to love that lively girl.

The students at Willow Marsh High had created a memorial on top of a hill, but I wanted something engraved in stone at the school so she'd always be remembered.

Jade clasped her hands together on top of her head, squishing her spiky, bright red hair. She'd had blue hair when I met her, but a couple of weeks after Corrine died, Jade showed up at school with red, spiky hair, just like Corrine had.

"That might actually get me to participate," Jade said, so quiet I almost didn't hear.

My gaze snapped to hers. She smiled at me—a tight-lipped Jade version—as tears glistened in her eyes.

Leya let out an audible breath of relief, then clapped her hands, her manicured nails clinking together. "I'm designing the T-shirts! And we have to make sure we do it before I head back to Skokie."

"Just move here." Graham dropped his arms from around me, came to my side, and stuffed his hands in his pockets. I stared at his bare arms. He wore hoodies religiously in the winter, but come summer, he only wore T-shirts. He tanned so easily, and for some reason, I wasn't expecting that.

"Wish I could." Leya twirled one of her many braids around her finger. "I've been trying to convince the parents, but they aren't feeling it."

It probably had a lot to do with all that went down when my dad and I first moved here. Ghosts, murders, and a madness growing inside me were legitimate reasons to be wary of a place. But Dad and I had grown attached to Willow Marsh in a way I couldn't explain to most people outside the town. Our souls were tethered to the haunted soil.

Jade came toward me, pausing at my side and clicking her tongue ring against her teeth. The ring was just another Corrine thing Jade had done like she was slowly becoming her. If a gold cross ended up around Jade's neck, I was going to have an intervention.

"Just let me know what I can do to help." Jade tugged up her hood, covering her spiky hair, her voice loud for everyone to hear. "Can we please go now? I've already overdosed on my vitamin D for the day." She took off down the hill, not waiting for a response.

"Don't you need to watch Nash?" Marcel called after her.

She grunted. "Don't remind me. Seriously, why did my mom go back to work? I hate watching my brother." Her voice trailed off as she disappeared down the trail.

Graham checked the time on his phone, keeping his voice low, as he walked backward toward Jade and Marcel. "I have to get to work, too."

I moved to follow when the darkness coiled around my ankle and seized it from the inside, stopping me in my tracks. It felt like a thick sludge set to boil. Clenching my teeth, I fought against it, trying to shove it away, but it was latched on tight. Each effort I made caused it to squeeze tighter, blocking all the blood from getting to my foot.

I stroked the side of my bronze family ring on my left

pointer finger, trying to relax. I repeated my mantra in my mind. *Control. Steady. Calm.*

The darkness nudged me like it was trying to communicate. The last thing I needed was another presence inside me, dictating my life. I thought it was all over after Delilah, but something happened down in the crypt when I'd destroyed the portal linking our world with the other side. I'd been trying to ignore it, telling myself it was all in my imagination.

But the sludge burning me from inside was definitely real.

Suddenly, everything around me shut off, surrounding me in darkness.

❧

Outside my window, a bird cawed, calling to me. I stepped out into the humid air, the ground warm on my bare feet. I trudged into the woods, following the whistling sound. It lured me in, the tragic tune twisting my heart in circles.

Tessa. My name swept by me, stroking my ears. I didn't recognize the voice.

I soon entered a clearing, the lush grass soft under my feet. As I stepped into the middle, the willow and birch trees around me began to rot, the branches bending and shrinking, releasing a foul odor.

Black fuzzy vines slithered up from underneath me as the grass disintegrated. The vines slowly wound around my legs, working their way up my body. Each move I made sent the vines into a frenzy, grabbing tighter and searing my skin.

Help us! Hundreds of voices, all full of despair and sorrow.

I opened my mouth, but the fuzzy vines laced between my lips, sewing my mouth shut.

Please, Tessa! So many voices of all different ages, begging and pleading.

A deep chuckle echoed all around me as the voices screamed, so wretched and horrid. The whistle of the bird turned shrill. My arms fought with the vines, my hands wanting to escape and cover my ears, but it only agitated the vines.

It's almost time, Tessa. The gravelly male voice grated my eardrums. *Be ready.*

The ground trembled, breaking into pieces as decaying hands reached through the earth, clawing their way up.

Be ready. The voice shook my bones. *We will rise.*

❦

The vision was sucked away, leaving me panting on top of the hill.

"Tessa?" Leya waved her hand in front of my face.

I focused on her bug sunglasses.

"You coming home with us, or you just gonna stay here for the rest of your life?" Sarcasm hugged her tone, but there was an underlying worry there.

I wondered how long I'd zoned out.

Suddenly, the darkness released its hold, clumped into a pocket, and slithered its way back behind my heart, where it loved to cozy up. I had to stop myself from shivering.

"I think we need to talk," I whispered, tightening the scarf holding my hair in a ponytail.

Last time, I'd tried to do everything on my own, and it just made things worse. I'd been trying to be more open and honest with Leya and my dad.

Thank goodness Leya always made it easy to talk to her.

She linked her arm with mine. "I'm all yours tonight, sugar."

"Is everything okay?" Graham appeared at my other side, concern embracing his eyes. With his short haircut, the green in his eyes seemed much more vivid. Also highlighted his long lashes. I thought I'd miss the shaggy hair but being able to see every inch of his hot face made up for it.

Graham was starting to know me almost as well as Leya. Almost.

"Yep." I gave him the sincerest smile I could before I linked my fingers with his and tugged him down the hill.

Inside, the darkness bubbled. It was small and quick, but I felt it. And I could have sworn it was laughing at me, like it knew everything was definitely *not* okay.

CHAPTER 2

The second Leya and I walked into the house, I smelled heaven. I had to leap over all the political signs in the hallway to get to the kitchen.

"This is like a relay of some sort." Leya's voice came out in a grumble behind me. "Good prep for the 5k, I guess."

My legs seriously got the best workout, just trying to maneuver around the house every day. Dad had stuff every-where. I had no idea running for mayor would require an obnoxious amount of marketing materials.

A loud thud echoed in the hall, and I turned to find Leya sprawled on top of some yard signs. She held one up. On it, written in bold blue, was: *Make Willow Marsh your safe haven. Vote for Alec Walker-Isaacson.*

"Your dad might need to rethink this one." With a grunt of effort, Leya got to her feet and straightened out her gold overall shorts. "He can't even keep your house safe."

Dad had a lot of reasons for running for mayor, but his main platform was to create a safe place here in Willow Marsh. A lot of shady deals went down, and the current mayor, plus the sheriff, always looked the other way.

While I agreed with Dad, the Willow Marsh way of living helped me get away with murder earlier this year. But I hoped to never be put in that situation again.

It would be tricky, getting a town to want a newcomer as mayor, but Dad was playing the Walker descendant card for everything it was worth. Joseph Walker was one of the three men that originally founded Willow Marsh, and it turned out that his wife? She was an Isaacson and my namesake.

I plopped down at a chair in the kitchen, snatched the paper bag in the middle, and fished out a bacon cheeseburger. Thick, juicy beef, crisp bacon, fresh tomatoes, two slices of American cheese, and probably an overkill of mayo made the burger basically heaven on earth.

I'd already taken a bite when Dad bent over, kissed the top of my head, then placed an ice-cold bottle of Dr Pepper in front of me. I quickly snapped a picture, holding the bottle in a 'cheers,' and sent it to Graham.

It had become a new tradition of ours to have a Dr Pepper every night and talk about our day, but with Graham now working at Craig's Auto Shop, and Leya being here to visit, our ritual had been put on the backburner.

Dad took the seat next to me, rubbing his calf and grimacing.

Leya was on the other side of the table, one hand holding her crispy chicken sandwich, the other holding a large onion ring. She worked back and forth at them.

Heathrow's Burgers was my favorite place in Willow Marsh. Since Dad started his campaign, the place had become a staple at our house. Thank goodness I went out on a long run every morning. It helped balance it out. A little bit.

"Is your leg bugging you today?" I used a napkin to wipe some mayo off my face.

Dad nodded as he peeled back the wrapper of his burger. "I've been too busy to go to physical therapy lately."

Earlier in the year, when I'd had my run-in with Reed Harrison—another founding family descendant—in a crypt below the town, the creepy man had shot my dad. It made me feel a little less guilty about killing Reed in the end. Although, most of it was the spirit that had taken over my body— Delilah Morgan. Her dad just happened to be the current mayor and was Dad's competition.

This town was so messed up, and it was sometimes hard to keep track of how everyone was connected. I needed to cover a wall in photos and names, connecting everything with strings like they did in those crime shows.

"Just have an intern do your leg exercises for you while you talk on the phone in the office or something." Leya finished off the onion ring and took a long swig of her Sprite. "Isn't that what they're there for?"

Dad chuckled. "They're there to help my campaign."

I pointed my burger at Dad, some sauce dripping onto the table. "You being able to walk could come in handy as mayor."

Dad picked up a steak fry and dipped it in ketchup. "If Franklin D. Roosevelt could be the president while in a wheelchair, I think I can handle being a mayor of a small town with a bum leg."

Leya wiggled her fingers in the air. "Sympathy votes!"

Dad already had enough of those.

With Dad running for mayor, every secret in our life was getting revealed. Like losing my mom and brother in a car accident—with me as the driver. I stared at the scar on my right hand, between my thumb and pointer finger. I knew I couldn't keep that one a secret forever, but it was one of those things I wished I could have told people myself. Not have them read it on the front page of the Willow Marsh Herald. I thought it at least meant I could stop hooking one of Amá's scarves over my hand to cover the scar. But with the new scar on my left palm, thanks to using a rusted knife to draw my blood to destroy the portal, the scarf had only switched hands. Thank goodness I only had to wear it out in public and not around my family and friends.

Seeing the scar was difficult for some residents of Willow Marsh. The fact that I'd killed Reed had mixed reactions from the citizens. Those connected to the Harrison family—like Reed's younger brothers Lars and Ace—wanted my head on a platter. Preferably one that was a relic from the Civil War that we'd found in the crypt. They thought it symbolic of the destruction the Walker line had rained down on Willow Marsh. The fact that Reed had killed many people—including Corrine—apparently didn't justify his death in their eyes.

Then there were the ones that praised me. People had approached me at the store or on the street and *thanked* me for 'ridding Willow Marsh of its scum.' I was a saint in their eyes for catching the killer of so many residents.

Dad's phone rang, and he checked the screen. "Oh, it's Marcel. I hope he has good news." Dad was already talking on the phone before he stood and hustled out of the kitchen.

Marcel had joined his campaign as an intern. I had no idea he had an interest in politics, but with the way his eyes lit up when Dad approached him, you'd think he'd just been asked to whittle a statue of Chadwick Boseman—his favorite actor.

Leya stood, stretching her arms over her head. "Ready to talk?"

"Yeah." I tossed the trash into the bin under the sink. "Want to go for a walk?"

"You mean, do I want to enter the creepy woods out back where supernatural things tend to happen?" She waggled a finger at me. "No, thank you. Your room will suffice."

My phone buzzed with an incoming text. I looked down to see a picture of Graham leaning against a car he was working on, wearing his blue coveralls, a smudge of grease on his cheek, and holding up a bottle of Dr Pepper in a 'cheers.' Man, he made auto-body work look hot.

After Leya and I changed into pajamas and settled onto my bed, I told her everything going on with my dark passenger and how it seemed to be growing.

When I finished, and her wide eyes had gone back to their normal state, she sat in contemplative silence before she spoke. "Have you told Rita?"

I stared at the dahlia on my family ring. "Not yet."

Rita was the local therapist and had helped me through losing my mom and brother and also with everything that happened with Reed down in the crypt. Rita believed me about the spirits, so I knew I could tell her, but it would worry her. I didn't want to add any drama unless it was necessary.

"I've been waiting for the right moment."

Leya nodded in understanding, running her fingers along her braided hair that rested over her shoulder. "Maybe we should do some research. See if there's a way to rid your body of it."

I leaned back against the headboard and picked up my late brother's ukulele that sat next to me on the bed. I chose one of Felix's favorites, "Could You Be Loved" by Bob Marley, to play.

"I've thought about that, but I don't want a repeat of last time."

Doing the séances had not only let Delilah take control of me, it had let the ghost of Roy Ellington—the third and final member of the founding families—into our realm and caused all sorts of problems. He was one crazy, messed-up man. Thank goodness he'd finally been sent to the other side, along with Delilah.

"Maybe you did something wrong during those séances."

"There's something else." I took a deep breath before I

told her about the vision I'd had on the hike.

Leya shook out her arms. "That's so freaking creepy. What do you think it means?"

"I'm not sure I want to know." I strummed the song, hoping it could calm my nerves. "But I have a really bad feeling in my gut that something bad is coming."

Leya's phone buzzed. When she glanced down at the screen, she smiled.

"What?" I asked, leaning to get a better look, my fingers pausing on the strings of the ukulele.

She showed me a gif on her phone of two puppies hugging. "So adorable."

Leya had been trying to talk her parents into getting a dog, but they'd refused. I noticed she really couldn't talk her parents into anything.

I smiled, then saw who had sent it. I snatched the phone from her, scrolling through tons of messages, mostly of cute dogs and puppies. "You've been texting Marcel?"

Leya took her phone back. "Well, yeah. He's become a friend from all this." She grinned at the gif. "He loves puppies as much as I do."

Even though it was innocent, I wasn't sure how Jade would respond to her boyfriend sending all these photos and clips to another girl. At least Leya would be going back to Skokie in a few weeks, and then maybe the texts would end.

The doorbell rang, saving Leya from any scolding comments.

I set down the ukulele and then trotted down the stairs, knowing Dad wouldn't answer the door. His voice drifted down the hall. Since Marcel was now texting Leya, Dad was probably talking to someone else.

I swung the front door open and instantly wished I had checked out the peephole first.

Blake Hayes.

CHAPTER 3

Blake's tight shirt clung to his muscles as usual, and his jet-black hair was combed to the side. His tropical scent attacked me. Funny that I used to find it intoxicating. But then I got to know the true Blake, and I suddenly hated any scent that smelled remotely like it.

The darkness inside me flared to life at the sight of him, worming its way behind my eyes like it wanted to get a better look. I tried to push it away, but it held firm.

I was tempted to slam the door in Blake's face, but then I saw what he was holding. A sword. The same sword I'd found in the crypt and took out with me as evidence of all the relics.

"You're looking beautiful." Blake's brown eyes wandered down my tank and shorts, and I found myself crossing my arms against my chest and wishing I'd remembered I'd changed into sleepwear.

"Save your ridiculous remarks for someone who cares," I said. "What do you want?"

Blake placed his free hand against his chest, mock hurt in

his eyes. "We haven't spoken in months, and this is how you greet me?"

"First," I said, not holding back the anger in my voice, "the fact that I haven't responded to any of your texts should be enough to tell you I don't want to see you." He opened his mouth, but I cut him off. "Second, last time we were together, you tried to rape me. You're lucky I haven't kicked you in the nuts repeatedly."

The darkness rippled, almost like it was laughing. It separated—tugging apart with a snap that made me flinch—each half slithering to an ear. It heated, warming my earlobes.

Blake's hand wandered down to his crotch in a protective way. "I didn't try to rape you."

I scoffed, doing my best to ignore the darkness, but some of its wrath crept into my mind. "You knew someone else was controlling my body. You knew I loved Graham. You knew I didn't want you!" I huffed. "Why am I even giving you the time of day?"

I placed my hand on the door, ready to close it, but Blake put his foot out to stop it from closing.

"Aren't you curious as to why I'm holding a sword?" He used his charming voice that used to make me fuzzy. But that was because of Delilah—my spirit passenger and his dead girlfriend.

Yes. "Nope."

I moved to shut him out, but he lifted the sword that time, pushing the tip against the door, and working his way inside my house. He wandered into the front room, stepping over political signs to get there.

"Love what you've done with the place." His gaze lingered on the wooden sign hanging above the fireplace.

Leya had made it for me when we moved to Willow Marsh. It had my family's motto on it. "Donde quiera que moramos, siempre seremos familia." *Wherever we dwell, we will always be family.*

Blake set the sword down on the coffee table. "These things are surprisingly heavy." He sunk into the couch, lifted his legs, and set his feet on the table.

I finally found my voice that had somehow vanished for a bit. "What do you think you're doing?"

He clasped his hands behind his head. "Why, yes, I would love a drink. Water will be fine."

I marched up to him, my fists clenched at my sides. The darkness seemed to move to whatever location inside me would get it closer to Blake. It nestled into my hands. "I'm not getting you anything. Get out of my house."

His thick eyebrow twerked up. "Or what? You'll call the cops?"

I hated that his dad was the sheriff.

I snatched the sword from the table, using both arms to lift it. "I'll cut off your manhood. Now. Get. Out. Of. My. House."

The darkness retreated from my hands, working its way back to its cave behind my heart, its heat subsiding.

"Hey, honey..." Dad came around the corner and into the family room, pausing when he saw Blake on the couch. If I thought I was mad, Dad looked like he wanted to straight up take the sword from my hand and drive it through Blake's chest. "What are you doing in my house?"

Blake's arrogance scurried away, and out came a cowering boy. He shot up from the couch, holding up his palms in innocence. "I was just dropping something off that belongs to your family." He nodded toward the sword in my hands, not lowering his. "That was Joseph Walkers. Thought you might want it."

I turned the hilt in my hand and noticed an engraving. Sure enough, Joseph's name was scrawled on there.

Dad growled, low and guttural. "You could have just left it on the porch, rang the bell, and then got the hell off my property."

I'd never seen this side of Dad.

Blake noticeably swallowed. "Yes, sir. I'll be leaving now." He wouldn't—no, couldn't—look me in the eyes.

He only made it a few steps before Leya bounded down the stairs, her smile evaporating when she saw Blake.

"Not you too," Blake mumbled.

Leya let out an animalistic roar, leaped over a pile of signs, and charged at Blake, hitting him so hard that they fell onto the couch. She pounded away on his chest, and he just let her. Dad and I didn't move to stop her. I think we both wanted to do the same. But Dad was running for mayor, and I had to be his charming daughter.

Leya, on the other hand, could beat the crap out of him. Which, when I finally saw how hard her punches were, I realized she could do some serious damage. Dad and I shared a look, and then we both sighed. We knew we had to stop her, so Blake walked out of our home on his own two feet.

Dad and I each grabbed one of her arms, tearing her away from Blake.

"You're a horrible human being!" Leya's chest heaved in anger. Just like Dad, seeing her this upset was unusual.

But in their eyes—and mine—what Blake did to me was unforgivable. If I hadn't been able to take control of my body and stop him, he and Delilah would have had sex, using *my* body, and my heart and soul would have had to suffer through the whole thing.

Blake slowly sat up, rubbing his chest. He flinched through the pain. "Nice to see you, too, Leya. So glad you could come visit."

Both Dad and Leya opened their mouths wide, ready to yell, but Blake got up from the couch, putting his hand up.

"I'm leaving." He shuffled toward the door as quickly as he could, stumbling over some signs as he did.

I felt peace again the second he crossed the threshold.

Leya ran to the door and ripped it open. "And don't ever come back here!" Then she slammed the door, flinching at the loud noise. "Sorry, Mr. Isaacson."

"Trust me. I was tempted to do the same." Dad pinched the bridge of his nose. "I think I need some ice cream."

Leya clapped her hands together, back to her peppy self. "Let's have shakes! I'll make 'em." She pranced into the kitchen like she hadn't just pummeled Blake. That was one of the many reasons why I loved her.

I woke in the middle of the night, needing a glass of water. I trekked quietly down the stairs so I wouldn't wake Dad and Leya, using the flashlight on my phone to light the way. The last thing I needed was to break a bone tripping over Dad's mayor signs.

When I turned toward the kitchen, I saw the sword still sitting on the coffee table. Why did Blake feel the need to suddenly give it to us? I didn't think he or his father would be sentimental like that, wanting to give us a piece of our family history.

The town had been torn on what to do with the relics I'd found in the crypt. Half wanted to sell everything and split the profit among the town so we'd all be rich. Mayor Morgan was on that side.

The other half wanted to open a museum, drawing in tourism to our small town. That way, the town could prosper, but we'd still be preserving history. Dad was on that side. So was I.

Tiptoeing into the family room, I tucked my phone in my

pocket and picked up the sword, turning it over in my hands. It was cool to think that my ancestor used it during the Civil War. I never thought I'd hold something so valuable.

The darkness pulsated behind my heart, stiff and ragged. It almost seemed to reject the sword, like it wanted nothing to do with it.

A whistle sounded down the hall, causing me to spin around. It didn't sound like Leya or Dad, and I hadn't heard either of them come downstairs. I really hoped it wasn't a vampire finch. I couldn't handle it.

Holding the sword out in front of me, I worked my way down the hall, keeping each step light and watching where I stepped. As I neared the bathroom door, the whistle came again. It was definitely human, not a creepy little bird. After a second, I recognized the tune. "Man in the Mirror" by Michael Jackson.

I tensed my muscles, trying to hold the sword still, but it trembled under my touch. I worried about what waited for me around the corner.

Control. Steady. Calm.

With a deep breath of courage, I stepped into the bathroom and almost dropped the sword.

A figure stared at me through the mirror, both his stance and smile lopsided. The disturbing twinkle in his light blue eyes brought back so many bad memories.

He wiggled his fingers at me in a wave. When he spoke, his tone was sweet and creamy, just like it had been when he was alive. "Hello there, Tessa."

Lowering the sword to my side, I lifted my chin, wanting to appear strong. "Hello, Reed."

CHAPTER 4

Reed Harrison watched me through the mirror, amusement mixing with the torment in his eyes. Four faint red lines resided on both his cheeks from when his eyes had bled in the elevator and he'd clawed at his face. The front of his flannel jacket was covered in dried blood.

Reed's spirit was way clearer than Ellington's had been. Maybe it was because Reed's death was recent. He hadn't had much of a chance to whither and fade.

I'd really hoped he'd moved on, but I guess I shouldn't have been too shocked to see him in my mirror. My eyes went to the sword in my hand.

"Blake." I hissed his name as a curse word. Had he known Reed was linked to the sword? Or had he just been prompted to bring me the sword? Either way, it was now in my possession.

"You're as bright as I remember," Reed said, clasping his fingers together. He pulled his hands up toward his mouth and pointed his index fingers at me. "Which lets me know I came to the right place."

"Hell didn't want you?" I lowered the sword to the ground, the weight getting to me. As soon as the metal touched the ground, the darkness inside me sprung to life, setting my blood ablaze. It broke into a few pieces, going behind my eyes, my right ear, and my right hand.

Reed chuckled, melodic and airy. "Let's just say my relationship with the other side is...complicated."

"I'll update your social media status for you," I said, backing out of the bathroom. "Just, please, leave me alone."

I swiveled around and almost let out a scream.

Reed stood in the hallway grinning at me, his head cocked to the side, the sword in his hand. I glanced back in the bathroom, only to see the sword still on the floor. But Reed was somehow holding it. Or a replica.

"Oh, sweet Tessa." Reed stroked my name, taking his time with it. "It's really fun in this dimension. I just imagined the sword, and poof. There it was." He flicked out his hand, and the imaginary sword vanished.

"How are you standing in front of me?" It took Ellington a long time to be able to communicate with me outside of a mirror.

Reed rubbed the side of his beard. "Not too sure on that one. I couldn't manifest at the Hayes' residence." He motioned to the front door. "Once the sword crossed that pretty threshold, suddenly, I was free." He bent toward me, trying to tap the tip of my nose with his finger. The smallest tingling sensation tickled my nose. "You, my dear, are quite powerful. It's astounding, really." With a wink, he turned and went into the kitchen, continuing with his whistling rendition of "Man in the Mirror."

I was torn on what to do. Wake up Leya and Dad? Call Rita? Or the least tempting but most practical option—go and see what Reed wanted.

Stroking my dahlia family ring for good vibes, I went into

the kitchen to find Reed sitting on the counter. Well, his spirit hovered above it.

"What do you want?" I asked, taking a seat at the table. I crossed my legs and folded my arms, trying to appear as closed off as possible. I hated this man. I couldn't believe I had to face both him and Blake in the same day.

Reed put out his bottom lip in a pathetic pout. "Oh, come now. After everything we've been through, this is how I'm treated?"

"Well, the last time we were together, I killed you, so you had to have known this wouldn't go much better."

He adjusted his flannel jacket, cackling the whole time. "Touché." Placing his palms on the counter, he leaned forward, his eyes for once showing the smallest amount of empathy. "How are my brothers?"

"Still as creepy as ever."

I'd hardly seen Lars and Ace since Reed's death. They'd locked themselves away from the world, but I couldn't shake the feeling that I'd be seeing them again. The Harrison family never let things drop. And I'd killed their brother.

Reed's thin lips twitched like he was torn between smiling and sneering at me. "You could at least give me some sort of update. You owe me that much."

I tightened the scarf holding back my hair, wishing I could use it to strangle Reed. "I owe you nothing."

"You killed me."

"Because you were about to kill me."

He hopped off the counter, sauntered over to the table, and leaned his hip against it, getting way to close for comfort. "Fair enough. I don't want to quarrel with you. We have business to attend to."

I scooted my chair back, creating some distance between us. Granted, he was just a spirit, but I still didn't like having him that close. I could almost smell the whiskey he loved so much. Although, before he died, he'd claimed the heavy drinking was a farce.

Reed rolled up his shirt sleeves, making sure they were perfectly done.

"Oh, you really do mean business," I said.

He grinned, showing off his teeth. "I need your help."

There was no way I was doing anything for this man. "Not going to happen."

He scratched his beard before clasping his hands together. "I'm in this predicament because of you."

"What predicament?"

He glanced over his shoulder, fear briefly flashing through his eyes. Whatever he was seeing was in his realm, not mine. He finally turned back toward me, rigid and panicked. "I'm not sure exactly what happened after you killed me, but I'm stuck in Nowhereville, and I want out."

"What do you mean, Nowhereville?"

"It's just a vast area of dreary landscape, everything gray and murky." He checked over his shoulder again. "There aren't many interesting people here, and it's dreadfully boring." With the way his voice hitched, I had a feeling there was more going on than he was telling me.

"Sounds perfect to me. Right where you belong."

His lips twitched. "I could help you in return."

I squirmed under his intense gaze. "Help me with what?"

With a lopsided smile, Reed pointed at my hands. I stared down at them, only to find them bright orange, like they were on fire.

CHAPTER 5

I jumped up from the chair, shaking out my hands, but they stayed glowing. "What's happening to me?"

Reed rolled out his neck like he was stretching it. "I've been hearing some chatter over here in The Gray, as I like to call it. If you be a good little girl, I'll tell you all about it."

The darkness radiated from my hands, the brightness contrasting with the name I'd given it. Maybe I could refer to it as literal hell. It swayed side to side, making the glow dance across my hands.

No matter how hard I tried, it wouldn't subside. The darkness had taken residency in my hands like there was no way to evict it.

"Now, I'm assuming you don't want to walk around like that," Reed said, his tone sugary sweet, his previous fear gone. He leaned to the side, his cloudy eyes watching my reaction. "Do you?"

I shook my hands again, but it only seemed to add to the fire inside. It seared my skin, the heat overwhelming, and I worried it would become permanent. I ran toward the sink, turned the faucet on cold, and shoved my red-orange hands under the water.

The only reaction I got was the darkness undulating, loving the waterfall, like it made its dance mystical. I snatched my hands back, turned off the water, and leaned against the sink.

"I can stop that, you know." Reed sat on the kitchen table, feet crossed, legs swinging like a child. "Make your life boring once again."

I held out my hands. "How could you stop this?"

The darkness felt like a part of me, like it had suctioned to every cell in my body.

"It just needs a little coaxing, that's all. And there's no way it's going to listen to you."

I lowered my hands to my side, not sure what to do with them. "And it would listen to *you*?"

Reed shrugged. "Most likely. Demon's pets can be difficult to reason with but give them the right treat, and they'll do as you command."

"What do you mean a 'demon's pet?'" I think I'd rather have Delilah back.

He glanced over his shoulder again, his panic returning. "Long story, doll, and I'm running out of time."

"So, how do I get it out?"

Reed waggled a finger at me. "Oh, no. You have to help me first. Then I'll help you."

The darkness shut off its heat, retreating to the cavity behind my heart, almost like it had grown bored. If it really was a pet, it would explain its erratic behavior. It had mood swings similar to a puppy.

My hands faded back to a light brown. Surprisingly, there was no aftermath obvious on my skin. I pushed away from the sink. "Save your breath, Reed. There's no way I'm ever helping you."

"You want to live with that inside you?"

"I'll figure it out on my own." Or maybe, I could contact Amá. With Leya's help, I might be able to keep it under control this time.

Reed chuckled and clapped his hands together. "Oh, you really are my favorite. Sad things ended as they did." He jumped off the table and sidled up next to me, folding his arms to match my stance. I hadn't even realized I'd folded mine. But I didn't budge, even with him taunting me. "Tessa, dear, save yourself the trouble. All I ask is a simple task, and then we'll get Nirah out of you."

Nirah? It had a name?

"How do you know it's this ... Nirah inside me?" The second the name left my lips, the darkness came to life behind my heart and hurried up my neck, going around and around, a trail of fire following it.

"From what I gather, she's one of the hardest pets to keep tame. Always slinking off to places she doesn't belong." He pointed at my neck. "Like inside you."

I touched my neck, wondering if it glowed like my hands had done. The heat startled my fingertips. "What do you need me to do?"

"Get me out of here."

"How could I possibly do that? It's not like I can just search for 'The Gray' on my GPS."

His jaw pulled tight. "I wouldn't be here if it weren't for you. You're a smart girl. Figure it out."

I wouldn't even know where to begin. "So, I get you out of there, and then you'll help me get rid of Nirah?" I cringed, hating giving her a name. It made it that much more real.

He swept out his hands. "Easy exchange."

Nothing that involved Reed Harrison was easy. I had a feeling the price I'd have to pay would be steep. I turned toward him, standing on my tiptoes to be eye level with him. "Not happening, Harrison. Try your luck somewhere else."

I made it to the foot of the stairs before he spoke.

"That's the thing. You're the only person I can reach out to. Everyone else is blocked." He tried to straighten a frame on the wall, but his hand passed right on through. "I'm now linked to this house. You can say no all you want, but I won't leave until you say yes." He closed his eyes, lifted his chin, and held out his arms. The floor rumbled beneath my feet. It started soft, but slowly grew, shaking the frames on the walls and sending the chandelier in the entryway swinging.

I gripped the banister for support. "Knock it off, Reed."

He swayed, the house moving along with him.

A family photo fell, landing on the stairs, shattering the glass.

"Tessa?" Leya's panicked voice came from my bedroom.

"Reed," I quietly hissed through clenched teeth.

He opened his eyes, flashing me his lopsided grin. His words came out in a sing-song voice. *"Say you'll help me, and I'll stop."*

My feet slipped on the ground, but I was able to keep myself up by holding onto the banister. Something crashed in the kitchen, glass by the sound of it. I knew he wouldn't stop, no matter how stubborn I was.

"Fine," I growled. "Just please stop."

The house came to a complete standstill.

Reed leaned forward, moving his hands like he was patting my cheeks. The air around my face warmed. "There's a good little girl." The wood floor creaked in the hall upstairs. "I think the relics would be a good place to start." Reed winked. "I'll be seeing you soon, doll."

"Wow." Leya stood at the top of the stairs. "That earthquake was insane."

"No kidding." Dad strolled up next to her, running his

hand down his face. He eyed me. "Why were you downstairs?"

I turned to where Reed had been, but he was gone. "Just getting a drink of water." I went partway up the stairs and picked the broken frame off the step. My family stared up at me, all smiling wide. I remembered getting the picture taken. Felix changed about twenty times before he'd settled on the baby blue shirt. Then Amá made the rest of us change so we'd all match.

"We'll get a new frame." Dad's soft voice shifted my attention to him. He sat on the step above me, holding a big piece of broken glass in his hands.

"I think something broke in the kitchen as well," I mumbled.

Leya leaned against the banister, folding her arms. "Are earthquakes common in Willow Marsh?"

Probably not. But that wasn't an earthquake. It was Reed and was probably only the tip of the iceberg of what he could do.

I hated that he was back in my life. I thought I'd never have to see the creep again. I should've known I wouldn't be that lucky. Not in Willow Marsh.

CHAPTER 6

Dad, Leya, and I sat around the kitchen table, having cereal for breakfast. I missed Amá's grand meals she'd make in the morning.

Leya frowned at her phone. "That's so weird."

"What?" I took a huge bite of Lucky Charms, knowing it was the closest I'd ever get to anything lucky.

"Marcel said he didn't feel an earthquake last night." Leya scrolled through her phone. "No one's talking about it online, either."

Eyebrows knitted together, Dad's thumb flew across his phone. "It's not listed on the government website."

Leya snorted. "Mayor Morgan probably told them to take it down. Wouldn't want to hurt his campaign."

I was torn between asking Leya why she'd texted Marcel and telling them it wasn't actually an earthquake. Did I really want to hide things from them again? How would that benefit me? Dad had started to come around to all the supernatural stuff.

I decided to take a leap of faith on my family. "It wasn't an earthquake."

Both Dad and Leya looked over at me. Their thumbs paused on their phones. Milk dripped from Leya's spoon that she held over the bowl.

Pushing my bowl away from me, I sat back in the chair. "I, uh, had a visitor last night."

Leya's gaze swept back and forth between Dad and me before she mouthed, *Graham?*

I rolled my eyes at her and shook my head.

She shrugged, her face saying, *What?*

Dad caught our interaction, his face growing dark. "What's going on? Have you been having people over in the middle of the night?"

I threw up my hands. "Who could I possibly have over that could shake an entire house like that? My friends don't have superpowers."

"Not that you know of," Leya muttered. "I could gain one here in Willow Marsh. I'm thinking anything is possible in this town."

Dad looked at me. "Spit it out."

I took a deep breath, trying to steady myself for their shock. "It was Reed."

Leya's spoon fell from her hand, crashing against her ceramic bowl. "Lord, have mercy. Please tell me you're joking."

Dad rubbed his hand across his jaw, looking like he was at a loss for words. Though he was getting used to strange things happening here, he surely did his best not to accept them, like ignoring them would make them go away.

"That sword Blake brought over? Turns out Reed was linked to it."

"I'm going to *kill* him," Leya growled. Then she held up her hand. "I'm talking about Blake." She tapped her bottom lip. "Which I guess was obvious since Reed's already dead." She tilted her head to the side. "Is it possible to kill him again? I mean, he's obviously not fully gone from our realm. But I guess that makes him a ghost. So, we need to kill his spirit?"

Dad finally found his voice. "What does he want?" He flinched like he couldn't believe he'd just asked that question. It meant admitting it was real.

"Apparently, he's stuck somewhere between here and the other side," I said. "He wants me to get him out."

"How is that your problem?" Dad asked at the same time Leya said, "Good. Let him rot."

I sighed. "That's what I said, but then he caused our house to shake and said he wouldn't stop until I did what he wanted."

Dad's phone buzzed. He checked the screen as he spoke to us. "What does he expect you to do?"

"He wants me to figure it out." I scratched at my chin. "He did mention starting with the relics."

Using her spoon, Leya swirled her cereal around in her bowl. "Half the relics are at the Hayes' home, which you're so not going over there. The other half are still in the crypt, and the sheriff has the key now. I highly doubt he'll hand it back over to you."

Dad stood, his thumb attacking his phone. "I have to go put out a fire. Looks like Mayor Morgan has created another smear campaign against me." He motioned to the open cereal boxes and bowls on the table. "Sorry to leave you with another mess."

"We got it, Apá," I said. He bent down and kissed my forehead. "What is it this time?"

Something flickered across his eyes, but I couldn't read it. "Nothing for you to worry about. We can talk about this Reed stuff later." He took a few steps before he paused in the doorway, looking back at me. "I hate to say this, but maybe there's an opportunity to kill two birds with one stone."

Leya shuddered. "As long as they aren't vampire finches. Those birds are the *worst*."

The one that had followed me when we first moved to Willow Marsh turned out to be linked to Ellington.

"What do you mean?" I asked.

Dad rested a hand on his hip, tiredness tugging at his eyes. I wondered if his fatigue would ever go away. He'd been running on empty ever since we'd moved here. "I could really use the sheriff's support if I want to win this election. He seemed to warm to you after everything down in the crypt."

He really had. The man had gone from being an overbearing jerk to looking at me with newfound respect.

Leya snapped her fingers. "Oh! Tessa, don't you wanna be a cop? Maybe you could see if he wants an intern."

I scrunched my nose, trying to remember ever talking about that. It didn't ring any bells.

"You want to be a cop?" Dad asked, surprise in his tone.

"Not that I can remember."

Leya waved a hand. "I think you said something in your sleep one time. But when you'd said it, I thought, 'you know, Tessa would be a good officer.'"

The idea was intriguing. I'd love to shadow Sheriff Hayes and see what he did every day. I hated the way the law was maintained—or lack thereof—in Willow Marsh. Maybe I could change that one day and become the sheriff myself.

Dad checked his phone again. "If it's something you want to do, Tessa, I'll support you. We could really use getting on his good side right now. Then you might have access to the relics and get Reed off your back." He grimaced. Dad would probably never get used to talking about the dead like they existed among us.

With a wave, he left Leya and me alone in the kitchen, the front door closing moments later.

Leya closed the box of Lucky Charms and took it to the

pantry. The whole kitchen looked much better now that Dad had updated it. It was a clean white with granite counters. A gigantic improvement over the orange and green seventy's theme they'd had before.

"So, what else is in it for you?" Leya took her bowl to the sink and rinsed it out. "You wouldn't help Reed without a really good reason."

"You might want to sit down." I waited for her to put the bowl in the dishwasher and then join me at the table before I told her the darkness was actually a demon's pet inside me, also known as Nirah, and how she could make me glow.

With each word, her eyes widened, and her jaw dropped. When I finished, she brushed her hands together like she was ridding herself of evil and stood up, pacing the kitchen.

"Girl, why do you attract this stuff?" She rubbed her temples, doing an about-face.

"It's not on purpose." I stared down at the dahlia ring on my pointer finger. It held a lock of my great-great-grandmother's hair and linked me to the other side in a powerful way. My blood held magic in it, thanks to my heritage. Both my parents contributed to that.

Nirah remained quiet behind my heart like she was sleeping. I wasn't sure if knowing who she was made it better or worse.

Leya took one of the many hairbands from her wrist and tied back her braids. "I really don't like the idea of you helping Reed. You know we can't trust the man."

"What else am I supposed to do?" I twirled my ring. "Maybe I could contact Amá."

"I think if you want to do that, we should reach out to Mrs. Morales."

Corrine's mom. She knew all about contacting the dead. I wondered if Rita would join us. We could have four people in the circle. If something went wrong, we'd have more hands on deck to hopefully stop the chaos.

I stood, grabbing my empty bowl, and taking it to the dishwasher. "I'm going to see if the sheriff is at the station. Why don't you call Mrs. Morales?"

It would be difficult for me to talk to her. Though it had been months, we were all mourning the loss of Corrine. Leya always had a good way with people, knowing the right things to say. She'd be able to talk to Mrs. Morales with an amount of empathy I couldn't muster right now.

I really didn't relish the thought of inserting myself into the Hayes' life, but if getting close to the sheriff could help my dad and get Reed out of my house, then I had to take the chance.

CHAPTER 7

The police station was in the heart of Willow Marsh, right on Main Street. In my light blue Corolla, I pulled along the curb, finding a parking spot a block down.

I'd been able to drive a lot more recently without any anxiety attacks, but I still couldn't drive with someone else in the car. I made Leya or Graham drive when we were together. Rita had been working with me, trying to get me over my fear, but the last time I drove with two passengers, they both died. It was going to take time.

I stood on the curb, purse hanging from my shoulder, staring at the glass front doors of the city offices where Rita worked. Below the building was the crypt that still held lots of treasures from the Civil War.

Nirah stirred, slinking out of her cave and finding a spot in my neck. She vibrated my skin, almost like she was purring. She heated my neck, causing sweat to break out along my hairline. It made the already muggy day practically unbearable. Add in the fact that I was wearing my hair down, no scarf to hold it back, plus a button-down blouse and slacks, there was a good chance I might melt into a puddle on the sidewalk.

But I wanted to make a good impression on the sheriff.

I made sure the scarf on my left hand covered my scar and walked the block to the station with my head high, confidence in my steps. When I arrived in front of the police station, a pair of ravens sat on the roof, both croaking at each other like they were in a conversation. They came to a sudden stop when they saw me, their tilted heads staring at me.

I hated birds.

"You dropped this, dear."

I spun to the side to see a gorgeous, albeit mysterious, woman next to me. There was something ethereal about her that made it seem like she was floating, not standing. Glitter lined her dark skin, and she had her black hair in long, beaded braids. She wore a knee-length black dress with a red belt around her middle. The deep red lipstick on her plump lips made her look fierce.

She held out my family ring. "I believe this is yours?" Her voice was calm and smooth, one that could instantly make you relax.

Confused, I took the ring from her. It had slipped off? How? It fit me so snugly. I guess I was sweating pretty badly. Maybe it had loosened enough to fall.

"Thanks." I slid it back onto my pointer finger, the metal surprisingly cool. The ring hugged my skin, and I shivered, despite the intense heat.

With a soft smile, she brushed past me and glided down the street. The ravens followed after her, keeping a little bit of a distance.

Nirah suddenly took a keen interest in my ring, slinking her way to my finger and circling around it multiple times like she was examining it.

I stared at the door to the precinct, remembering why I was here.

The second I stepped into the building, the air conditioning greeted me, and I wished I could kiss it.

Smoothing out my blouse, I went to the front desk and smiled at the clerk, clasping my sweaty hands in front of me. "Is Sheriff Hayes here?"

The clerk looked up from her paperwork, her spectacles perched on the tip of her long nose. With her gray hair and wrinkles, she was probably in her late sixties or early seventies. She had her hair pinned back in a bun. If Sheriff Hayes accepted me, I might have to do the same. It was professional and would keep my bushy hair off my sweaty skin.

"He's in a meeting right now, dear," the lady said. "It should wrap up soon, though, if you'd like to wait." She leaned forward, reaching out to grab my hand. Nirah quickly zoomed away from my finger, shooting her way to my neck. "Oh, my, that ring is beautiful."

"It's a family heirloom," I said with pride.

She ran her wrinkly fingers over the bronze on the side and then the dahlia on top. "It's breathtaking." She released my hand and sat back in her seat. "I don't think I've met you before. But your pretty face sure looks familiar."

"Tessa Isaacson."

Her blue eyes twinkled in a knowing way. I waited for her to mention Reed, the crypt, or anything pertaining to it. That was where the minds of most people in the town went. Thankfully, it was for the *other* reason people knew my name. "Your father is running for mayor, isn't he?" When I nodded, she glanced over her shoulder to make sure we were alone and then placed a hand next to her lips to block her mouth. "I'm not allowed to get too political in this place, but I'm voting for your dad. It's about time Willow Marsh got some fresh blood around here." She wiggled her drawn-on eyebrows.

"I've seen the posters. Your father is very handsome, which is a major upgrade from the current mayor."

I held back a laugh. "He'll be honored to hear he has your vote. Can I give him your name?"

"Oh, where are my manners?" She took her glasses off her nose and let them fall against her chest, a gold chain keeping them in place. "When I get talking about handsome men, I tend to lose my concentration." She held out her hand. "Grace Heathrow. Most people in town call me Gracie."

Now it was my turn for my eyes to twinkle. I gave her cold hand a soft shake, trying to be kind to her bones. "Heathrow? As in Heathrow Burgers?"

She nodded. "My husband, Willy, opened it years ago when we were newlyweds. I thought he was crazy for wanting to open a business, telling him it would never last. He proved me wrong, just like so many times over the years. There isn't a thing that man can't do once he sets his mind to it."

I thought back to when we first moved here. "I could have sworn it was a Willy Heathrow that fumigated our home."

Gracie grinned. "That would be Willy Heathrow, Jr. Wanted his own business, just like his father. It was our second son, Duncan, that took over the burger joint once my Willy retired." She chuckled. "Although, Willy still sneaks over there a couple of times a week to work the grill. I think he will until the day he dies."

"Well, his burgers are the best I've ever had. I'd marry them if I could."

"I'll make sure to tell him. It'll make his day."

A door opened, and two men stepped out of an office. Sheriff Hayes and Mayor Morgan. They were exchanging pleasantries, acting like they were old friends. Which they probably were.

Mayor Morgan was the epitome of the star high school quarterback, where life hadn't treated them well after they graduated. He'd gained a lot of weight and wore it low. There wasn't much left of his thinning hair. His dark eyes had bags so big you'd think cotton balls had been stuffed under his skin.

He'd helped his team win state back in his prime. There were trophies and pictures all over Willow Marsh High. But he'd torn his ACL his sophomore year in college, ending his football career.

With the way he smiled wide and tried to flirt with Gracie as they neared the front desk, he definitely hadn't lost his charm.

Although I could tell Gracie's smile was strained, so maybe he wasn't as charming as he thought.

The mayor's smile didn't skip a beat when he saw me standing there. He held out his hand, his other holding the cowboy hat he always wore. "Ah, the girl who gets away with everything. How's your father doing?"

I bit back a snide remark. Dad wanted to stay professional and not stoop to low blows and squabbles.

"Getting excited for the election, sir." I shook his hand with way more force than I had Gracie's, making him grimace. "We've really grown to love Willow Marsh and are excited to help make it the best place to live." That was as diplomatic as I could be.

Nirah had wriggled down my arm and almost got to my hand before I was able to snatch it away from the mayor. I wasn't sure what she was capable of doing, and the mayor probably wasn't the best candidate for a test subject. Especially not with witnesses, one being the sheriff.

Mayor Morgan laughed as he looked at his hand in surprise. I hadn't gripped it *that* hard. Then I noticed a tiny red mark—almost like a burn—on his index finger. I wondered how he'd gotten it.

He quickly covered his irritation and slapped the top of my shoulder. "Hope you didn't take offense to my post this morning. You know how politics go. Well, see you around." He slipped his cowboy hat onto his head and left the station.

Sheriff Hayes shook my hand. His jet-black hair was slicked to the side, and his thick eyebrows were in desperate need of attention. It was becoming difficult to tell there were two of them. But he was still a handsome man, just like his son, Blake.

The sheriff had perfected his confidence, so he didn't exude arrogance like Blake did. Maybe one day Blake could work to that, but he had a long way to go.

"What was he talking about?" It probably had something to do with the smear campaign Dad had mentioned this morning.

His jaw twitched. "Just a jab about Reed Harrison's death. I got him to take it down."

"Specifics, please." I couldn't hold back the annoyance in my tone. I was sick of Mayor Morgan dragging me into all of this.

Sheriff Hayes thought for a moment before he finally spoke. "He doesn't like the fact that you weren't arrested for Reed's murder. He said with your dad as mayor, more people could die, and there would be no repercussions."

Nirah's anger seared into me, and I had to bite back my tongue, so I didn't tell the sheriff what I really thought of Mayor Morgan. Dad had warned me this would happen. I closed my eyes, taking a deep breath. *Control. Steady. Calm.*

"What brings you in here?" The sheriff's gruff voice brought me back to reality.

"I was hoping to talk to you in private."

Sheriff Hayes stepped back and motioned for me to go

into his office. He smiled at Gracie. "Hold my calls for a little longer."

His office was lacking his usual distinct smell—cigarette smoke. A quick scan of his desk showed he didn't have an ashtray.

I took a seat in a cushioned chair in front of his desk, setting my purse on the wood floor. "Did you quit smoking?"

Sheriff Hayes had shut the door and was sitting down in his leather chair on the opposite side of the desk. He scratched the side of his jaw for a split second and then stopped. He normally had stubble but was now clean-shaven. He sighed. "Making some life changes. Remi's idea."

Remi was his wife and Blake's step-mom. I'd only met her once, and it was brief, and never the way I wanted to meet her—or anyone. It was the night Blake and Delilah almost used my body to have sex. Remi had found us half-naked in his room. Thank goodness she interrupted when she did.

"One whole month without a cigarette." He opened his desk drawer and pulled out a piece of nicotine gum before popping it in his mouth. "It hasn't been easy. Been smoking since I was twelve."

"I'm surprised you're still alive then." I briefly closed my eyes, scolding myself. I needed to be polite.

But Sheriff Hayes chuckled. "Remi always says the same thing." He sat back in his chair, lifting his foot to rest it on his knee. "Let me guess. This visit has something to do with a certain election coming up."

"Actually, there are two things I wanted to talk to you about." I reached down into my purse, my hand fumbling until I gripped a piece of paper. As I went to pull it out, my ring caught on the lip of the purse. I expected the ring to twist around my skin, but it stayed in place like it was molded to me. With a frown, I tried to rotate my ring. Nothing happened. I looked closer, noticing the bronze had embedded in my skin. How was that possible?

"Is everything okay?" Sheriff Hayes asked.

"Uh." I wasn't sure. But I really didn't want to discuss my predicament with the sheriff.

I quickly cleared my throat and placed a map of Willow Marsh on his desk. "I was hoping to do a 5k in honor of Corrine Morales. The money raised would go for a memorial for her at the high school."

The sheriff slid the paper close to him, looking it over. "This is the route, I assume?"

"Yes."

He nodded. "I think that's a great idea. We can block off the roads and direct traffic. Just let us know the date and time."

That was easy. "Thanks." I set another paper on the table. "That's all the information about it. I've already talked to some local businesses about sponsoring it."

He skimmed the page. "I'm sure Gracie can get Heathrow Burgers to donate money or maybe give you some coupons to put in the packets."

"That would be great." I quickly changed the subject, wanting to get it over with. "I was also wondering if you've ever taken an intern."

Sheriff Hayes looked taken aback. "Can't say that I have. You interested in becoming a cop?"

I crossed my legs and set my clasped hands on my lap. I didn't want to fidget. "After everything that happened when we moved here, I like the thought of protecting people from going through what I went through."

His lips ticked, but I couldn't tell what it meant. Did he agree? Did he think I was questioning his ability as a sheriff?

"What are you thinking this internship would entail?" he

finally asked, his voice low and gruff, which was typical for him, so I tried not to read too much into it.

I sat tall. "Basically, shadowing you. Seeing how things are run. What a day in your life involves. Do some ride-a-longs."

He slowly nodded, taking it all in. He was chewing his gum in the front of his mouth, his intent eyes on mine. I wished I could dive into his mind and rake through his thoughts. It had to be weird to him for me to ask, given our history.

Sheriff Hayes was pretty much my enemy after stepping foot into Willow Marsh. Not because he was a terrible person or anything, he just ran the town in a political way, turning a blind eye to the law sometimes. I think a lot of our disagreements stemmed from the fact that neither of us knew each other's histories.

"This isn't exactly common," he finally said. "I'm not sure how the citizens would feel about a mayor candidate's daughter tailing me."

"This has nothing to do with my dad. This is a high school student interested in a future in law enforcement and reaching out to a respected sheriff for insight."

His lips ticked again, but it turned into a smile. "Well, when you put it that way."

Was he actually going to say yes?

"But I still don't think certain people in the town will agree."

My hopes dropped a little. I needed to be bold. He respected that. "Since when did you start worrying about what people think? You've always run this town with the citizen's best interests at heart. You do what you think is best."

"How is letting you intern for me what the town needs?"

I kept my voice steady. "Because it shows you turning a victim into an advocate." I eyed the pink dahlia on my finger. "You're helping me take back my life."

Sheriff Hayes rubbed at his mouth, thinking. He kept his deep brown eyes on me the entire time. He finally pressed a button on his work phone. "Gracie, Tessa is going to need a visitor badge for the office. She's going to be interning for us."

His lips twitched into a smile, which I returned. I was one step closer to getting Reed Harrison out of my life.

Again.

CHAPTER 8

When I left the police station, I immediately tried taking off my ring. It wouldn't budge. My skin didn't hurt or look irritated. The ring was just firmly in place like it had taken permanent residency.

I thought back to that strange lady in the street. Did this have something to do with her? But what could she have possibly done to make my ring embed in my skin?

My phone vibrated. I had a few texts from Graham.

Graham: *Can you do something tonight?*

Graham: *I need to see you. It's been forever.*

Graham: *Yeah, we saw each other yesterday but no one-on-one time.*

Graham: *Are we still a couple, or has something changed?*

Graham: *You found someone else, didn't you?*

A smile broke out on my face, knowing he was joking. Honestly, with Leya visiting and Dad's campaign, I hadn't made much time for him lately.

Me: *Yep, sorry, found someone else. Didn't know how to tell you.*

Graham: *Makes sense. You're the hottest girl in town. I knew you'd move on.*

Me: *Yep, as soon as we parted ways yesterday, I went on the prowl.*

Graham: *Sounds about right. Well, it was nice while it lasted.*

Me: *Nice? That's all you got for me?*

Graham: *Yeah, okay, it was amazing. Wanna take me back?*

Me: *Sure. Those sexy green eyes always draw me right back in.*

Graham: *So, tonight?*

I didn't want to leave Leya alone. Maybe Jade would hang out with her. But that meant the possibility of Marcel being there, and I wasn't sure how I felt about that.

But I needed to spend some time with Graham if I wanted our relationship to work.

Me: *Pick me up at six.*

I peeled the top of my blouse away from my sweaty skin and shook it out. I was ready for fall to come.

After tossing my phone into my purse, I fished around until I found the keys to my car.

"Just the girl I wanted to see," a man's smooth tone said from behind me.

I closed my eyes and took a deep breath, steeling myself. I knew exactly who it belonged to, and he was one of the last people I wanted to see.

Ace Harrison. Reed's youngest brother, and honestly, the most put-together of the bunch. I spun around and stuffed a smile on my face.

Ace's flannel short-sleeve shirt was pressed and tucked into his blue jeans, showing off his large, silver belt buckle with a snake on it, the fangs bared. He grinned, lopsided like every Harrison. He was clean-shaven, highlighting his long, square jaw. His gelled hair was brushed to the side. I glanced down, expecting to see his tan work boots, but instead found brown cowboy boots, new and polished. He'd cleaned up in the time since his brother died. Confirmation people did better without Reed in their life.

Nirah circled around inside, finding a spot near my belly button, like she wanted to be near the snake on Ace's belt.

I took out a scarf from my purse and tied back my hair, wanting it off my neck. "Need me to take out your other brother?"

Ace flinched, surprised by my comment. I'd surprised myself. I meant to just think it, not say it out loud. Nirah vibrated in a chuckle. Had that been her doing? It was like Delilah all over again. At least with Delilah, she could communicate with me, so I knew what she was thinking. Although, that wasn't always pleasant.

"I'd be grateful, sweetheart. If it weren't for me, Lars would have killed you a long time ago." Ace flipped on a smile, but his eyes remained empty like usual. "I was hoping I could pick your brain."

It was my turn to flinch in surprise. "About what?"

He glanced around and then took a step toward me. "It would be better in private."

"You're out of your mind if you think I'd go anywhere alone with you. Especially after admitting Lars wants to kill me." I bit my tongue. Another thing I'd meant to think, not say.

But he just chuckled and motioned to the café across the street. "Let me buy you lunch."

"Do they have Dr Pepper?" I wasn't hungry, but if I could get a free soda out of the situation, it could possibly be a win.

"If they don't, I'll go find you one." Ace swept his arm out, telling me to cross the street first.

I headed into the café, hoping I wouldn't regret it.

He tried to get me to sit at a table in the back corner where it was empty, but I slid into a booth near the window. I wanted witnesses.

Ace slinked onto the bench like a snake, his cloudy blue eyes on mine. "You're looking very nice today. All dressed up."

Next to me on the table was a napkin with utensils on it, so I slipped it in front of me and twirled the napkin in circles with my finger. "I was thinking the same thing about you. I'm digging the new boots."

He kinked his head to the side, his smile coy. "You sure know how to flatter a guy."

The waitress cautiously approached the table, her hazel eyes sliding back and forth between Ace and me. "Can I get you two something to drink?" Her eyes kept sweeping between us, probably trying to piece together why the two of us were having lunch.

"I'll have a Dr Pepper," I said, still twirling the napkin.

"Coke for me." Ace leaned toward the waitress and tapped the table. "With a lemon, please."

She offered a strained smile and quickly shuffled away from the table.

Nirah worked her way to my shoulder, wrapping her hot, slimy entity around my bones like she belonged perched there.

"Why are we here, Ace?"

He leaned back, one arm draped across the back of the bench, the other resting on the table. "I heard you're close with the other side."

I lifted one shoulder in a shrug. "I'm friends with the Hastings and I'm dating a Dixon. So, yeah, you could say I'm close with the side of the town that hate the Harrisons."

His chuckle was light and musical. "Not in this town, silly girl." He leaned across the table, his face going serious. "I mean with the dead."

Again, what I was thinking just popped out of my mouth. "There's no way I'm contacting Reed for you."

Ace's smile returned as the waitress came back with our sodas. Her eyes never stopped flickering between us as she set down the cups. I was impressed she could do it without spilling any of the soda because she never even looked where she was setting them. Same with the straws. She pulled them from her apron, eyes on us, and set them next to the cups. Then she scurried away.

I snatched the straw closest to me, yanked off the wrapper, placed the straw in the cup, and took a long sip. The ice-cold liquid cradled my dry throat, but I noticed something off right away. It was Pibb, not Dr Pepper. But it would do for now.

"That's the thing." Ace squeezed his lemon into his Coke before dropping it in the cup. "I think he's already reached out to me."

My lips paused on the straw, my wide eyes on Ace. I finally let the straw slide from my lips. "What do you mean?" That wasn't possible, was it? Reed was linked to the sword that had been in the Hayes' home, and he had finally manifested when I touched it in my house. He couldn't travel.

"He's been coming to me in my dreams." Ace stared out the window, his eyes distant. "For a little over a week. Everything about it feels so real." He swallowed, his large Adam's apple bobbing along his long neck. "He tries to talk to me, but his voice comes out like static." His eyes found mine. "Do you really think it's Reed? Or have I gone crazy?"

This time I was able to stop myself from saying he'd been crazy since the day he was conceived. But just barely. It wanted to escape my mouth so badly. Nirah stirred like she wasn't happy with me.

Reed had told me he couldn't connect with anyone else, and I was his only option.

"That lying S.O.B.," I said through clenched teeth.

Ace twerked his head. "Excuse me?"

"So, you haven't heard a word he's said?"

If Ace's eyes were capable of emotion, I'd say there was something close to hope in his now. "It was him?"

"Maybe."

The thought of Reed communicating with his brothers terrified me. Ace and Lars were capable of horrendous things, just like Reed. Their ringleader would be back, and the town could be in for a world of hurt, especially when one of them had nothing to lose.

"What does this mean?" Ace moved his straw up and down in his cup. "Why would Reed still be here?"

"Probably just misses his baby brothers so much."

If Ace heard me, he didn't register it. "Do you think something is wrong? Like he can't cross over?"

No way I was telling Ace that Reed was stuck between realms. Reed blamed that fact on me, and I didn't need another Harrison thinking that.

"Pretty sure hell would welcome him with open arms." I took a sip of soda. "His lair is probably as he left it before he came to earth."

Ace looked at me, his face passive. "You believe in a life before this?"

I squirmed in my seat. "How about we not talk religion? Listen, I'll take care of Reed. Don't you worry your psychotic little head about it." Nirah was going to be the death of me. She'd completely removed the filter from my mouth.

Ace just blinked, still void of emotion. "Can I help?"

"No." I finished off my soda and stood just as the waitress came back.

"Do you want anything to eat?" she asked.

I straightened my blouse. "Nope. My disturbing prince is paying. Also, next time someone asks for Dr Pepper, let them know you have Pibb instead. They aren't the same." I hurried out of the café, eager to get away from Ace.

If Reed communicated with his brothers, I had much more to worry about than him stalking my home.

CHAPTER 9

I'd barely gotten back in my car when my phone rang.

"Pick me up." It was all Jade said before she hung up.

"Nice to talk to you, too, Jade," I mumbled before starting the car.

The Jenson family lived near the center of town, not far from Main Street. It was a cute, one-story cottage, the outside in pristine condition. Her mom and dad loved to garden and kept the paint job and everything else up to date. The other residents in Willow Marsh could learn a thing or two from them.

As I pulled into the driveway, the garage rumbled open, revealing Jade's bedroom. After they had Nash, they'd given him Jade's room and turned the garage into a room for Jade. They'd offered to install a wall, but Jade liked the idea of having a garage door in her room.

Nash came running up to me the second I got out of the car, his blond curls bouncing. "Hey, Tessa!" His tongue stumbled on the S's in my name. He threw his small arms around my legs.

I ruffled his hair, the soft locks tickling my skin. "Hey, Nash."

"We're bringing Mom lunch!" He grinned, showing off two missing bottom teeth and a swollen lip.

I cupped his chin with my hand. "What happened?"

"Fell off my bike." He bounced on the driveway. "The tooth fairy gave me five dollars!"

Jade sulked out of her room, wearing a backpack and her hooded denim jacket. She reached up, grabbed the cord hanging from the garage door, and shut it. "Five dollars. For a couple of teeth. It's insane."

Nash pointed his thumb over his shoulder. "She's a little cranky because the tooth fairy only left her fifty cents." He shrugged. "But that was forever ago! Back when there were dinosaurs."

Jade opened the passenger side door and tossed her backpack inside. "Let's just hurry and get this over with. I've been binge-watching *Stranger Things*."

Nash opened the back door of the car, grunting from the effort. "For the gazillionth time."

I paused, watching them both get in my car. I hadn't driven with anyone in the car with me since the night of the crash.

Jade tapped the hood of the car. "Tess, let's go."

"You want me to drive you somewhere?" I finally squeaked out.

Jade arched a dyed-red eyebrow. "Uh, yeah. What did you think I meant by 'pick me up?' That I wanted to ride on the back of your bicycle?"

Nash giggled. "That would be funny!"

Jade turned toward his voice, snapping her fingers. "Booster seat." She jogged to the front of the house, coming back with the seat and putting it in the back of my car. She helped Nash into the seat and buckled him in.

When I still hadn't moved after she shut the door, she tugged on the bottom of her jacket. "Tess, suck it up or whatever. It's going to be fine. We're only going a couple of miles. You know I wouldn't get into a car with just anyone." She glanced inside the car where Nash was playing the air guitar. "Especially with that runt. He's annoying, but I do love the kid."

Jade rarely spoke of her brother—or her family—before Corrine died. In fact, I hadn't even found out she had a brother until months after meeting her. But with Corrine gone, a switch flipped in Jade. She'd been spending more time with her family, which had been nice. I'd grown fond of her family, especially her brother.

I nodded. "Only a couple of miles. I can do this." I could do this. I mean, I couldn't avoid driving without anyone in my car forever.

Amá would want me to do it. She'd be encouraging me the whole way. So would Felix.

Control. Steady. Calm.

"I won't even say anything rude if you drive like an old man." Jade jogged over to the passenger side. "But we have to leave now. Mom doesn't have a huge window for lunch." She got into the car, slammed the door, then leaned across the center console to look at me. "Let's go!" The muffled sound of her being inside the car did nothing to drown out the impatience in her tone.

With a deep breath, I opened the door and slid into the driver's seat.

"I want to be a pilot when I grow up." Nash was sitting behind me, swinging his legs in the seat. "What do you want to be, Tessa?"

"A girl with a backbone." Jade reached over and turned the keys in the ignition for me. "Kick anxiety right in the face, Tess." I glanced over at her, and her eyes softened. "Just don't overthink it." She flipped on the radio, not turning it too loud. She settled on an R&B station she knew I liked. "I want to be a paramedic."

"Really?" I couldn't hide the surprise in my tone. She'd never mentioned that before. After buckling my seatbelt, I reversed out of the driveway, checking every mirror about twenty times.

Jade slunk down in her seat. "I like the thought of being able to save someone who's about to die."

I thought back to Corrine. Leya and I were there when she got shot, but there was nothing we could have done to save her.

"That would be awesome!" Nash said. "I can fly you around!"

Jade grinned over her shoulder at him. "That's brilliant."

"What about you, Tessa?" Nash asked with an unwavering eagerness.

I turned onto the next street, keeping at a slow pace. "A cop, actually."

"Cool!" Nash clapped his hands together, then threw his fists into the air. "We could work together! It's gonna be so much fun!"

A few minutes later, I pulled in front of *Craig's Auto Shop* in one piece. Nash unbuckled himself and was out the door in seconds.

I glanced across the console at Jade. "Thanks."

She shrugged. "Yeah. Whatever." The smallest smile pulled at the corner of her mouth before we got out of the car. I'd never tell her because it would make her mad, but I liked this new version of Jade.

We found Nash squatting near a Chevy truck, peering underneath it. "...and Tessa's going to be a cop, so we're going to save people together! Like heroes!"

Lola Jenson rolled out from underneath the truck, grinning at Nash. She pressed her greasy glove against his nose, leaving behind a smear. "Sounds like a great plan." She stood, brushing off her coveralls that were a hair too big for her small frame.

Jade and Lola had the same delicate faces with soft features, which always made me laugh because nothing about them was soft. They were two of the toughest women I knew. Lola had her long, blonde hair thrown up in a sloppy bun.

"I hope this means you brought me lunch." Lola took off her work gloves and tucked them into her back pockets. "I'm starving."

"We made tuna sandwiches!" Nash said. "With extra—"

"Volume, Nash," Lola said with a shake of her head.

"—pickles," Nash whispered so softly that it was barely audible.

Lola rolled her eyes. "This boy only knows two levels."

Jade handed her mom the backpack. Lola took Nash's hand, and together they walked toward a grassy path in front of the shop.

"It seems like this job has been good for your mom," I said, glancing around to see if I could spot Graham. He was working today.

Lola had never been a grump or anything, but I'd noticed how happy she was now that she was working full-time again and doing something she loved.

"I know. It's been great at home." Jade kicked at the ground, bringing my attention back to her. "A lot less yelling." She looked up, her mouth open like she was about to say something, but then her gaze locked behind me, and her jaw fell.

I whipped around to see what had rendered Jade speechless.

A guy in his late teens, maybe early twenties, stood there in dirty coveralls, downing a bottle of blue Powerade. His brown hair was a disheveled mess, and a long grease stain ran down his firm cheek.

I turned back to see Jade still gaping.

"Do you know him or something?" I asked, stepping back so I could see both of them.

"Gopher?" Jade squeaked out.

The guy lowered his arm and used the other to wipe at his mouth. The annoyed look in his eyes switched to excitement when he saw Jade. "Spade!" He tossed his empty bottle into a trashcan and jogged over to us, wrapping Jade up in a hug. "Man, it's been forever." He pulled back, looking her up and down. "When did you grow up?"

"When did you get back?" Jade sputtered.

I'd never seen her so flustered before. She'd gone rigid at his touch.

"A couple of months ago." The guy was tall and lean, his jaw sporting a little bit of growth. "I'm surprised your mom didn't tell you."

Jade's eyes narrowed in on her mom sitting on the lawn, completely unaware of us as she ate with Nash. "Me, too. She knows how much—" She blanched, tucking her hands into her pockets.

The guy tugged on one of the strings hanging from her hood. "Nice jacket. I have one just like it." He rested his hands on his hips. "A little hot for it, don't you think?"

In a matter of seconds, Jade had ripped off her jacket and then clutched it in her hands like she didn't know what to do with it. She wore a tight tank top, which definitely caught the guy's attention.

I stood there, watching the two of them interact. This guy looked incredibly glad to see Jade. She looked like a mix of stunned, confused, and embarrassed.

I held out my hand to him. "Tessa."

The guy blinked, tearing his gaze from Jade. "Oh, hi." He

wiped his hand off on his coveralls—probably adding more grease instead of taking it off—and then shook my hand. "Topher."

"Hence the gopher," I said.

Topher shoved Jade on the arm. "You have buck teeth in elementary school, and no one ever lets it down."

"They look amazing now." Jade's eyes went wide, realizing she'd said it out loud.

I was really enjoying this flustered version of Jade. I'd never seen it before.

"So do you," Topher said, his gaze back to her. "Loving the red hair. I mean, the blue was always nice, but it's fun to mix things up now and again."

"Totally." Jade smiled. Like a real, happy girl smile. Nothing tight-lipped or forced.

When they just continued staring at each other, I cleared my throat. "Do I get to find out why you called her Spade?"

Topher winked at her. "Just an inside joke."

Jade blushed. Her cheeks actually turned red, and I wanted to snap a picture so badly.

"And you two know each other how?" I asked.

"Just from living here in Willow Marsh," Topher said, his eyes on Jade.

She stared up at him with a longing that took me by surprise. It was that exact moment that I remembered Jade had a boyfriend. Granted, the two weren't getting along, and I was pretty sure Marcel and Leya liked each other.

I wasn't sure how to broach the subject of Marcel with Leya. Anytime I hinted at it, she snapped at me. But I knew her better than anyone, and that look she got in her eyes whenever she received a text from him practically screamed she was smitten with the guy.

Taking Jade out of the equation, Leya and Marcel would make a cute couple. They got along great. Marcel and Jade had been fighting more, and honestly, they didn't quite go together. From what I'd been able to pry out of Jade, they started dating because "he was there and convenient."

I had some major work to do.

"Tessa."

I spun around to see Graham standing there in his coveralls, one earbud perched in his ear, the other hanging against his chest. I could faintly hear heavy metal coming from the earbud. I went to throw my arms around him, but he stepped back, looking over his shoulder at Craig, the man who owned the shop.

Clearing his throat, Graham folded his arms. "Did you drive all of you over here?"

I nodded, looking back and forth between him and Craig, whose eyes were drilling holes into the back of Graham's head. "Uh, yeah." I stepped closer to Graham, lowering my voice. "What's with Craig?"

Graham sighed. "He's an ex of my mom's. I wouldn't have gotten this job if Lola and Topher hadn't talked him into it. I think he's just waiting for me to screw up so he can fire me."

I checked over my shoulder to see Jade and Topher standing incredibly close, chatting away.

"Speaking of Topher," I said, turning back to Graham. "What's happening right now?"

Graham pulled back in surprise like he couldn't believe I didn't know. "Jade has had a crush on him since elementary school."

I threw out my hands. "How come no one tells me these things? You guys have to remember I didn't grow up here."

Graham blinked rapidly, drumming his fingers along his folded arms. "Oh. Yeah. Sometimes I forget you don't know everyone like we do." His jaw twitched, and it seemed like he was holding back a smile. "So, you drove with Jade and Nash in your car?"

I couldn't help the smile that broke out on my face. "Yes. I didn't want to, but you know how Jade is."

"Yep." His blinking eyes looked over my head, not making eye contact with me. He was holding something from me.

I set my hand on his arm. "I do appreciate how hard you and Leya have been helping me. I think maybe I just needed a rude, out-of-the-blue approach."

He slowly smiled, putting one of his hands on top of mine. "Guess we hadn't tried that tactic. Until now."

It all clicked into place. "You guys did this on purpose, didn't you?"

Graham shrugged. "We'd tried everything. Jade once mentioned kidnapping you and forcing you to drive somewhere with us, but Leya and I thought this version would be better."

Much better. The kidnapping would *not* have gone over well.

"Graham!" Craig yelled from the garage. "Your break is over!"

Graham's smile faded. "See you at six." He leaned down, quickly brushing his lips against my cheek before he jogged into the garage.

I turned my attention back to Jade and Topher. Whatever was happening between them, I needed to put a stop to it.

"We should probably get going, Jade," I said. "I'm sure Marcel wants to meet up or something."

Jade's eyes widened in horror like I'd just announced her biggest, darkest secret.

Topher's smile faltered. "You're still with that guy? The scrawny kid with the glasses?"

I folded my arms, waiting for Jade to tell him she was with Marcel, but she said nothing. Just stared at the ground.

"Well, it was nice to meet you, Topher, but we really need

to get going." I took Jade by the arm and yanked her toward her mom and brother. "What was that?"

"What was what?" Jade mumbled.

"You were totally checking him out, and you have a boyfriend."

"Shhhh!" Jade looked over her shoulder to make sure Topher hadn't heard. He'd been too busy checking out her backside to notice.

I stopped. "Jade, break up with Marcel."

Her head snapped back to me. "What? Why?" She glared. "Has he said something?"

"No." I rubbed my forehead. "It's just obvious you two are over each other. Just put everyone out of their misery and move on."

Jade's hands balled into fists. "Marcel and I are fine. Drop it." She stormed off before I could say another word.

CHAPTER 10

Leya had gone over to watch a movie at Jade's place. Jade had to watch Nash again—something she'd been doing a lot this summer—so she didn't want to go anywhere. Nash required way more energy than Jade had. Leya also had a five-year-old brother, so she knew exactly how to release the energy in a positive way.

Thankfully, Marcel was working with my dad tonight on the campaign, so nothing awkward would be happening.

I'd hoped that once Leya headed back to Skokie, things would fizzle, but I was starting to think that wasn't going to happen. If anything, their communication would increase.

Graham's Ford truck rumbled in front of the house at exactly six o'clock. I opened the front door as soon as I heard his truck. I'd switched into a jean skirt and a pink tank top, topping the outfit off with my pink Chuck Taylor's. I'd almost worn my hair down—Graham liked it that way the best—but it was too hot, so I forced my thick hair into a high ponytail, using Amá's pink and green floral scarf to hold it in place.

Graham opened the front door of his truck, his blinking eyes finding mine. His T-shirt was more snug than usual, highlighting the fact that he'd been working out. I wasn't sure what made him start, and I didn't want to ask because I was pretty sure it had to do with Blake Hayes. Graham's resident earbuds dangled against his chest, always ready to be popped in.

I ran down the stairs and threw my arms around his neck. Graham lifted me off the ground, holding me close. Breathing in his pine scent took me to a heavenly place, grounding me in all the chaos my life had to offer.

Nirah had gone to sleep behind my heart, apparently not interested in my night out with Graham. For that, I was grateful. I didn't need her interruptions.

When Graham finally set me down, his lips were on mine before I could say anything. He kept one hand on the small of my back, the other cupped around my neck. His breath was minty fresh, his lips soft. I'd pull him closer, but there wasn't any more room left between our bodies.

When Graham and I first started dating, everything with him was hesitant. I was his first girlfriend. Two months into our relationship, he'd confessed I was his first kiss as well. For someone who didn't have any experience, he was a pro at it.

As time went by, he loosened, every hug, kiss, and hand-hold becoming natural for him.

I paused our kiss, our lips barely apart. "It's nice to see you, too."

He rocked me back and forth, keeping his voice low to stop his stutter. "I feel like we've hardly seen each other recently—alone."

It was only going to get worse now that I'd become an intern for the sheriff. But I only planned to do that a couple of hours a day since Leya was still here. I wasn't sure how Graham would react to my news. I was still trying to process it myself.

I kissed his jawline. "Well, it's just you and me tonight. What do you want to do?"

He arched an eyebrow, amusement tugging at his full lips. Man, I really wanted to kiss them again. His fingers drummed along my back. "It's a surprise."

Taking my hand, he steered me toward his truck, opened the passenger side door for me, and sneaked a kiss on my cheek before he closed the door. I loved how he treated me with respect. Always a gentleman. I somehow struck the jackpot with him.

As I slid to the center seat, I spotted a raven sitting on our roof, looking at me. Its head cocked to the side, almost like it was challenging me in a mocking way. I quickly buckled up, trying to ignore the worry blooming in my heart. It didn't mean anything. It was just a stupid bird.

Graham hopped in the truck, turned the ignition, then put his arm on the bench behind me so I could snuggle into him. I focused on his warmth, letting the worry melt away.

We drove down the quiet streets, listening to heavy rock music. It tended to keep Graham's nerves at bay. I was slowly getting used to it, though it wasn't my favorite genre. I preferred R&B, something with a smooth beat I could dance to.

Graham pulled off the highway, taking us down a dirt road. He was headed toward the lake. I'd only been there a couple of times since I'd moved here. I thought it odd that no one really swam in it or anything. The water was pretty, and from the top, looked clean. Sometimes people took small boats out onto it, but that was it.

As we neared the lake, Graham parked the truck near a willow tree, holding his door open so I could hop out on his side. I immediately went to the shore, my steps unsteady on the rocky ground.

The lake was massive. I could barely make out the trees on the other side—they were just a green blur.

I took a deep breath, loving the smell of water mixed with the trees. The sun reflected off the surface.

"Help me?" Graham stood off to the side, yanking on an old, green tarp on the ground.

I jogged over and took hold of an edge. "What is this?"

Dirt flew up at every yank, causing me to cough. I shuffled down the side, trying to see why it wouldn't budge.

"There's a boat under here," Graham whispered.

When I got to the back, I bent down, my leg lifting behind me. "Looks like it's stuck on a branch."

A small grunt escaped Graham. I turned to find him staring up at the sky, hands on his hips, muttering something under his breath.

"You okay?" I asked.

He didn't lower his gaze. "You're in a skirt, Tessa. I'm trying to be honorable here, but you're making it difficult."

Man, I loved this guy. "I'll tell you when I'm done."

It took some acrobatic work, but I shimmied over the bush, using the boat as support until I could wrap my hand around the end of the tarp and disentangle it from the branches.

"Go for it!" I said.

With some flourish, Graham tugged the tarp off in one motion, the fabric crinkling in the wind, before he was able to bunch it up and set it on the ground.

Together we pushed the boat until half of it was in the water. Graham grabbed a blanket and a picnic basket from the back of his truck.

"Oh, a picnic," I said, helping him put the supplies in the boat. "On a lake." I took in the old, wood boat, the romance slipping away. "Uh, will this hold us?"

He grinned, easing my worry. "She'll hold up just fine. We just need to make it to the center of the lake."

Once I scrambled into the boat, Graham joined me. We both untied an oar from the side and then rowed out to the center.

It was a little cooler out on the lake. The humidity had jumped, but with the light breeze passing through, it almost felt nice.

As we neared the center of the lake, I noticed a small piece of land protruding from the water. It was a small island, maybe twenty by twenty feet. When we reached it, Graham hopped out and tugged the boat, so the front was partly on the land. Then he helped me out.

While he set up the picnic, I took the time to take in the scenery, loving the view. I spun in a slow circle, looking at all the willow and birch trees surrounding the lake. The sun was on its descent, turning the sky orange. With the water all around us, it was beautiful.

Graham's arms suddenly wrapped around my waist, and he pulled me into him.

"This place is amazing." I placed my hands over his, linking our fingers. "Why don't more people come out here?"

"There are lots of rumors about this lake," he said, his voice low. "People in this town are way too superstitious."

With all the weird things that happened in Willow Marsh, I wouldn't blame them.

He kissed the side of my head. "Let's eat."

Graham and I ate our meal, watching the sunset. He'd brought turkey sandwiches and juicy watermelon, along with a couple of Dr Peppers. When we'd finished, he spread his legs so I could sit between them, my back pressed against his torso.

The stars slowly came to life, lighting up the cloudless sky. The lake rippled with the breeze. With the sound of the water, the gorgeous sky, and being in Graham's arms, I wished I could pause the moment forever. It was perfect.

"Are you ready for the best part?" Graham whispered in my ear.

"It gets better than this? How is that possible?"

Graham stood and then extended his hand, helping me up. He came up behind me so he could wrap his arms around me. "Just watch."

A few minutes passed with nothing happening. I almost turned around so I could at least get some kisses while we waited, but it suddenly began.

Little balls of yellow light popped up around the lake, slowly filling the area until we were surrounded. Lightning bugs. They swirled around, almost in a dance, a buzz in the air. I didn't realize I was moving closer to them until Graham tugged me back, so I didn't walk right into the lake.

The yellow swirls were mesmerizing. The lightning bugs seemed to be buzzing in unison like they were playing a song for us. There was a faint hum in the distance, almost like someone singing, but I had to be imagining that part.

"Told you it was amazing," Graham whispered in my ear.

I turned around so I could look up at him. He stared at me, his normally quickly blinking eyes calm. The light from the lightning bugs lit up his green eyes.

"How did you find this place?"

He brushed his nose against mine. "A couple of weeks ago, I went on a walk around the lake and noticed the lightning bugs. After a few trips back, I noticed they came out at the same time every evening."

"It's incredible."

He was silent for a few beats before he spoke in a hushed tone. "I love you."

Lifting onto my tiptoes, I pressed my forehead against

his, trying to keep my breathing in check. My heart raced. "I love you, too."

Then our lips were one, molding together in soft, slow movements. He tasted sweet, like fresh fruit. My hands slid around his neck and then up to his hair. I used to love gripping his locks while we kissed, but they were gone. Something I was still getting used to.

Both his arms were wrapped around me, holding me tight and sure. So many bad things had happened since moving to Willow Marsh, but Graham made up for that and then some.

The breeze whirled around us, my ponytail swaying. It was soft at first, then it increased, turning faster and faster until it made Graham and I lose our balance, and we stumbled a few steps. The scarf holding my ponytail ripped off, disappearing into the wind.

When we broke apart, lightning bugs surrounded us, creating a wall.

"Tt...Tessa!" Graham sounded panicked.

I looked at him, but he was staring at my skin. When I glanced down, I yelped in surprise. I was glowing, bright like the lightning bugs, from every inch of my skin.

CHAPTER 11

Nirah had come to life, but I'd been so wrapped up in the kiss that I hadn't noticed. She'd separated into multiple pieces, wrapping herself around my bones and purring in excitement.

The heat inside my body felt like I was standing in the middle of a firepit. Yet, I wasn't sweating.

Graham had his hands clasped on top of his head, his eyes wide in awe, with a slight trace of fear. I couldn't imagine what he was thinking.

I shook my arms, but it only caused the glow to brighten. The lightning bugs continued their circuit around us, blocking us out from the world. Inside our little tornado, the breeze had stopped, the air calm.

"Ww...what's happening to you?" Graham licked his lips, his blinking out of control.

"I don't know." It had to be Nirah's doing, but I had no idea what she was trying to do, or how the lightning bugs fit into the equation.

Suddenly the tornado of lightning bugs blew away from us, like they were being sucked by an invisible vacuum. They resumed their dance over the lake before they started popping, exploding like small, yellow fireworks.

"What the..." Graham trailed off, watching the disgusting show in horror.

My stomach flipped as the lightning bugs disintegrated until they were all gone. The lake water rose high into the air, bubbling and producing steam. It towered into the sky, blocking all lines of sight. The water sputtered, threatening to rain down on us.

Graham threw his arms around me, holding me close. We were standing on the tiny island in the middle of the lake, with no way to escape. If all the water collapsed at the same time, would it wash us away?

The sizzle of the boiling water was loud. If the water didn't wash us away, it would certainly scald us, leaving us with permanent damage.

My body was still a human glow light. Was there a way I could stop it? Could Nirah? She squirmed inside me, loving the show. She was probably encouraging it, if not the main source.

Below me, the earth trembled, vibrating my bones and jostling us around. I clung to Graham, trying to stay on my feet. My thumb stroked my family ring, hoping for some strength. Some direction.

I briefly closed my eyes. *Amá. I need your help.*

The ground undulated like a mighty roar. My feet flew out from underneath me, and Graham and I tumbled to the ground. Little sprays of water shot from the bubbling wall of water, searing my skin on contact. Graham threw his body over mine, shielding me as best he could.

Nirah fought inside me, wriggling around like she was being suffocated. The glow of my body grew until I had to squeeze my eyes shut, the light unbearable.

Seconds later, the water stilled before it plummeted back

to the earth, landing with a splash all around us. I buried my head into Graham's chest, waiting for the water to reach us. But it never did.

When I opened my eyes and turned my head, the lake was completely still. My glow had vanished.

"You've got to be kidding me," Graham hissed under his breath as he rolled off me.

I followed his gaze to the boat. It had shredded into hundreds of pieces, completely unusable. Pain pricked my skin. All over, like a bad case of chicken pox, were little red dots from the water. Graham looked worse.

I stood and pulled my phone from the back pocket of my jean skirt, but I had no service.

Graham checked his phone as well. "No bars."

"So, we're stranded on an island that no one ever visits." I rubbed my arms, even though it was hot out. The whole experience had set my hair on end. "Did you tell anyone you were taking me here?"

A tiny spark lit in Graham's eyes. "Leya knows."

"At least someone does."

The spark left his eyes. "TT...Tessa, ww...what just happened?" His gaze traveled my body like he was waiting for it to glow again.

With a sigh, I sat down on the blanket. It hadn't budged the entire time, which I once would have found odd, but everything in Willow Marsh was odd.

My thick hair was heavy against my slick neck. On top of everything else, I wasn't sure what upset me more—the fact that I couldn't pull my hair back in this heat or that I'd lost one of Amá's scarves.

Graham joined me, keeping a noticeable distance and checking out the spots on his arms.

I composed myself before I told him about Nirah and Reed. I even mentioned how my family ring had molded to my skin. Graham blinked wildly the whole time, his jaw hanging open, his fingers drumming along his legs.

When I finished, he rubbed his eyes. "You have another *thing* inside you?" He almost sounded annoyed.

"Wasn't like I asked her to join me," I said in a defensive tone.

Graham played with the earbuds hanging against his chest. "Did you have another séance?" Now he sounded like a scolding parent.

"No!" I took a deep breath. *Control. Steady. Calm.* "I think it all started in the crypt. When everything was going down with the box and Ellington, I think she worked her way inside me."

He groaned. "Is this ever going to end?"

I stood, brushing off the back of my skirt. "Maybe you should be asking, 'Hey, Tessa, how are you doing with having another entity inside you?'"

He jumped to his feet, the motion aggressive, but he still kept his voice low so he wouldn't stutter. "I'm sorry, this is all just a little much, you know? There's been something constantly going on since I met you."

I folded my arms against my chest. "Sorry to inconvenience you with all these things happening to me that *I didn't ask for*!" So much for my mantra.

His anger fell away, and he pulled me into his arms. "You're right."

I sunk into him. "I need you, Graham. You're my rock in all of this, and I don't need you chipping away."

His warm lips kissed my forehead. "Any idea what to do this time around?"

"No," I said into his chest. "Don't freak out, but I'm planning on reaching out to Mrs. Morales to see about contacting Amá."

I steeled myself for his tirade, but it didn't come. Instead, he rubbed my back.

"I think that's the safest way to do it." He hesitated before he added the next part. "Would you like me to come with you?"

I pulled back enough to look at him. "Thank you for offering, but I wouldn't put you through that. Leya will go with me, and I'll ask Rita to join us."

He nodded. "Sounds like the right people to have there." He stroked my cheek with his thumb. "Just promise me you'll be safe."

"I'll let Mrs. Morales do all the work."

His eyes went to the broken boat. "Looks like we might be here a while. Unless you want to swim all the way back to shore."

I glanced at the still lake, remembering what it looked like just minutes ago. "Yeah, no thanks. So not diving into that water anytime soon."

We lay down on the blanket, arms wrapped around each other.

"You know, this would be romantic if all that craziness hadn't just happened."

He grinned. "We still have all night to forget."

I tried to move my arm to punch him in the gut, but he held my arms in place. "You better keep your mind in the right place, buddy. I'm not ready for ... that."

He kissed the tip of my nose. "You know I would never take advantage of you, right? Or pressure you?"

My mind wandered back to the night Delilah had taken complete control of me while in Blake's bed. If his step-mom hadn't walked in, they could have gone all the way, using *my* body.

Graham was nothing like Blake.

"I know." I gently kissed his lips before I snuggled into him.

Thank goodness I'd ended up with the right guy.

CHAPTER 12

I woke to find a bright light shining on us. I lifted my hand to shield my eyes, trying to see who it was.

"Who is that?" Graham grumbled.

We'd fallen asleep at some point. It was still dark in the sky, so morning hadn't come. Our bodies were tangled up on the blanket.

Graham propped himself up on his elbows, squinting at the light. Then his eyes shot wide open, and he scrambled to his feet, kicking me away.

"What has you all wound tight?" As soon as I stood and got out of the direct light, I saw why he freaked out.

A boat floated just to the side of the small island, the words *Willow Marsh Sheriff* painted on the side.

Sheriff Hayes stood on the boat, his arms folded, bushy eyebrows raised, and amusement tugging at his lips. Dad was on the other side, hands balled into fists, his angry eyes on Graham.

Graham took a step back, hiding behind me. "He's gg... going to kk...kill me, isn't he?"

I tried to reach back and take his hand, but Graham snatched it away from me.

"It'll be fine," I said. "I'll explain everything."

"Land ho!" Leya's bubbly form came into view, somewhat blocking my dad. "I've always wanted to say that."

Jade stood next to her, laughing so hard that her hands were pressed against her stomach, which was rare for her. She clapped her hands, collecting herself. "This is the best thing that has ever happened to me." She saluted Graham. "It was nice knowing you."

Leya's smile faded. "What happened to you two? You both look like you have a rash."

Dad cleared his throat, demanding everyone's attention. "Tessa, on the boat, now."

Graham tugged on the back of my tank top. "Do you think if I jumped in the lake, I could make it to the other side before they caught me?"

"No way." I turned around, patting him on the chest. "Suck it up, Buttercup. Just act cool, like nothing happened."

"Nothing *did* happen," he said through clenched teeth. "Well, between me and you. But we can't really explain all the lightning bugs, either." He threw his head back. "I'm so screwed."

"Tessa!" Dad bellowed.

"Yes, sir." I spun around and marched to the boat, letting Sheriff Hayes help me onboard.

Nash lay sleeping on a bench, awkwardly wearing a life vest like they'd tried to wrestle it on him as he slept. Leya and Jade must have really worn the kid out.

Leya tried to talk to me, but Dad took my arm and steered me off to the side so we could talk alone.

"You have some serious explaining to do, young lady." Dad ran his hand down his face. "What on earth were you thinking coming out here alone with him?"

I put my hands on his arms. "Dad, relax. We just had a picnic. The boat got damaged, so we couldn't take it back to shore. And our cell phones don't have service out here."

His jaw twitched. "That would explain why you didn't answer your phone." He held up my arm, looking it over. "Why *are* you covered in a rash?"

I glanced over my shoulder to make sure the sheriff wasn't listening. "I'll explain everything once we're at home. Just brace yourself for the supernatural."

Dad groaned. "Not again."

"You sound like Graham."

He harrumphed. "Maybe that boy isn't so bad after all."

"He's not, Dad. He'd never do what Blake tried, I promise."

Dad wrapped me up in his arms. "I'm just glad you're okay. I was worried sick when you didn't come home."

"What time is it?"

Dad released me and checked his watch. "Almost three in the morning." He pointed a finger at me. "Way past your curfew, young lady."

I wrapped my hand around his finger and lowered it. "Stop calling me 'young lady.' It's weird."

"Well, you are a young lady." He patted my cheek. "We're having a serious discussion when we get home."

I smiled up at him. "And ice cream?"

A smile broke out on his lips. "And ice cream." His smile dropped, and he glared at Graham, who swallowed noticeably and hid behind a laughing Jade.

"Dad, you're going to traumatize him."

Dad pulled me in for another hug. "Good. I want him to think about me every time the two of you are alone."

I scrunched my face. "Gross. That's so weird."

Dad kept his arms around me all the way back to the shore. He had a small talk with Graham—out of earshot—

before Graham got in his truck and left. I wasn't sure what Dad had said, but Graham wouldn't make eye contact with me.

Sheriff Hayes came over to me, rubbing his jaw. "Can you be at the office at eight?"

"That's only a few hours from now."

He rested his hands on his hips, right above his gun and taser. "If you want to be a police officer, you better get used to it. Besides, I want to know why the lake lit up like the 4th of July tonight."

I hadn't thought about other people noticing. It was awfully bright and loud.

After everything in the crypt, I'd told Sheriff Hayes everything that happened. I'd tried to be vague about all the supernatural stuff, but he could tell I was holding things back. Even though there was a chance he'd think I was crazy, I told him everything that had gone down with Ellington.

Sheriff Hayes had been quiet for a good five minutes after I'd finished, his face showing no emotion. But when he'd finally talked, I could tell he believed me. I wondered if anything had happened like that in Willow Marsh before, but I didn't ask at the time.

"You want to know the truth?" I asked. Maybe if he knew, he could search the relics so I wouldn't have to go into his house. The sheriff had grown on me, but I still despised Blake and wasn't sure if I could ever forgive him.

Amá would want me to—she was the most forgiving person I'd ever known. But Blake had crossed a major line, and he didn't seem at all sorry.

The sheriff rubbed his eye. "I'm not going to like it, am I?"

"Nope."

He sighed. "I'll bring the coffee."

"I'll just bring a Dr Pepper for myself."

"I actually have some in the office."

I pulled back in surprise. "Really?"

Sheriff Hayes popped a piece of nicotine gum in his mouth. "Best soda out there." He patted my shoulder. "See you in a few hours."

I turned toward my dad's car when my skin pricked, the sensation of being watched rippling through me. Spinning in a slow circle, I scanned the trees surrounding us, trying to spot anything out of the ordinary. As my gaze swept past two birch trees, a glowing pair of eyes made my head snap back.

A larger-than-life wolf watched me through the trees, its dark fur blending with the night. Its intense eyes bore into mine, making my hands clutch onto the bottom of my skirt. A raven was perched on its shoulder, only visible thanks to its beady yellow eyes.

"Tessa?" Leya called out.

I turned to see her and Dad watching me. Jade and Nash were already in the car.

"Let's go," Dad said.

With a slight nod, I looked back at the trees, but the wolf and bird were gone.

CHAPTER 13

Jade insisted on coming home with us. I'd warned her that my story involved practically everything she hated—the paranormal, romance, pets, and Reed—but she wouldn't take no for an answer.

I changed into my pajamas, tied my hair back with another scarf, and went back downstairs, curling up on my abuelo's chair. Leya and Jade were on the couch, Leya's feet kicked up in Jade's lap. Leya was the only person on the planet who could set her feet in Jade's lap and not have Jade punch her for it. Marcel couldn't even get away with it.

Dad brought us each a bowl of ice cream and then sat down on the loveseat next to a conked-out Nash. His blond curls clung to his round, sweaty face.

I took a bite of my rocky road, thinking of Felix. It was his favorite flavor.

Nirah had gone dormant ever since the lake like she was tuckered out from all the ruckus. It was like I had a deranged puppy living inside me.

"I want every detail." Leya had changed into her pajamas,

an oversized T-shirt and pink shorts. "Starting from when Graham picked you up."

Dad pointed his spoon at me. "Please don't."

Jade nodded. "I agree. You can tell Leya all that sappy stuff later. Just tell us what went down on the island." Her lip curled in disgust. "Unless it involves clothes coming off. Keep that part for Leya, too."

Leya wiggled her eyebrows at the same time Dad grunted.

"The clothes stayed on, Apá. I promise."

Leya winked at me, which, unfortunately, Dad noticed.

"She's kidding, Apá. I'll just tell you about the lightning bugs."

I dove into the story and watched as their reactions switched to total awe. It really was a sight to see, but kind of difficult to explain.

When I finished, Leya set her empty ice cream bowl on the coffee table. "So, what does this mean? Are the lightning bugs symbolic of something?"

"It means," Reed's sugary drawl came from near the fireplace, "that things are about to change in Willow Marsh."

Dad leaped from his chair, his ice cream bowl shattering on the wood floor, and I cringed from the noise. Nash turned onto his back, one arm covering his eyes and his leg dangling from the side of the couch. But he didn't fully wake. Man, he was a deep sleeper.

Dad ran his hand down his face, shaking it out and blinking fiercely, but Reed was still there when he looked at the fireplace again.

Reed's ghostly-self leaned against the mantle, his feet crossed at his ankles. He wore the same flannel jacket, jeans, and tan work boots from the night he died, blood stains included.

Jade's jaw was dropped, her wide eyes not blinking. She'd been moving to set her bowl on the coffee table when Reed appeared, so she was frozen leaned forward, her arms outstretched and hands gripping tightly onto the bowl.

Leya had shrunk into the couch, trying to make herself as small as possible. She kept pulling at an imaginary blanket like she wanted to cover herself.

I took the blanket folded on the back of my abuelo's chair and tossed it at Leya. It just hit her face and then landed in her lap, Leya frozen in place like Jade.

Seeing a ghost hanging out in your living room was a lot to take in.

I leaned my elbow on the armrest, resting my chin in my hand and slightly hating how used to this I was getting. "Reed, did you have anything to do with what happened tonight?"

He smoothed out his flannel jacket. "Sorry, doll, but no. Nirah sure played a big part, though."

A groggy Nirah turned in a circle in the cavity behind my heart, adjusting her sleeping position. It really had worn her out.

"I fear what Andras has planned is much grander than I imagined," Reed said.

"Who's Andras?" I asked.

"The demon, Tessa. Master of Nirah. Do keep up."

"What's he planning?"

Reed lifted one shoulder in a shrug. "Still trying to piece that all together. Things aren't quite as clear where I am. It's like walking around in a haze, with voices murmuring around you. I've heard some whisperings of his plans for Willow Marsh, but I have nothing concrete yet."

I shifted in the chair so I could see him better. "You sound like you actually want to *help* us."

Reed sighed, way over the top. "Tessa, doll, you forget how much I love Willow Marsh. I may hate a lot of the residents." He motioned to me and the others in the room. "But I still have family here. My roots are deep."

I narrowed my eyes at him. "Speaking of your family, Ace said you've been coming to him in his dreams. I thought you said you hadn't been able to contact anyone, and I was your only hope."

Reed clapped his hands together. "That worked? I couldn't tell if he saw me or not. Besides, we couldn't communicate, no matter how hard I tried. You're still my only option."

Jade finally unfroze, setting her bowl down on the coffee table and sitting back on the couch, her movements slow. She scooted toward Leya and snagged some of the blanket for herself. I was expecting some snide commentary from her, but she remained quiet.

"Reed Harrison is in our home," Dad said in a low, shaky tone. He stood next to the loveseat, the shattered remnants of the bowl around his feet.

"Way to catch up, Daddy dearest," Reed said in a condescending tone. "And he's running for mayor." He tipped an imaginary hat at Dad. "Good luck with that."

"Is there a way you can figure out what this Andras demon is up to?" I asked.

Reed scratched at the side of his beard. "I'm trying, doll. It's going to take some time, though. The man has a huge following."

I tilted my head to the side. "You know, I really thought you'd be among that crowd."

Reed tsked. "Come now. There's no need for low blows. I may not be perfect, but I am a man of honor." He quirked an eyebrow. "Honor might not be the correct word here."

"No. Definitely not. But you are loyal to your family. I'll give you that." I tried to twirl the family ring around my finger but then remembered it was embedded in me.

"Now isn't a time to dawdle, Tessa, dear," Reed said.

I turned my focus back to him. "So, what do we do?"

Reed pushed away from the mantle and took a seat on the loveseat where Dad had vacated, his arm resting on the back of the couch. Reed kicked up his leg, resting it on his other knee. "I'll scout around on this side, see what I can gather. I do hate to say this, but you might need to reach out to your mother. You're going to need all the help you can get if you plan to win this battle." He tried to tickle Nash's bare foot, but his ghostly hand slid right through.

Dad held up his palms. "No way. Tessa is not—"

Reed flicked his hand out toward him, Dad's voice shutting off, his lips still moving. Dad placed his hand against his throat, trying to speak, but nothing came out of his mouth.

"You can reach out to my brothers as well," Reed said. "They'll be willing to help."

"There's no way I'm working with your brothers."

Reed cocked his head. "This town has been divided for too long. It's time for everyone to band together and make sure Willow Marsh stays intact."

"This so doesn't sound like you," I said. "Are you feeling okay?"

"Let's just say I have a new perspective in death," he said, buttery smooth. "All those things I cared about while I was alive seem so petty now."

Maybe people could change. Maybe there *was* forgiveness on the other side. But Reed had killed innocent people. There was no forgiveness in that. I needed to tread carefully around him. After all, he could be working *with* Andras.

"Fine." I glanced down at my family ring. Maybe I could soak it in something. Or maybe Mrs. Morales would know why it had suddenly become a part of me.

"Tessa?" Reed sounded impatient.

I looked at him. "I'll reach out to my mom and see if she knows anything. Let me know what you find."

Reed suddenly leaped from the couch, his ghostly figure fading in and out. His panicked eyes sought out something behind him.

"Reed?" I asked. "Are you okay?"

He licked his lips wildly as he backed up and then turned like he was pressing his back up against something. He moved his attention back to us and smiled wide at everyone. "Just fine, thanks. It was a pleasure to be with you all tonight. I'm afraid I must run now. But don't you worry, I will return shortly. Nighty night." He faded until he was gone.

"What just happened?" Dad asked, his voice now free and his face pale.

I was about to speak when my phone rang. I glanced down to see that it was the sheriff calling, so I answered. "Hello?"

"Good, you haven't gone to sleep," Sheriff Hayes said. "Meet me at Duncan Heathrow's place."

The line went dead.

CHAPTER 14

We all rushed to change out of our pajamas before we left. I told them the sheriff just asked me to come, but Dad and Leya were dying to know what was going on. I couldn't blame them. I was dying as well. Jade finally took Nash home so he could sleep in his own bed.

I'd never met Duncan Heathrow, but from the few interactions I'd had with his mom at the police station, I could tell they were a nice family.

We pulled onto the street where Duncan lived ten minutes later. The area was lit up with flashing lights, every police cruiser, fire truck, and ambulance in Willow Marsh on location.

Dad had to park at the end of the block. We all piled out of the car and worked our way through the crowd.

Sheriff Hayes met us a house away from the Heathrow's, his face grim. He popped a piece of nicotine gum in his mouth.

"What happened?" I asked.

"We got the call right after I left the lake." Sheriff Hayes rested his hands on his hips. "Their daughter has gone missing."

I glanced past him to see all the Heathrows standing outside on the well-lit lawn. Duncan and his wife were in tears, their other two kids huddled around them. Gracie and her husband were there, too, Gracie holding her daughter-in-law close, her own tears escaping.

"How old is she?" Dad asked, a strain in his tone.

"Nine," Sheriff Hayes said.

My breath hitched. Same age Felix was when he died.

"Do you have any leads?" Dad asked.

Sheriff Hayes' eyes sought mine. "Tessa, I need you to come with me into the house." He glanced at my dad. "The rest of you will have to wait out here."

He turned toward the house, and I followed, surprised he'd take me with him. I wanted to intern, but I didn't think he'd actually let me see a crime scene, and so quickly.

The sheriff lifted the yellow tape so we could duck underneath it.

"He's back!" The raspy, shaky voice came from behind us. I turned to see an old man, the top of his head bald, the sides lined with white hair. His cane seemed to be holding up his hunched body. He pointed a wrinkly finger at the sheriff. "Mark my words, Hayes. He's back."

Sheriff Hayes patted the old man on the shoulder. "It's not what you think, Lloyd. Go home and rest."

"I've been resting for years!" Lloyd bellowed. "Now, we need to act."

"What..." I trailed off when the sheriff held a hand up to stop me.

Sheriff Hayes waved a couple of fingers at a deputy. "Deputy Rafferty, could you please take Mr. Cromwell's statement for me? I need to head inside."

Deputy Rafferty jogged over to Lloyd with a grin, like he knew what he was about to get into.

The sheriff motioned for me to go under the yellow police tape, the look in his eyes telling me not to ask about Lloyd. I'd just ask Jade about it later. She knew everything that went on in Willow Marsh.

As we neared the Heathrow's, Duncan was blabbering to another deputy, his words fast and slurred.

"Why are you just standing around?" Duncan asked. "You should be out there looking for her!"

Gracie eyed me as I walked past, her eyebrows knitted together, probably wondering what I was doing there. I wish I knew, too.

Above us, the caws of ravens could be heard. Squinting my eyes, I looked up at the dark sky, trying to see past the bright lights that had been brought in by the sheriff's department. My eyes trained on a few ravens circling the perimeter like a bad omen.

Sheriff Hayes handed me some booties and gloves when we got to the front door, making me put them on before we stepped into the house.

Sheriff Hayes eyed my ring. "You might want to take off your ring. The gloves are pretty tight."

My ring did not want to come off. It wouldn't even twist.

I sighed. "It's suctioned to me at the moment."

It took some wrestling, but I finally got the glove over the ring and onto my hand.

The front room was littered with blankets and pillows, and the coffee table was pushed off to the side.

"They watched a movie tonight," Sheriff Hayes said next to me. "Had a little camp out here before Duncan and Steph carried the kids to bed." He motioned to the dining room near a sliding glass door. "This is where it gets weird."

The door was open, letting in a small breeze. I took small

steps toward the opening, crouching down in front of a gaping hole in the screen door. It had been torn to shreds like claws had ripped through.

"What did this?" I asked.

The sheriff squatted next to me. "Not sure." He motioned to the claw-like tears. "But those are practically the size of a bear's."

I scanned the backyard, seeing the outlines of willow and birch trees lining the edge of their property, leading out into the darkened woods.

"You need to see the bedroom, Tessa."

I followed him up the stairs, noticing a small trail of blood running along the carpet. I kept to the side, watching where I stepped. As we entered the hall upstairs, the carpet started to squish under my feet.

Warm liquid soaked through the bottom of my Chuck Taylor's. "Is this water?"

"Yes, and we have no idea where it came from." Sheriff Hayes motioned to the open door. "This is Chloe's room."

I stopped in the doorway, surveying the room. Pictures of gymnasts lined the walls surrounding her four-poster bed. Gold and silver medals hung from the posts, dangling in the air. There were wooden shelves lined with trophies and ribbons.

And it was incredibly muggy, the air thick and wet.

"She's talented," Sheriff Hayes said, leaning against the doorframe. "Been doing gymnastics since she could crawl."

Taking a tentative step inside the room, I looked toward the bed. The sheets, bedspread, and mattress were torn into pieces. Small drops of blood were scattered around. A small patch of Chloe's floral nightgown hung from the side of the bed.

With all the damage, I expected to see more blood.

"There's not much blood," I said. "That's odd, right?"

"That's the first thing I noticed, too," Sheriff Hayes said from beside me. "Gives me hope that she's still alive."

Everything in the room was drenched like it had rained, which I guess could have washed away the blood, but the water didn't look tainted at all.

Nirah stirred in the cavity behind my heart, waking from her deep sleep. There was a moment of quiet from her before she sprang to life, heating me from the inside. I leaned against one of the bed posts, trying to keep myself from falling over.

"Are you okay?" Sheriff Hayes asked.

I pressed a shaky hand to my forehead. "Lightheaded."

He sighed. "The first crime scene is always tough."

Blinking away the spots in my vision, I looked up at the sheriff. "Why did you bring me here?"

He motioned to the bed, which was when I finally noticed two key things. One, the entire bed was covered in dead lightning bugs. And two, among all the ripped material, lay a green and pink scarf. My hand went to my hair. It was the scarf I was wearing at the lake. The one I thought I'd lost.

"I only know one person who wears those scarves, Tessa. Not to mention, Duncan and Steph mentioned they saw a blinding light coming from the bedroom, reminding me of the lake lighting up tonight. Happened about the same time."

My gaze snapped back to him. "You can't possibly think I had something to do with this."

He shook his head. "I'm obviously aware of your alibi. I'm just trying to figure out how all this got here."

"And *why*."

Nirah danced around inside me, a newfound life in her. I stared at my skin, waiting for it to light up, but it remained the same.

I wasn't sure if I should mention it, but I figured it would be best to tell him anything that seemed suspicious. "When we were about to leave the lake, I swear I saw a pair of golden eyes staring at me through the trees. Belonging to a big animal, like a wolf or something." But slightly bigger.

Sheriff Hayes swore under his breath. "This can't be good."

I looked up at the sheriff. "I'm afraid this is just the beginning."

"The beginning of what?" he asked.

My stomach coiled so tight I had to lean against the bedpost for support. "I wish I knew."

CHAPTER 15

Sheriff Hayes and I went outside behind the house so I could tell him all about my Reed encounter. We went to the edge of the property line, partway into the woods. We'd left the coverage the back porch lights had to offer.

The sheriff was silent for a few minutes after I'd finished.

He tossed a piece of nicotine gum in his mouth. "I thought we'd seen the end of Reed Harrison."

I scoffed. "Are you really surprised he tried to find a way to haunt our lives after his death?"

"Not really." He adjusted his sheriff hat. "Are you sure you want to contact your mom? Last time things got a little out of hand."

I leaned my back against a birch tree. "What other option do we have? If anything, I think talking to Mrs. Morales will help."

"Do you think she's in the right state of mind to help?"

Losing her daughter was hard on Mrs. Morales. Corrine was a bright light in Willow Marsh. She made everything better. Then there was the issue of working with Reed. He'd killed her daughter. No way she'd want to help that man. But she'd want to help Willow Marsh. She wouldn't want her daughter's death to be in vain.

I wondered if we could reach out to Corrine as well. Or would that be too emotionally difficult for Mrs. Morales?

Sheriff Hayes' eyes were unfocused on a root protruding from the earth. "Do you think more attacks are going to happen? Like what happened with Chloe Heathrow?"

I thought back to my vision of all those people screaming for help. "Unfortunately, yes."

"Any reason why it was the Heathrow's? And why their daughter? Is there a way to know who they're targeting?"

I stroked the side of my ring. "I'm not sure. Maybe Reed will be able to find out. But if things continue as they are, you might have to think about evacuating the town."

He rested his hand on his waist, right above his gun. "I don't want to do anything rash until we know what we're dealing with."

"We're dealing with a demon." I stared at the dahlia on my ring. "It doesn't get much worse than that."

"That's if we believe Reed. Can we really trust the man?"

No, we couldn't. But my vision had felt *so real.* Like it was a forecast of what was to come. "Let me reach out to Mrs. Morales today, and we'll go from there."

The sheriff nodded. "Let me know how it goes." He stared out into the trees. "They definitely didn't prep us for this in the academy. This is way out of my jurisdiction."

"I feel the same way. But here we are. I hate to say this, but I think what happened down in the crypt was just a battle before the war. Something big is about to go down, and I think our main goal should be getting as many people out alive as we can." I paused. "Hey, Sheriff, has anything like this happened in Willow Marsh before? You've taken this surprisingly well, all things considered."

He rubbed his jaw. "There have been rumors of supernatural type stuff over the years, sightings and whatnot, but there's never been anything concrete that I know about. My grandma used to tell me all sorts of crazy stories about ghosts when I was a kid." He suddenly stiffened, his hand sliding to his gun.

I followed his gaze but didn't see anything between the thick birch and willow trees filling the dark woods.

With slow steps toward the east, he pulled his handgun out from its holster, his finger sliding against the side. Even though his eyes were trained ahead, he walked cautiously, not making a noise.

I mimicked his steps, keeping them light and steady. If he heard me behind him, he didn't make any indication.

A snarl ripped from the south, making both the sheriff and I turn.

A gigantic black wolf stood a few yards away. His golden eyes were huge, almost the size of saucers. They contrasted with the darkness of night, making them glow.

With a shaking hand, I turned on the flashlight on my phone, so I could see the animal better. He was easily twice the size of a normal wolf. Maybe three times. He'd somehow gotten bigger. His thick fur stuck out all around him like he was electrified. His yellow fangs were bared, easily long enough to rip a limb off with one bite. Saliva dripped from its mouth, landing on the dirt.

The wolf's eyes trained on me, the snarl rising.

Around us, the wind picked up, whipping fiercely. Quarter-size drops of rain fell from the sky, pelting me, but I couldn't move. I was entranced by this wolf. It wasn't until the sheriff's hand landed on my shoulder that I realized I was moving toward it.

"Tessa!" The sheriff yelled over the roar of the storm. "We need to get out of here."

"We can't outrun it!"

"I know. I'm going to run to the left, trying to get its attention. You go right once he has his sights set on me."

Before I could say anything, the wolf sprang toward us. I took off toward the right, running parallel to the Heathrow's house.

Gunshots echoed through the woods, barely audible over the storm. Rain beat against my face and arms as I ran, sprinting as fast as I could. I glanced over my shoulder to see the wolf barreling toward me. The sheriff continued to fire, but his bullets just ricocheted off the wolf and fell to the ground. This was no ordinary wolf.

Inside, Nirah woke, igniting a fire in my veins that made me run faster. I leaped over a fallen tree, my Chuck Taylors sliding across the mud on landing. I quickly regained my footing and pushed harder, knowing I needed to lead the wolf away from people, especially if this was the same one that had taken Chloe.

Turning north, I headed deeper into the woods. Lightning lit the dark clouds above, lighting the path in front of me. Tree branches scratched along my arms as I ran, stinging my skin.

Fog slowly rose from the earth, covering the ground and rising, inch by inch. When it got to my waist, I dared to look behind me again. The wolf's glowing eyes stood out from the fog, a smaller gap between us than I hoped.

The fog reached my chest, and it wouldn't be long until I couldn't see at all. My feet connected with rocks and branches on the ground, making me stumble and lose my traction. I fell forward, my palms slamming into the muddy earth and jolting me. Scrambling back to my feet, I put my hands out in front of me, trying to feel around. The fog went well above my head, cloaking me in endless gray.

I needed to find a place to hide, and quick. Keeping my

hands out, I walked forward until my hands brushed against the bark of a tree. I wrapped my arms around the trunk and shimmied up, trying to get as far off the ground as I could.

Wind and rain attacked me as I climbed, almost making me lose my grip a few times. But then I'd hear the snarl of the wolf, and my urgency would skyrocket. I reached a group of branches I could settle on, trying to keep as still as possible.

The thunder and wind covered up the sound of my labored breaths. I worried my pounding heart could be heard through it all, though. It beat so fast and hard, like it was on the verge of exploding.

You can't hide forever, Tessa, a deep, rumbling voice said. *I will find you.*

Shrill cries filled the air, making me cringe.

Tessa! Tons of people screamed my name, so loud and full of pain. *Help us!*

Wind shook the tree, making me cling on tight. Nirah slid to my arms and legs, helping me coil around the branches. Right below me, a howl pierced the air, and I shuddered. My only hope was that the wolf couldn't see through the fog, and the smell of the storm covered up my scent.

Minutes passed and the storm raged on. My muscles burned, and I knew I wouldn't be able to hold on much longer. The entire tree jerked with the wind, each jolt causing my heart to slam into my throat.

Closing my eyes, I repeated my mantra over and over again in my head. *Control. Steady. Calm.*

If only the storm could do the same.

My fingers and arms slipped across the wet bark, my muscles starting to give out.

The storm came to a slow stop, the weather calming and the fog evaporating. When it all cleared, I looked down, dreading what I'd find, but the wolf was gone.

CHAPTER 16

My wobbly legs carried me back toward the Heathrow's house. With every rustle of a tree or a snap of a twig on the ground, I jumped, holding out my phone with the light on and frantically scanning the area for a wolf.

"Tessa!" Sheriff Hayes came into view, jogging toward me, maneuvering between the willow trees, and I let out a long breath of relief. "You're okay." He stopped when he got to me, his arm reaching out like he wasn't sure if he should hug me or not.

I was equally excited to see him, but we so hadn't reached that level of a relationship.

Both our phones beeped, killing the awkward moment.

Sheriff Hayes stared at his screen, then swore under his breath. "You have got to be kidding me."

The fear inside me melted into anger. Mayor Morgan had sent out a city-wide text alert about searching for Chloe in the woods behind the Heathrow's house at the crack of dawn. The same area where the sheriff and I were standing and had an encounter with a wolf.

"I'm taking he didn't talk to you about this?" I asked.

Sheriff Hayes shoved the phone back in his pocket. "Nope." He rubbed his forehead. "I can't call it off without alerting everyone that we have a larger-than-normal wolf stalking the area."

"I think it's gone." I folded my arms close to my chest. "We still have a couple of hours before dawn. Hopefully, it will be far away by then."

Sheriff looked at my mud-covered clothes. "Maybe you should go home and change. Meet me back here right before dawn. We're going to have to erase any signs of the wolf and our chase." He sighed. "If we can."

That was a lot of ground to cover and not much time. It was too dark to do it now, so it would have to wait for the sun to wake up. Dawn was just around the corner.

I filled Dad and Leya in on everything that happened on the way back to the house. I left them mulling it over in the front room so I could go upstairs and take a hot shower. As I peeled off my wet, muddy clothes and left them in a pile on the ground, I replayed all the crazy events that had happened.

Reed showing up in the house. Lightning bugs exploding at the lake. My skin glowing bright red and orange. Nirah living inside me. My family ring molding itself to my skin. Chloe missing. A gigantic wolf chasing me through the woods.

I turned the water as hot as it would go, practically scalding my skin. I'd once thought having Ellington haunting me and Delilah taking possession of me would be the worst thing that could possibly happen to me.

It paled in comparison to what I was up against now.

I stared at the dahlia on my ring. Why wouldn't the ring come off? I'd hoped the water might loosen it, but it was hanging on for dear life.

After fifteen minutes, I forced myself to turn off the

water and stepped out of the shower, grabbing the towel hanging from the rack and throwing it around me. Fog filled the bathroom, steaming up the mirror.

With my palm, I wiped across the glass, clearing a small section.

Reed's form stood behind me, smirking at me through the mirror. Letting out a yelp, I spun around, clutching my towel tight around me.

"What are you doing here?" I asked.

"You invited me." Reed's gaze traveled my body.

I shivered, despite the heat in the bathroom. "I *never* invited you."

He swept out a hand. "You grabbed the sword, which made me manifest, and now, here I am."

"That doesn't mean you can follow me into the bathroom." I did nothing to control the anger in my voice.

Reed frowned. "You're not as pretty when you're upset." He leaned forward, trying to tap my nose with his finger. "You should stick with smiling."

I swatted at his hand, but it only went through his transparent figure.

Reed leaned against the wall, folding his arms. "I was just coming to check on you after your encounter with Andras. It had to be upsetting."

I furrowed my eyebrows as I leaned my back against the bathroom counter. "What are you talking about?"

Reed rolled his eyes. "My, my, Tessa, it's only been an hour since he chased you, and you've already forgotten."

I pressed my hand to my forehead. "Andras is the wolf? Is he some sort of shapeshifter?"

He tapped his fingers together. "Ah, so you *do* still have a brain."

I ignored his comment. "What about that raven that was with him at the lake? Is the raven a shapeshifter, too?"

"Yes, but I haven't been able to find out her name." He pouted. "The people here can be so untrusting."

My hand went to my hip. "Can you blame them?"

"There has to be *some* level of trust." Reed stared at the dahlias on the shower curtain. "How arrogant must he be if he thinks we will blindly follow him, no questions asked?"

"Are we talking about you or Andras?"

He tsked, his cloudy eyes finding mine. "Oh, come now, Tessa. Will we ever get passed this—" He swept out a hand. "—rift between us."

I pulled my towel tighter around me. "No. Now, get out of my bathroom."

With a wink, he faded into nothing.

✦

A little before dawn, I made Dad and Leya join me when I met up with the sheriff. We had a lot of ground to cover before the town showed up.

We found Sheriff Hayes in the woods. His confused eyes settled on the muddy ground. When I approached his side, I followed his gaze but couldn't see anything out of the ordinary on the ground.

Leya peered over my shoulder. "What are we looking at?"

I stepped back, scanning the area. It was ... clean. Like no attack had happened. I turned to the sheriff. "Are we in the wrong spot?"

He slowly shook his head. "We were right here. This is where it started."

"Which way did you go?" Dad asked. "Maybe the sheriff and I can go one way, and Tessa and Leya can go the other."

The sheriff and I exchanged a wary glance, but we both finally nodded, heading in opposite directions into the woods.

The wolf had chased me along this path. Its huge paws

should have been embedded in the earth. My shoe impressions should have been there, along with a long streak where I skidded across the mud.

"How is this possible?" I muttered.

"Are you sure we're in the right spot?" Leya asked with an edge to her tone. "I mean, it was completely dark."

We continued scanning the area until we finally met back up with my dad and the sheriff.

They'd found nothing.

We'd found nothing.

No trace of the wolf, the chase, or me sliding and falling to the ground.

Almost like it had never happened.

Sheriff Hayes popped a piece of nicotine gum into his mouth. "I really picked the wrong month to quit smoking."

"We both saw the wolf," I said. "And Reed confirmed it's Andras. We need to somehow find him and put a stop to this madness."

Leya linked her arm with mine. "How do we even hunt a shape-shifting demon?"

"If Mrs. Morales doesn't have what you need," Sheriff Hayes said, "you should hit up the library. Maybe you'll have some luck there."

Leya furrowed her eyebrows. "They have books on how to hunt shape-shifting demons?" Her tone went down a notch. "This town is so freaking weird."

The sheriff sighed. "No, but they might have books on legends of Willow Marsh that Mrs. Morales doesn't have."

I thought back to that old man outside the Heathrow's house. "What about that man? Lloyd? He was yammering on about "him coming back" or something."

"Lloyd Cromwell?" Sheriff Hayes let out a strained laugh. "That man is off his rocker. Ignore him."

"Yoo-hoo!"

I spun around to see Barbie waltzing towards us with Fluffsies in the crook of her arm. She was dressed head to toe in pink hiker's gear, her hair and makeup done like she was ready for a night out on the town. Graham came up behind her, keeping a noticeable distance.

Barbie's gaze ran over the sheriff, then Dad, before her focus went back to the sheriff. "Is there where the search party is being held?"

Leya leaned toward me, her voice low. "She does know a search party isn't an actual *party*, right?"

I choked back a laugh.

"Well, this should be a fun day," Sheriff Hayes mumbled.

Fun was the last word I'd use to describe anything involving Barbie. I glanced down at the scarf wrapped around my hand to cover my scar. An overwhelming need to take it and strangle Barbie came over me, startling me.

Nirah vibrated under my skin in a laugh. *She* was the one that wanted to strangle Barbie, not me. I needed Nirah out of my body, and soon. The last thing I wanted to do was kill my boyfriend's mom. Or anyone, for that matter. I had a sinking feeling that if I didn't get Nirah out soon, someone would end up dead by the use of my hands.

Again.

CHAPTER 17

At the break of dawn, a huge crowd gathered in the Heathrow's backyard. Duncan was outside, but his wife, Steph, and his mom were inside with the other kids.

Mayor Morgan made a show of greeting Dad and the sheriff, talking about the travesty Willow Marsh had seen, almost in a mocking way. There was nothing organic about the guy. He was a trained puppet, putting on a vomit-inducing show.

The mayor's daughter, and Delilah's older sister, swept me into her arms like we were long-lost friends. Everything about her was drama.

"Oh, Tessa," Paisley said, hugging me tightly. "This is all so heart-wrenching."

I squirmed out of her embrace. "We'll find her."

Her blue eyes lit up, her hands squeezing my arms. "Are there any leads?"

I wasn't about to tell her about the wolf. With her love of always assuming the worst, I wanted to appear optimistic. "Not yet, but I know we'll find something soon."

"Oh, sweetie." Paisley pouted, stroking my cheek with her hand. "To be so young and innocent. These cases never turn out well."

Man, I wanted to punch her right in her self-righteous face. She was only a few years older than me.

Mayor Morgan cleared his throat and held up a hand, saving Paisley from a beat-down. "Can I have everyone's attention?" He waited until it was completely silent before he spoke in a booming voice. "Thank you for taking time out of your busy schedules to come help search for our sweet Chloe Heathrow. We haven't a second to waste. We'll split up into groups and search these woods behind Chloe's home."

"What exactly are we looking for?" Barbie asked as she scratched under Fluffsies' chin.

Mayor Morgan turned to the sheriff, motioning for him to speak like he'd agreed to help with the search.

Sheriff Hayes quickly popped a piece of nicotine gum in his mouth, chomping away, the anger behind his eyes apparent, before he stepped forward. "Look for any signs of Chloe. She was in a pink floral nightgown when she was taken."

Duncan choked back a sob as his dad rubbed his shoulder, trying to console him.

The sheriff cleared his throat, almost like he himself was holding back tears. He tucked his thumb into the top of his pants, his hand gripping his belt like he wanted to punch something.

When he spoke, his voice came out shaky at first. "Everyone split into groups of two to four. Spread out and try to cover as much ground as possible."

Mayor Morgan leaned forward. "Surely, we should be looking for disturbed earth or signs of a struggle, right, Coop?"

Sheriff Hayes nodded stiffly, his glaring eyes on the mayor.

"Yes, that's correct. Look for anything out of place, anything that looks suspicious."

Mayor Morgan held out a hand. "Remember that no clue is too small. If you think you find something helpful, bag it." He looked at the sheriff. "You have plastic bags for these occasions, right?"

Sheriff Hayes looked like he might explode.

Dad went to the sheriff's side. "I think it's best to let the deputies bag any evidence, take any pictures, or tape anything off. They're trained professionals."

"Alec is right," Sheriff Hayes said. "Just holler if you find something."

Mayor Morgan narrowed his eyes but didn't say anything. Smartest thing the man has ever done.

The sheriff clapped his hands. "Let's head out."

As everyone headed into the woods, Jade and Graham caught up to Leya and me, so I filled them in on everything. Jade knew at least some of it, but Graham had no idea what had happened since we left the lake.

Graham threw his head back and stared into the sky, speaking quietly to keep his stutter at bay. "A shape-shifting demon? Is a typical wolf too much to ask for?"

Jade chuckled. "I'd give anything to go back to a normal, boring Willow Marsh."

"There you are!" Marcel jogged over, smiling at Jade. Wait, no, he was smiling at Leya. His smile faltered when he saw Jade glaring at him. Marcel cleared his throat. "Why are all of you standing around? Did you find something?"

"Not quite," Leya said, smiling at him.

I pinched her arm, making her yelp.

Marcel nodded. "It's okay. You don't have to tell me."

Thank goodness he thought I was mad at Leya for spilling what we'd been talking about and not about the fact that she was checking Marcel out in front of his girlfriend.

Jade's snarl disappeared, and her eyes went wide.

I turned to find Topher and Jade's mom heading toward us. Topher's sultry gaze was on Jade.

Marcel looked back and forth between Topher and Jade, a frown forming on his lips.

"I'm so not in the mood for this," I whispered. Love triangles, well, a square, in this case, were awful. Too many emotions and confusion.

Taking Graham's hand, I tugged him and Leya away from the group. "We're going to go search."

"There's no point in searching," Leya said, glancing over her shoulder at Marcel. "We know we aren't going to find anything."

I kept tugging her along until we were out of sight of the others. I spun on her. "Leya, stop. No more flirting with Marcel."

Leya gasped. "We were *not* flirting. We just shared a smile."

Graham looked between Leya and me. "What's going on?"

I folded my arms and sighed. "To sum it up, Marcel and Leya like each other, and Jade and Topher like each other."

"When did Jade and Marcel break up?" Graham asked as he peeled his damp shirt away from his chest. These humid summers were brutal.

I shook my head. "They didn't."

Graham wiped some sweat from his brow. "This is awful."

Leya threw up her hands. "It's not that big of a deal."

Graham smiled softly. "I was talking about the weather."

Leya lowered her hands, setting them on her hips. "Oh."

"Isn't it always like this?" I asked.

"It's never been this humid in my life," Graham said. "This summer seems ten times worse than usual."

"That's pretty fitting for Willow Marsh, isn't it?" I couldn't control the sarcasm in my tone.

"Why hasn't he broken up with her?" Leya looked back in the direction of Marcel and the others, even though we couldn't see them.

"Because he doesn't have a death wish," Graham said.

"Jade has to be the one to end it," I said. "I'm working on it. Things have just been a little crazy lately."

The squish of mud sounded behind me. Footsteps grew closer, more than one person by the sound of it. I didn't think much of it until I heard the humming. A chill ran through me, knowing the source.

Lars and Ace.

CHAPTER 18

Lars and Ace appeared among the trees, coming toward us. Ace wore a lopsided smile, Lars an empty gaze.

I found myself clutching my fist, resisting the urge to remove my scarf.

Seriously, Nirah, knock it off. We're not killing anyone.

Nirah shuddered in what felt like disappointment.

Ace strolled over to us, the tilt in his saunter reminding me of Reed. He looked up at the cloudy skies, his crooked smile growing. Sweat beaded around his face. A few of the beads slid down his cheeks and neck, soaking into the top of his red tee. "Lovely day, isn't it?" Ace's melodic voice made me shiver.

Leya folded her arms and looked Ace up and down. "Are you for real? This is the absolute worst." She blew out a long breath. "I could really use a beach right now. Or even a pool."

Ace's gaze went to Leya, causing her to shrink into me. His lips twitched in amusement. He was turning more into Reed every day. Or maybe he'd always been that way, but with Reed out of the picture, I could focus more on Ace.

Although, Reed wasn't out of the picture. Not entirely.

Lars whistled, the tune chilling. His milky eyes were fixed on Graham, though he seemed to be looking right through him.

Ace tucked his thumbs into the top of his pants, on either side of his large belt buckle. "Tessa, darlin', we need to speak with Reed."

"He's dead," Leya said.

Lars tilted his head to the side, his emotionless eyes settling on Leya. "Are any of us ever really alive? Maybe we are all floating through each day, never really grounded in life."

"What does that even mean?" Graham whispered under his breath.

Ace leaned toward me. "Yes, my dear brother has departed, but beautiful Tessa here can reach out."

Graham shook his head. "She's not doing a ss...séance for you."

"Ss...séance," Lars repeated. He bounced on the tip of his toes, his arms spread out, flicking the air in sharp thrusts. He whistled a deep melody, synchronizing the tune with his movements.

I looked at Ace and pointed my finger at Lars. "Does he come with a muzzle?"

Ace completely ignored my question. "I need you to ask Reed something for me."

"It doesn't work like that," I said.

"And even if it did," Leya said, one hand on her hip, "she wouldn't help the likes of *you*." Her tone was firm, but she shook next to me, her other hand clinging to the side of my shirt.

Ace clasped his hands together. "But this is oh so important."

"I'm sure whatever it is can wait until you join Reed in hell," I said.

Graham choked on a laugh. Nirah wriggled inside me in a lively mood.

Ace's face remained serious. "Oh, but it can't. This is of the utmost importance."

"Listen, Ace—" I started.

"Everything is of the utmost importance to you." Reed's silky voice cut through the forest.

I spun around to find Reed's ghostly figure leaning against a birch tree, his feet crossed at his ankles.

Reed looked toward the sky. "It seems a tad too warm for summer, no?" His image flickered until he disappeared.

"Reed?" I took a step toward the tree.

"Reed?" Ace appeared beside me, so much hope in his tone. "Is my brother here?"

I furrowed my eyebrows. "You didn't see him?" I pointed at the tree. "Just there?"

"Wait, Reed was here?" Leya asked, clinging to my arm. "Like, here, here?" Her frantic gaze swept the area.

I turned to her, a frown forming on my lips. "You didn't see him, either?"

Reed had shown himself to others before, in my house. Was he stronger there because the sword was there?

Reed's image flickered back, standing right beside me. I jumped into the air, my hand flying to my chest.

"Something's wrong," Reed whispered, a fear in his voice that surprised me. "Something's very, very wrong."

"What do you mean?" I asked, keeping my voice low like him.

Reed checked over his shoulder. "This isn't right." His entire being went staticky like there was a bad connection. "He's ... closer ... help ... ." His tortured words cut in and out, along with his body.

"Reed? What's going on?" I was surprised at the worry in my tone. Worry about his well-being, which made no sense.

Ace's face appeared before me, way too close for comfort. "Is my brother here? I have so many——"

Placing my hand on his face, I shoved Ace away from me, turning my focus to Reed's crackling form.

"Talk to me, Reed," I said. "What's going on over there?"

Reed's head whipped back and forth, the motion almost unnatural, turning farther than normal. "They're ... coming ... ."

"Tessa!"

The voice startled me, and I found myself turning in circles, frantically searching for the source. I hadn't heard that sweet voice in months.

"Corrine?"

"Tessa!" Corrine's terrified voice echoed all around me. "Save us!"

"Corrine!"

"What's going on?" Leya asked, tugging on my arm. "What are you hearing? Seeing?"

I turned back to Reed. "Corrine is with you?"

Reed's flickering head bobbled. "Yes ... others ... died ... here ... ."

His head cocked to the side, almost like it was broken, the angle abnormal. Reed's face changed, morphing into another man with red eyes, the skin on the top of his head stretching until he formed two horns.

"I'll be seeing you soon, Tessa," the deep voice rumbled, causing every hair on my body to rise, goosebumps breaking out all over. With a wicked grin, he winked at me before he let out a breath, the force sending me flying backward, my back colliding with a tree.

The last thing I saw before I blacked out was Corrine's beautiful face, sobbing and full of fear.

When I came to, Leya and Graham were kneeling at my side, fussing over me. I could hear Lars whistling in the background, the muddy earth beneath his feet squishing like he was dancing.

Ace's face appeared above me, his empty eyes blinking quickly. "What did my brother want?"

Leya hissed at him. "Back off, Ace. No one cares about your stupid brother." Her gaze swept to me, her eyes softening. "Tessa? Are you okay?"

Groaning, I let Graham and Leya help me into a sitting position. My back throbbed in pain.

I wet my dry lips. "Looks like things are getting worse in The Gray. Bad enough that even Reed is terrified." I looked at Leya. "Corrine is there with him."

We sat there in silence, taking that in. Corrine was stuck in The Gray. With Reed. Andras.

It changed everything.

Leya finally broke the silence. "Did Reed say anything else?"

I wrapped my arms around my legs. "Reed's words kept cutting off, so I couldn't catch everything. All I caught was: "Yes. Others died here.""

"Others?" Graham whispered. "Who else is with them?"

"I don't know." I thought back to when all those people screamed my name, screamed for help. Was it everyone stuck in The Gray?

Leya rubbed my arm. "Maybe everyone that has died in Willow Marsh?"

Graham's face went pale, his whisper barely audible. "Greg." He swallowed. "Trenton."

Greg was Graham's older brother, and one of Reed's many victims.

Trenton was Graham's friend. He and his family disappeared months before Dad and I moved to Willow Marsh. We'd bought their house.

And I'd found their bodies in the woods.

All of them killed by Reed.

My body trembled at the thought of all of them being stuck in The Gray. I really didn't care about getting Reed out of there, but if Corrine, Greg, Trenton, and all those other poor souls were stuck there, I had to do something about it.

I looked at Leya. "We need to talk to Amá."

CHAPTER 19

Mrs. Morales couldn't meet us until later that evening. I parked in the dirt outside her workplace. She had a tiny hut on the outskirts of town for her business. She was a medium. She'd wanted to build her hut near the center of the magic in Willow Marsh—the picturesque clearing above where the crypt was located—but she couldn't get a building permit. She settled with another high magic area, right near the east entrance to Willow Marsh.

Seconds after getting out of the car, my tank stuck to my skin from sweat, the heat stifling. My thick hair was pulled back with one of Amá's scarves. Leya had her braided hair in a bun, keeping it off her neck. Illinois got hot, but not like this.

The night was quiet, the only sound coming from Leya's flip-flops.

"I should have worn shoes," she grumbled. "I don't want to ruin the vibe."

"Just don't walk during the séance, and you'll be fine."

She shoved my arm, a smile on her thick, glossy lips.

The door to the hut was open, a sheer curtain billowing out with the breeze. We pushed it aside and stepped inside.

The first thing I noticed was how much cooler it was in the hut. The temperature had dropped by at least twenty degrees, but I couldn't hear an air conditioning unit going.

The hut was a simple square with bookshelves on three of the walls. They were full of knickknacks and books, mostly dealing with the other side. In the center of the hut was a short willow tree—like an actual tree—a round piece of glass mounted to the top to create a table. Four tree stumps surrounded the table.

The only light came from string lights running along the edge of the ceiling, all the way around the hut.

Rita occupied one of the stumps. Her brown, curly hair hung to her chin, her resident spectacles perched on top of her head. Everything about Rita was soft. Her features, her presence, and her voice. She put me at ease every time I saw her.

Around her neck was a gold chain with a single pearl, matching her wedding ring. She saw me eying the necklace and touched a hand to it.

Mrs. Morales sniffed, bringing my attention to her. She had long, black hair going down to her waist. Her brown eyes and facial features reminded me of Corrine. They looked so much alike.

I wasn't sure if I should tell her Corrine was stuck in The Gray. Maybe I'd wait until after the séance.

She wiped at her nose with a handkerchief. "Sorry, my emotions..."

Rita patted her hand. "We're all so sad about Chloe. I just hope they find her alive."

Mrs. Morales dabbed under her eyes, wiping away the tears. "They will." She waved her handkerchief and then came to me, taking me into her arms. "Tessa, it's so good to see you." She pulled back and placed her hands on my cheeks. "How are you, dear?"

"I've been better," I said. "At least I can say my life is certainly not dull here in Willow Marsh."

She kissed my cheek and then hugged Leya. "Look at the two of you girls. So bright and beautiful." She cupped her hand under Leya's chin. "You have a bright future ahead of you. Just stay focused, and you will soar."

Leya smiled. "I like the sound of that."

Mrs. Morales motioned to the stumps. "Come. Sit down. We have a big night ahead of us." She swished out her flowy skirt with a flourish as she took her seat.

I held out my hand so she could see my ring. "Before we start, I was hoping you could look at my ring. It has basically suctioned itself to me, and I'm not sure why."

She took my hands in hers, examining the ring. Something flickered in her eyes, but I couldn't quite tell what. She softly smiled. "I think I may know, but let me do some research before I go saying anything. Now, I know some of your story, Tessa, but we need to start at the beginning. Back to the night you lost your mom and brother."

I started back in surprise. I wasn't expecting to go into so much detail about my life. I thought we would just reach out to Amá and see if she knew what Andras' plans were for Willow Marsh.

Leya crossed her legs. "Well, we better get comfortable then. There's a lot to tell."

Mrs. Morales got up for a moment to get us all bottles of water. When she sat down, her face was a mix of serene and business. She pointed her index finger at Leya, showing off a gold ring with a large ruby on top. "Make sure she doesn't leave anything out."

"Don't worry," Leya said. "That's why she brings me everywhere she goes."

All three of them turned to me, so I dove into my story. It had become easier to tell now that the truth was out there. Me taking a handful of anxiety pills, driving through a bad storm with my mom and brother in the car, a deer suddenly being in the road, me swerving to miss it, the car rolling. Neither my mom nor my brother made it out alive. Just me and the scar on my hand did.

I'd had nightmares for months, but after everything with Ellington, Reed, and the crypt—me destroying the box that would connect the living world with the dead—the nightmares had ended. They no longer needed to haunt me.

Amá had been there in the crypt. She told me the crash wasn't my fault and that I needed to forgive myself. She let me know that she and Felix were in a safe place, and that everything was going to be okay. She'd also informed me that I belonged in Willow Marsh.

I'd never doubted her since.

Surprisingly, Leya only had to break in a few times with some more details. I spilled everything that had gone on.

When we'd got to Corrine's death, Mrs. Morales put her handkerchief to her mouth, choking back her sobs. I couldn't imagine what it was like to lose a child.

How on earth would I tell her that her daughter was stuck between realms?

Mrs. Morales set a bunch of red candles on the table, lighting each of them. We'd tried to help, but she shooed us out of the way, saying she needed to be the one to do it. I think it was her ritual that she didn't want to break.

The smell of cinnamon wafted up from the candles, filling the hut with the scent. The four of us clasped hands, and Mrs. Morales began.

CHAPTER 20

Mrs. Morales took a deep breath, her eyes closed, and tilted her chin up. "Ariela Isaacson, we come to you tonight with full hearts and minds, only the purest of intentions." She paused, letting the words sink in. "Ariela, we need your help. Willow Marsh needs your help. If you're here, give us a sign."

We waited in silence. Minutes passed with only the sound of our breathing and the smell of cinnamon greeting us.

What if Amá couldn't come? If she had fully crossed over, could she come back? What if she couldn't hear us? I wanted to speak up, say something to catch her attention—maybe my voice would help—but I didn't want to risk anything bad happening.

Amá and I had always been connected in a powerful way. No matter where she was, I didn't doubt she'd be able to feel me and know I was reaching out to her. But there was a chance that she was busy in heaven. Our trial might have seemed so minuscule compared to what she faced every day.

Suddenly, the temperature dropped another twenty

degrees. Goosebumps broke out along my skin. My breaths came out in little, white clouds, just like everyone else at the table. Leya shivered, her hand shaking in mine.

"Someone is here," Mrs. Morales whispered. She raised her voice. "Whoever is there, please make yourself known."

Air swirled around me, my ponytail whipping with the wind. The family ring on my finger heated, warming my cold skin.

Tessa. The whisper of my name brushed along my ear, the sound sweet and motherly.

Yet, it wasn't my mom. I didn't know how, but I knew it wasn't her. I opened my mouth to say something, but Mrs. Morales tugged on my hand, warning me to stay quiet.

"Ariela." Mrs. Morales paused, understanding crossing over her face. She kept her voice calm and even. "Whoever is there, is something bad coming to Willow Marsh?"

Yes. The female voice echoed around the hut.

I glanced down at the willow tree under the table to see the leaves frosting over. Leya and I exchanged a look, worried at what it meant.

"Is Andras behind it?" Mrs. Morales asked.

Yes.

"Can it be stopped?" Mrs. Morales was leaning forward, eager for the response.

Silence.

Is that a no? Leya mouthed to me.

Behind me, a book fell off a shelf and thumped onto the ground. I tried to turn around without letting go of Leya and Mrs. Morales' hands.

A breeze swept into the hut, rapidly flipping the pages of the book until it abruptly stopped. All at once, the candles went out, the remaining light coming from the light strands hanging around the border of the hut. They flickered a few times before they settled, getting brighter than they had been when we first arrived.

Mrs. Morales stared at the lights on the ceiling. Her eyebrow quirked in surprise.

The temperature went back to normal, the branches of the willow tree thawing out, little drops of water landing on the wood floor of the hut.

Once Mrs. Morales gave me a head nod, I dropped their hands and picked up the book, bringing it back to the table.

Rita and Leya moved the candles out of the way so I could set the book in the middle.

Mrs. Morales checked the spine of the book. "Myths and Legends of Willow Marsh." She smoothed out the book, reading the page the book had opened to. "It's the legend of the lake."

Rita nodded. "Oh, yes. A legend that has been disputed over the years." She glanced at Mrs. Morales. "But I've never questioned it. I've come to accept that anything is possible in this town."

"What's the legend?" I asked.

Mrs. Morales took a drink from her water bottle. "It begins well before the Civil War, well before Willow Marsh was founded. All the way back to the sixteen hundreds.

"There was a group of settlers that broke off from the Virginia Company in Jamestown. They traveled all the way into the territory now known as West Virginia. They found this quaint little area with a beautiful lake. With all the birch trees surrounding it, they named it Birch Lake."

"Which is now Willow Marsh," I said, stroking the side of my ring.

"Yes," Mrs. Morales said. "The settlers slowly built a community here, prospering from the luck they had with the land."

Leya folded her arms on the table. "Like, because of the magic here?"

Mrs. Morales gave a brisk nod. "Exactly. The soil was rich and plentiful, the lake clean and pristine. They thought they'd stumbled across Eden." Her eyes were unfocused on the book. "In a way, they had. But just like in the Garden of Eden, a serpent showed up, tainting the minds in the town. Neighbors turned on one another, rage burning in everyone's hearts. They messed with each other's crops until all the food was ruined."

"Then things turned savage." Rita took the reading glasses on her head and set them on her nose, turning the book toward her so she could flip the page. "The hunger drove the residents mad. There were murders, adultery, greed, and jealousy."

"That's awful," Leya murmured.

"It gets worse," Mrs. Morales said, her voice somber. "Much worse." She nodded at Rita, who flipped another page in the book.

Rita pushed the book toward Leya and me so we could see it. There was a painting of the lake, surrounded by little children. They were all clasping hands, their eyes vacant.

"One night, all the adults woke to a strange humming coming from outside," Mrs. Morales went on. "They slowly gathered outside, but not after noticing that their children were not in their homes. They followed the humming, taking them to the lake. The water boiled, steam rising from it. They watched as their children entered the water, faces clenched in pain, but none of the children turned back. It was like they were hypnotized."

I put a hand to my mouth, sick to my stomach.

"Most of the parents ran after their kids," Rita said. "They dove into the lake, trying to rescue them, but it swallowed them all up."

"The others ran," Mrs. Morales said. "They gathered their things and fled in the night. One gentleman stayed behind, writing an account of everything that had happened, and condemning the land, before he, too, left."

"Some say it was bad luck that drove the children to the lake." Rita scratched the top of her forehead, right below her tight curls. "Some say it was Andras." She opened her mouth and then paused. She shot an unsure look at Mrs. Morales before finally speaking. "There is another part of the legend that isn't in any of the books."

Mrs. Morales nodded. "Yes, I've heard it, too."

"What is it?" I asked.

Mrs. Morales leaned forward. "Rumor has it, a coven of witches came to the area and sealed off the lake, putting a protection spell over it."

Leya blew out a loud breath. "Now there are witches involved. What else does this town have in store for us? Vampires?"

Rita tugged at the pearl dangling from her necklace and smiled softly. "Vampires aren't real."

Leya leaned toward me. "A hundred bucks and a lifetime of foot massages says they are."

I rolled my eyes but didn't take the bet. Willow Marsh was full of surprises.

"The spell supposedly stopped Andras from ever crossing into our world," Mrs. Morales said.

If that were true, how was Andras here now? Did someone break the spell?

"No one dared come close to this area again." Rita folded her arms on the table.

Mrs. Morales scoffed. "Not until Roy Ellington showed up. He thought himself greater than a legend."

That didn't surprise me. The man was arrogant.

"I also think he liked the challenge," Rita said. "He probably thought he could fix it so they wouldn't fall into the same trap the settlers had."

"How do you fix magic?" I asked. "Or basically Satan himself?"

"You don't." Mrs. Morales' gaze went to the book. "But you can fight against them."

I followed her gaze, looking at the picture, all those children walking into their doom. "Do you think Andras is planning a repeat? That this could happen to all the children in town?"

The town needed to be evacuated. If there were only a handful of us left to fight the darkness, we would have fewer casualties.

There was the option of all of us walking away, but wouldn't the cycle just keep on repeating itself? If we had the chance to stop it, shouldn't we take it? Not to mention, we'd be leaving Chloe, and all the others stuck in The Gray, behind.

Mrs. Morales shut the book. "I think we need to be prepared for the worst. We'll need to do some research and see if there's any way to fight this." Her gaze swept over all her books. "There has to be something here that could help us."

"Couldn't we, like, I don't know, drain the lake or something?" Leya played with a few of her braids that hung from her ponytail. "No one can drown themselves if there's no water, right?"

Mrs. Morales sighed. "Unfortunately, I don't think it's that simple. I think the epicenter is below the lake. With no water, Andras would just find other elements to work with. He could start a fire and completely destroy the town."

Leya made an 'O' with her mouth.

"That would be much worse," I said.

Rita stood, stretching her arms above her head. "Well, if we can't stop whatever is coming, maybe burning Willow Marsh to the ground would be the only option."

Burn Willow Marsh. That would ruin so many lives.

There had to be another way.

CHAPTER 21

The next morning, I recounted everything to Sheriff Hayes. It was weird to talk to him so openly about it and have him attentive and offering suggestions.

Sheriff Hayes sat back in his chair and sighed. His gaze went to the window. "I hate that it's come to this, but maybe we should evacuate. I'll hold a town meeting tomorrow tonight." He looked at me. "Do you think your father would be on board with that and be at my side? It might be a good way for him to garner votes."

"Why, Sheriff, it sounds like you're backing my dad." I thought it would be difficult to sway the sheriff to our side, but maybe not.

He scratched at the stubble on his chin. Dark rings were under his eyes. This whole thing must have been eating him alive. "Willow Marsh has been run the same way for years: through fear and money. And look where it's got us. More deaths than I care to admit. A divided town. Greed and bribery." He clasped his fingers together and rested his hands against his stomach. "We can't continue to survive like this. We need change. We need someone not corrupted by this town. Someone without connections that will sway their way of thinking."

"Make Willow Marsh your safe haven."

He nodded. "Your dad picked the perfect slogan for his campaign. That's what we need right now."

His phone rang, and by the expression on his face, it wasn't going to be a happy call. I tried to tune out his end of the conversation, not wanting to eavesdrop. I took the moment to stand, going to his bookcase and looking at the pictures of his family.

My insides coiled at the sight of Blake and his step-mom in a picture. The first time I'd met her, I'd been half-dressed in Blake's room. Definitely not the greatest first impression. For a while after, she'd glare at me when she saw me around town. One day, though, it stopped. She started looking at me with sympathy. It made me wonder if Blake or the sheriff had said something to her.

Still, it was weird to see her.

"Ready for your first ride-a-long?" Sherriff Hayes appeared at my side. "We got a call about a situation at the Harrisons."

I held in a groan. Not really the people I wanted to see, but there was still a spark of curiosity, wondering what had happened.

"Guess so." I smoothed out my blouse. I'd opted for the bun like I'd seen Gracie do. She'd complimented me when I'd shown up this morning, a twinkle in her aging eyes.

When we walked out into the foyer, Gracie offered a sympathetic smile. "Good luck at the Harrisons. You'll need it."

The sheriff tipped his hat to her, and together, we left the precinct.

I'd never been by the Harrisons before. I avoided it at all costs. It would just bring back memories that I didn't want to relive. Plus, Ace and Lars still lived there, and they were two of the creepiest men I'd ever met.

They had a decent-sized home, close to the woods, and on the complete opposite side of town as my house.

It was built like a cabin, the light wood kept in good condition. The two-story structure, from the outside, looked rather cozy. They had a long, gravel driveway leading up to the front of the house and a three-car detached garage off to the side.

Ace Harrison sat on the porch swing, his arm resting on the back of it, one foot kicked up, the other on the ground, slowly pushing the swing forward and backward. His lopsided grin greeted us, his eyes cloudy.

"You brought a guest," Ace cooed. "How lucky for us."

The front door banged open, and Lars stepped out, his emotionless eyes landing on the sheriff, his head quirked to the side. His thin white T-shirt had a couple of holes.

"Where is your backup?" Lars asked, voice monotone.

Sheriff Hayes adjusted his holster. "I didn't think the break-in required more than me."

A break-in? I hadn't pressed the issue on the drive over with the sheriff, so I still didn't know what had gone down. Who would break into the Harrison's house, and what could they possibly want?

Lars' empty eyes turned to me, grazing me over like the object I knew he saw me as. It was how he viewed everything. Just items that could be taken apart and thrown away like trash. I instinctively took a step back, creating a buffer zone with the creep.

"What are you doing here?" Lars asked, still flat and detached.

"She's my intern," Sheriff Hayes said sharply. "Why don't you walk me through what happened?"

Lars' tilted head slowly turned back to the sheriff. "Follow me."

It took a lot of effort to get my feet to move. I didn't relish the thought of stepping into the Harrison household. When Ace stepped up behind me, close enough that I could feel his heat, it made my decision for me, and I hurried into the house. I should have brought mace or something to protect myself.

The inside of their house was typical for a hunter. Animal rugs lined the wooden floors. Deer, buck, bear, and even buffalo heads filled the space on all the walls. It smelled like the woods, sap from trees, and wild animals.

The front room had a high, arched ceiling, going up two stories. Flannel blankets were draped over the leather couches. A brick fireplace was on the east wall, the brick reaching all the way to the ceiling. Antlers created the chandelier that hung down.

I stopped in front of a massive bear head on the wall, the mouth wide open, teeth razor sharp. Somehow, the eyes held a bit of life, like the bear wanted to devour me.

"This is my favorite part." Lars stood to the side of me, his hands stuffed in his jeans' pockets, his calculating eyes taking in the bear. "Most people like the thrill of the hunt. I prefer the moment we get them back here, and I can drag them into the garage and take them apart piece by piece." He stroked the side of the bear's head. "They're a fascinating puzzle, bears." He turned to me. "Have you met one?"

"A bear?" I shook my head. "Can't say that I have."

He nodded just once like this was a completely normal conversation, and he hadn't heard the sarcasm in my voice. "They're amazing." He leaned his body to the side, getting closer to me. "It's tricky to keep them full of life when they're dead, but it's all in the eyes. They're the window to one's soul."

I glanced up at his pale eyes that lacked emotion and knew exactly what he meant. The man's soul was as empty as his gaze. His lips pulled into a tight smile.

When the sheriff cleared his throat, Lars spun around on his heel—hands still in pockets—and headed toward the kitchen, the sheriff following.

Ace clasped his hands behind his back and leaned toward me. "I prefer the hunt. When you're skinning an animal, you know what you're going to get. There's no element of surprise. But when you're out in the woods, hunting your prey, there's a buzzing excitement of wondering when you're going to spot it and if you'll be able to catch it. Will it outsmart you? Or will you outsmart it?"

"What did Reed prefer?" I asked.

Ace stood tall, sharp chin tilted up, pondering. He thought long and hard about it until he finally spoke. "All of it, I think. The hunt, the skinning, and the stuffing."

That didn't surprise me.

Ace swept out his arm, motioning me to head into the kitchen. I hurried in there, not liking the thought of being alone with Ace for an extended period of time.

Lars stood near the back door. Arms folded, his feet were shoulder width apart as he watched the sheriff work.

Sheriff Hayes was squatting near the door, inspecting the shattered glass that covered the tiled floor. There was a fist-sized hole in the window on the door.

"No blood. They wore gloves." Sheriff Hayes stood back up. "Do you have any cameras?"

"No," Lars said. "We never like to see what's coming."

The sheriff twerked an eyebrow at that but didn't say anything. "And neither of you heard anything?"

"I fell asleep with the TV on," Lars said.

Ace moseyed up next to me, way too close for comfort. But I stood my ground, not wanting to show any weakness. These men were trained to sniff that out.

"And I had my white noise playing," Ace said.

I looked at him. "White noise?"

Ace nodded. "Yes. I need something to calm the soul so I can sleep. My preferred sound is a rapid-firing machine gun."

The sheriff and I exchanged a perturbed look. That was beyond disturbing.

"Was anything taken?" Sheriff Hayes asked, breaking the uncomfortable silence.

Lars took off without a word, heading through the laundry room to get to the other side of the house. There was an office in the back corner, more stuffed dead critters decorating the space. A large, wooden table sat in the middle, taking up most of the room. Built-in shelves lined the bottom halves of the walls.

Lars approached an elk head, pulling it away from the wall and revealing a safe. Blocking it with his body, Lars spun the lock, finding the right combination and opening it up. He backed away so we could see.

Manila folders, guns, and trinkets, like watches and rings, were stuffed inside.

"What are we looking at?" Sheriff Hayes asked.

Lars kinked his head, confused by the sheriff's question. "Why, something is missing."

"What is it?" I asked. And how did they even notice? There was so much stuff in there.

"A memory card," Lars said. It was so brief, but I swore his eyes flitted over to me when he said that.

I thought back to when I'd found that camcorder under the floorboards at the Willow Marsh Inn. It had footage showing Reed and his brothers killing Delilah Morgan because they thought she was a descendant of Joseph Walker when in reality, I was the descendant.

I'd hid the memory card in my room months ago, but I hadn't checked the spot since. He couldn't have been talking about the same card. If he was, that meant he'd taken it from me, and now someone had taken it from him.

Impossible.

"What was on the card?" Sheriff Hayes asked.

Lars' lips twitched, but he didn't say anything.

Ace had to speak up. "Just a camping trip with us and Reed. It's one of our last memories of him, and we'd like the card back."

If the camping trip he was referring to was them dragging Delilah out into the woods, torturing, and then killing her, then we had very different ideas of camping.

"Can you get it back for us?" Ace asked.

"I'll see what I can find," Sheriff Hayes said. "But there isn't much to go off here. I can brush the safe for prints, but like I stated before, I'm pretty sure the intruder wore gloves."

They would have been stupid not to. Although, breaking into the Harrisons was the epitome of stupid. You'd have to have a death wish.

"Wonderful." Ace grinned. "Would you two like some lemonade? Special family recipe."

CHAPTER 22

Thank goodness the sheriff turned down the invitation for lemonade. We got into his cruiser and pulled away from the Harrison's house.

"That place gives me the creeps," Sheriff Hayes said, looking at the house through his rearview mirror.

"Those men give me the creeps." I shook a shiver out of me. "I might have an idea of what memory card they're talking about, but we need to stop by my house to see if it's possible."

The sheriff stole a glance in my direction. "Would you like to enlighten me?"

I'd never mentioned the footage to the sheriff. After Reed had died, I felt like justice had been served. And, honestly, I just wanted it all over. Bringing out the tape would indict Lars and Ace, which would be two more Harrisons after me. One was more than enough.

I let out a breath. "Greg Dixon accidentally recorded Reed Harrison killing Delilah Morgan."

Sheriff Hayes' jaw tightened. "And you're just *now* telling me this?"

Because I didn't know if I could trust the sheriff to do the right thing. The Harrisons had him wrapped around their finger back then.

"I thought about it," I said, "but what difference would it make? Reed is dead."

"It's still evidence of a crime, and both Lars and Ace were involved." He flipped on his lights and raced toward my house, weaving around cars like we were in a high-speed chase.

"It doesn't matter how fast we get there," I said, holding onto the dashboard. "It's either there, or it's not."

He didn't slow down, and he didn't say anything.

Once we pulled into our driveway, he slammed on the brakes, the tires squealing on the concrete.

I ran straight for my room and dove into my closet, crawling to the back corner where I kept a box of valuables. When I found it, I pulled it out and set it on my bed. Sheriff Hayes watched from over my shoulder as I opened the box and checked its contents.

Amá's wedding ring was still in its case, along with all her expensive jewelry. If someone actually took the card, they passed up on all these valuables. I dug to the bottom of the box where the memory card should have been.

"It's gone," I said.

One of the Harrisons had broken into my house, came into my room, gone through my closet, touched all Amá's jewelry, and then took the card. The thought of their grubby hands on her jewelry disgusted me more than them taking the card.

The sheriff sat down on my bed. "Tell me exactly what's on the tape. Don't leave a single detail out, even if it's minuscule."

"I can do you one better."

After putting the box back in the closet, I pulled out my laptop and found the video, playing it for the sheriff.

Greg had gone hiking, using his camcorder to record the scenery. He'd heard a gunshot and went running in that direction, which in hindsight, was incredibly stupid. He should have run in the opposite direction. But he'd found Reed, Lars, and Ace towering over Delilah on the ground. They thought she'd been a descendent of Joseph Walker, one of the founders of Willow Marsh. But she wasn't. So, they shot her in cold blood.

Then they killed Greg. But not until after he was able to escape and hide the camera with the footage.

Sheriff Hayes looked away from the screen and popped a piece of nicotine gum into his mouth. "Who else would want that video? And how would they know the Harrisons had it?"

"I have no idea." I shut my laptop and leaned against the bed. "I didn't even know they had it."

"Send me a copy of the footage. That way I can open an investigation and get it sent to the state crime lab for authentication." Sheriff Hayes stood. "How about I drop you off at your dad's headquarters? Tell him about the town meeting tonight and ask if he'll join me."

"What are you going to do in the meantime?" I asked.

"See if I can figure out who has the card before Lars and Ace do."

If he didn't, whoever stole the memory card was as good as dead.

❧

Dad had rented space on Main Street. It was abuzz with all his volunteers, some chatting on the phones with residents, trying to drum up donations, others working on flyers and handouts.

Marcel jogged over when he saw me come in. He held out a small, wooden ukulele with strings and all. "I whittled this for you."

I took it in my hands, looking it over. It was perfect. Felix loved to play the ukulele. I still had his and would play it from time to time, but I wasn't nearly as good as him.

"Thank you," I said, hugging Marcel. "This is amazing."

He just shrugged it off. "I had some free time the other night." He looked down, shifting uncomfortably like he wanted to say more, but wasn't sure if he should. He rubbed the back of his neck, the short sleeve of his dress shirt riding up, revealing his tattoo. It was just a simple design, nothing flashy or meaningful from what I could tell.

He saw me staring at it and tugged his sleeve down. "Biggest mistake of my life. I swear Jade can talk me into anything."

"Does it symbolize anything?"

"No, which makes it even worse," Marcel grumbled.

I glanced over at my dad, who was talking in his small office on the phone. It might be a few minutes before I could speak with him. It was as good a time as any to ask Marcel about his relationship with Jade. I couldn't get a word out of her.

"How are things going with Jade?" I asked, keeping my voice low. There were lots of people around us, but they were hard at work, not paying us any mind.

Marcel sighed, checked over his shoulder, and then pulled me off to the side, away from all the traffic. "Things have been...rough lately. Jade's been on edge."

I tucked the ukulele under my arm. "Jade's always on edge."

"Not like this." Marcel adjusted his square-rimmed glasses. "Before Corrine passed away, Jade was snarky with me, yeah, but only in public. She was a whole different person when we were alone. But now, she never turns the snark off."

I didn't want to overstep my bounds, but it felt like Marcel needed to talk about this honestly with someone. "Why did you and Jade get together in the first place?"

He leaned against the wall, folding his arms. "It's not like we have a lot of options around here. It started as just kissing, but then we were labeled a couple by everyone at school, so we ran with it." He glanced to the side, a far-off look in his eyes. "I think Corrine's death has made Jade rethink things in her life. She wants to live life to the fullest."

"But she can't do that with you."

He shook his head. "Nope. We're just too different. It was fine when we were in middle school when we were still trying to figure out who we were." He rubbed the back of his neck, swallowing. "Honestly, I'm terrified to break up with her. I think it has to be *her* idea."

"Maybe I can plant some seeds in her head or something." I touched his arm. "It'll work out in the end."

He kept rubbing the back of his neck like he was nervous. "Has, uh, Leya ever said anything about me?"

"She talks about you a lot," I said, trying to hold back my smile. "But if you mean in a romantic way, no." His face fell, so I quickly went on. "Not because she *doesn't* like you like that, just because you're Jade's boyfriend. She would never do that to Jade."

His eyes lit up with hope. "Maybe I should just break up with Jade. Get it over with."

"No. I think you're right about it having to be her idea. Especially with the state she's in right now. I'll work on it, I promise. Just keep your hands to yourself in the meantime."

Marcel held up his palms. "I wouldn't dream of cheating on Jade. Or anyone."

"And that's what makes you a classy guy."

I smelled Dad's cologne before I saw him. He came up and side-hugged me. "Tessa, did you come to help?"

"Ha, no. You know politics isn't my thing." I straightened out his baby blue tie. "But I am here on behalf of the sheriff."

"Why don't we talk in my office then?" Dad said.

I smiled at Marcel before I joined Dad in his office. He closed the door behind me. I set the ukulele down on his desk and then picked up the frame. It held a picture of our family the Christmas before we lost Amá and Felix.

"What does the sheriff want?" Dad asked, taking a seat in his chair.

I set down the frame and hopped onto the desk, my legs hanging over the side. "He wants to evacuate Willow Marsh." As Dad's eyes widened, I told him all about the legend of Birch Lake and how we fear a repeat will happen.

By the end, Dad was slumped in his seat, running his hand down his face. "Where would everyone go?"

"That, I don't know," I said. "An extended camping trip? I think the most important thing is getting them away from the lake. And this town."

Dad loosened his tie. "And you're planning on staying." He said it as a statement, not a question.

"I think I have a better chance of stopping it than anyone else." I looked at my family ring, caressing the side with my thumb.

Dad's gaze went to the ring as well. "Do you even know how?"

"Not yet. Mrs. Morales is going to do some research." I hated the next words out of my mouth. "And with Reed's help, we might be able to figure it out."

"I hate this so much," Dad grumbled.

I leaned forward, placing my hand on his arm. "I know, but we only have two options here. Walk away or fight to protect Willow Marsh. I know you love this town as much as I do."

"I do. But how do we even know something that big is going to happen? Reed could be playing with you."

"He may be using me, but that doesn't explain Chloe being abducted, the boiling lake, or all the lightning bugs exploding. Something sinister is going on whether we like it or not."

When the word *sinister* crossed my mouth, Nirah stirred inside me, coming to life. She slithered out from behind my heart and looped around my throat, squeezing a little. My hand went to my throat at the same time the earth rumbled, shaking the entire building. The picture frame rattled to the end of the table, falling off before I could catch it.

"We need to get out of here," Dad said, trying to walk through the earthquake. He kept stumbling on the way to the door, the quake getting stronger with each passing second.

I hopped down from the table and tried to move toward Dad, but the ground roared, making it difficult to move. I held onto the table, trying not to fall over. Dad held out his hand for me, but he was too far away.

Cracks and bangs sounded outside the office, furniture crashing to the ground. People's panicked screams echoed out on the main floor. A filing cabinet fell in front of the door to Dad's office with a heavy thud, blocking our exit.

The earthquake stopped as quickly as it had started. Everyone stayed frozen for a moment, waiting for more.

Once we thought the worst had passed, Marcel and some of the other workers went to move the filing cabinet so we could escape Dad's office.

I stared at Dad, worried that it wasn't a regular earthquake. The look on Dad's face told me he was thinking the same thing.

My phone vibrated, and I looked down to see Leya's face lighting up the screen. "Hey."

"What was that?" Leya screeched.

"An earthquake?" I didn't mean to form it in a question. It just came out that way.

Leya huffed. "You know that wasn't an earthquake. Nothing in this town is natural." She took a long breath. "There's some damage at the house. Broken furniture and stuff. You might want to come check it out."

"We're on our way." I ended the call.

I snatched the ukulele from the floor and checked it out. A string had popped loose, but other than that, it was fine.

As soon as we were freed from Dad's office, we headed out of the building, climbing in Dad's car and hurrying home. Lots of people were outside of their homes and workplaces, looking around in fear and confusion. With how crazy the earthquake had been, I expected a lot more damage, but so far, everything we passed looked minimal. Nothing that couldn't be repaired or replaced.

I texted Graham and Jade to make sure they were okay. Graham came back with a simple "yes," while Jade texted me a thumbs-up emoji.

Leya was waiting on the front porch, holding two pieces of wood close to her chest. As soon as I got out of the car, she spoke.

"The sign broke." She sniffed. "The one I made for you with your family's motto."

I rushed up the porch steps and carefully took one of the pieces from Leya. It had cracked down the middle.

Dad came up behind me, looking over my shoulder. "All we need is some glue, and we'll have it back together in no time." He ran his hand down his face. "How bad is the damage inside?"

Leya shrugged. "Some broken dishes and lamps, stuff like that. Not sure about any damage to the house itself."

My phone buzzed with an incoming call from the sheriff.

I quickly answered. "Hello?"

"You better meet me at the lake," Sheriff Hayes said, his tone defeated.

CHAPTER 23

We had to park way back from the lot near the lake. They had the area taped off, not allowing anyone through. A cluster of citizens stood just beyond the tape, all trying to get Sheriff Hayes' attention.

As we approached, a deputy lifted the tape so we could duck underneath. When Leya tried to go through, the man held up a hand. "Only the Isaacsons are allowed back here."

Leya clenched her fists, glaring at the man. "I'm a member of the family."

The deputy furrowed his eyebrows in confusion, his gaze wandering over Leya's pink shirt that said *Haitian and Proud.* He opened his mouth, probably to protest, but Sheriff Hayes walked up and spoke.

"Let her through," he said. "She won't let up until we do, and we don't have time."

"Sheriff!" Lloyd came close, grabbing onto the tape with one hand, the other leaning on his cane. "I told you he's back! He's up to his old tricks."

The sheriff rubbed his forehead, squeezing his eyes shut like he was trying to hold in his anger. "Not right now, Lloyd."

He lowered his arm and looked at me and then my dad. "Follow me."

"Andras will not stop until he has his way!" Lloyd bellowed.

I stopped in my tracks and spun on my heel to face Lloyd. "Did you say 'Andras?'"

Lloyd nodded vigorously. "Yes, the demon himself. He destroyed this town once, and he's about to do it again!"

"Tessa," Sheriff Hayes said in a tight voice.

I pointed at Lloyd. "You and I need to have a talk when I'm done here."

Lloyd's white, bushy eyebrows shot up in surprise. Then he licked his lips and nodded. "Yeah, okay. And you can call me Cromwell. Most people do." He backed away, using his cane as a support, and going quiet.

Sheriff Hayes' lips ticked into a small smile. "If I'd known that would get the man to shut up, I would have done that forever ago."

I shrugged. "Some people just need to be heard, Sheriff."

"If law enforcement doesn't work out for you," Sheriff Hayes said, "maybe you should follow in your dad's footsteps and run for mayor."

"Any leads on the memory card?"

He shook his head. "Haven't had time." He motioned toward the lake. "Wait until you see this."

We followed the sheriff down the trail, heading toward the lake. I gasped when I saw what had happened.

All the trees surrounding the lake had fallen, lying flat on the ground. It was like something had come through and bulldozed them.

"How is this possible?" Leya whispered.

"The quake," I said.

Dad ran a hand down his face. "How could an earthquake

cause all the trees to fall in a perfectly circled pattern, and there's no other major damage to the city?"

I threw up my hands. "How did Reed show up in our living room the other day? How did the lake boil and the lightning bugs explode? We have to go off the assumption that anything can happen in this town."

The sheriff put his hands on his hips and surveyed the area. "What I really want to know it what it means."

"It's like the entire area around the lake has been cleared," Leya said, a quiver in her voice. She looked at me. "A child taken, and now this? Is what happened in the sixteen hundreds going to happen again?"

The thought sent my stomach rolling. I couldn't imagine all the children in the city dying like that. I didn't even want to think about it.

I pressed a hand to my stomach, looking out at the lake. Graham and I had seen it boil. Had that been a test run by Andras?

A raven landed on a nearby birch tree, cocking its head and cawing. Its crows turned into a melody, something about the silky tone intoxicating. I found myself moving toward the lake, each step slow and steady, moving at the beat of the raven's song.

"Where are you going?" Leya asked.

Nirah stirred inside me, slithering out from behind my heart and breaking into multiple pieces, traveling all throughout my body. I opened my mouth to respond, but a thick section of Nirah coiled around my throat, cutting off my ability to speak. For a moment, I thought she was trying to stop me from talking, but I realized she was trying to yank me back. Away from the lake.

Nirah soon seized all my limbs, stopping me from moving forward. The bird continued with its song, the melody commanding me to go to the lake. My muscles fought against

Nirah as she tried to regain control of my body, but she held firm.

The air around me began to swirl, slowly whooshing around my body, creating a barrier around me. The wall of wind expanded, going wide and tall, blocking me off from those around me. I could faintly hear Leya and Dad calling my name, but it sounded far down a tunnel, away from my grasp.

The raven landed on my shoulder. How had it gone through the tornado?

It sang its song directly into my ear, causing Nirah to shake with fury. Nirah warmed me from the inside, and my skin began to glow, getting brighter with each passing second. My muscles attacked Nirah with everything they had, making her relinquish some control.

The song lured me toward the lake, everything around me moving out of the way to let me through. Fallen trees lifted off the ground and flew through the tornado wall and out of sight. The water parted, clearing a path toward the center of the lake, where the small island lay.

Nirah surged through me, using everything she had to control my body. I froze at the edge of the lake, my muscles and Nirah in a heated battle, and my entire body glowing.

The raven's song grew louder, piercing my ear drums. I slammed my palms against my ears, trying to dull the sound. The raven's beak pecked at my hand, biting through my skin, but I held my hands firmly against my ears with the help of Nirah.

Nirah was helping me, but I couldn't figure out why. She was Andras' pet. She should be helping *him*. Unless Reed lied to me about that.

My knees gave way, and I fell to the ground, causing me to release my hold on my ears so I could put my palms out to catch myself.

Suddenly, everything around me stilled. The raven ended its song and flew down the path, heading toward the island. Swirls of colors attacked my vision moments before everything went black. I couldn't see anything, though my eyes were open.

I could feel a presence before me, but when I reached out, there was only air. It sounded as if the wall of wind had disappeared, and not a soul was around me. The energy in me slowly drained, leaving me weak and tired. Not being able to hold myself up any longer, I fell onto my side, curling into a ball on the ground.

All the fight in me drained. My entire being felt hollow like my spirit was gone, and just my bones and flesh remained on the shore.

What was happening to me? I could still think. My brain was still active, but I couldn't move any muscles. Couldn't see anything. Couldn't *feel* anything. I couldn't even sense Nirah inside me anymore.

Had she gone? Taken my soul and slithered away?

The thought terrified me.

I laid there for what felt like hours. Days. Time made no sense. The dull void just went on for eternity, ticking by slowly. Quickly. I wasn't sure.

Would I remain like this forever? It was a fate worse than death.

I tried to think about something. Someone. But my mind was empty of memories.

Where was I?

Who was I?

What?

...

A rush of energy erupted inside me, flinging my body onto my back. A bright orange light took over my vision, so bright and vivid.

My senses slowly came back to me, and the feeling in my body. I could smell fire. My mouth was dry.

My vision cleared, everything around me coming into focus. The birch trees. The red and orange sky as the sun began to set. Wait, wasn't it late afternoon?

The air around me was thick and stifling. The orange glow was coming from me. My body was still lit up. I tried to feel around me, only to find air on every side. I wasn't on the ground. I was floating.

I was dreaming. I had to be.

Or dead.

Was I dead?

Tessa. The male's scratchy voice took me by surprise. I'd heard it before. Seen his intense red eyes. *The answer to my prayers.* He laughed, the rumble vibrating every inch of me. *You're ready.*

His presence left, bringing me back to the reality around me.

"Tessa," Leya's shaky voice sounded nearby. "Tessa, say something!"

"What's going on?" Dad asked.

"How is this possible?" Sheriff Hayes asked.

They were with me. So, I wasn't dead?

"Okay," Jade said, an edge to her voice, "I've seen some crazy stuff in my life, but this surpasses all of it. This is downright freaky, and I'm so over it."

When had Jade gotten there?

"It's wild," Marcel said, his tone full of awe.

"Sticking with freaky," Jade said. "I mean, she's floating. Tessa is *floating.*"

Everything happened in a matter of seconds. My body fell back to the earth, hitting the ground with a thud. I took a huge gasp of air as I sat up, my eyes wide.

Dad, Leya, Sheriff Hayes, Jade, and Marcel were all in

front of me, their jaws hanging in shock. Behind them were deputies, firefighters, and paramedics, all frozen in terror.

What was everyone doing here?

I brought a hand to my head. "What happened?"

Leya dropped to her knees and threw her arms around me, sobbing. She said something, but it was a jumbled mess. I couldn't make out any of the words.

Dad kneeled beside me, pressing his lips to my forehead.

Then Jade was there, wrestling Leya out of the way so she could hug me. Jade held onto me firmly.

"Don't *ever* do that again," Jade said with so much fury that it made me flinch.

"Do what?" I asked.

She pulled back and looked at me. "We have some serious talking to do."

"We have much more than that," Dad said.

The sheriff came forward, popping a piece of nicotine gum into his mouth. "I *really* picked the wrong month to quit smoking." He crouched down. "We need to do some research. Now. This is getting out of hand."

I glared at all of them. "Will someone please tell me what's going on?"

Dad held out his hand and helped me to my feet. He glanced over at Leya. "Call Mrs. Morales and tell her to meet us at the library."

"They're closed," Jade said, checking her watch. "It's a little after eight."

Eight? Where had the time gone? Wasn't the town hall meeting at eight?

"I've got a set of keys," Sheriff Hayes said, standing back up. "I'll run home and get them and then meet you there."

Dad ran his hand down his face. "I need a drink."

I nodded. "Me, too."

Dad narrowed his eyes at me.

I pulled back a little. "We're talking about Dr Pepper, right?"

"Right." Dad cleared his throat. "That's exactly what I meant. I could really use an ice-cold Dr Pepper."

"Sure, you did." Leya held out her hand, helping me to my feet.

CHAPTER 24

The library was on the corner of Main Street and Center, the old, brick building matching everything else in the town. White columns stood in front, adding charm and a colonial feel.

A few streetlamps lined the park strip in front, lighting up the sidewalk and our path to the front door.

An eerie quiet greeted us when we went stepped into the library. A horrible feeling settled into my stomach, one of dread.

"She's not answering her phone or responding to texts," Leya said, staring at her phone. "I mean, you'd think Mrs. Morales would have her phone set to ring with everything going on."

I checked my phone again to see if I had a response from Graham. Everyone but him had been at the lake. Leya said she tried to get a hold of him, but she couldn't, so I tried myself.

He wasn't responding to me, either. Whatever Dad had said to him after the incident at the lake must have really spooked him. I wanted to question Dad, but we had more important matters at hand.

Like why I had been floating in the air, my whole skin glowing bright. According to Dad and Leya, the wall of wind had blocked their view of me. They tried everything they could to penetrate it, but nothing worked.

Hours had gone by, but all of them powerless to help. The sheriff postponed the townhall meeting since so many people were at the lake.

When the wall finally dropped, they saw me curled on the ground near the edge of the shore.

"You weren't breathing." Dad was leaning against the front desk at the library. "Paramedics tried to work on you, but it was like your muscles were locked into place. They couldn't get you out of your curled-up position."

Leya wrapped her arms around me, squeezing tight. "We thought you were dead."

"I felt dead," I whispered. "It was like my soul had been sucked out of me."

Leya shivered against me. "That's awful."

"For thirty minutes, paramedics tried everything they could." Sheriff Hayes was leaning against the front desk next to dad, his hands resting above his belt as he chewed on a piece of gum on his front teeth. "But with you curled up, they really couldn't do much."

Leya lowered her arms from around me. "All of a sudden, you were floating back into the air. Your back arched and you glowed like an angel or something."

I had no idea how to process that.

"What happened on your end?" Jade had her arms folded, her body turned away from Marcel like she was closing him off. If it bothered him, he didn't show it.

I jumped up, sitting on the front counter near my dad. "It was ... weird. There was this bird. Its song pulled me toward the lake. I tried to fight against it, but my body had a mind of his own."

Leya frowned. "I didn't hear a bird."

"Neither did I," Dad said.

Everyone else shook their head, telling me they didn't hear it, either.

"It was piercing loud to me." I cringed, remembering the shrill sound at the end as the bird pecked at my hands. I looked down, seeing little red marks all over my hand. I hadn't imagined it. But for whatever reason, I was the only one who could hear it. "Nirah tried to stop me. She basically seized my limbs, trying to stop me from moving forward."

Jade held up a palm. "I thought that ... thing ... inside you was *helping* Andras." She stuck out her tongue. "I can't believe I just said those words."

"I thought so, too," I said. "I could feel her anger, though, directed at the force pulling me."

Dad rubbed his eyes with his thumb and forefinger. "None of this makes sense."

"Hello, people." Leya walked backward toward the rows of bookshelves. "We need to be doing some research. That's why we came here."

"Leya's right," Marcel said. "We're wasting time."

Jade moved toward the front door. "I'm going to see if Mrs. Morales is at her house." When she got to the door, she placed her hand on the glass and looked over her shoulder at Marcel. "Oh, and we're done." She turned and left.

Marcel let out a long breath of relief. "Oh, thank goodness."

Dad looked at me, confused, but I just shook my head. The break-up was perfectly Jade.

Sheriff Hayes clapped his hands together, catching everyone's attention. "We only have a little bit of time before the meeting at nine. Let's split up." He glanced back at the door where Jade had exited. "Poor word choice. Let's fan out."

I immediately went to the witchcraft section they had in the back corner. The area was cloaked in darkness, the light in the aisle out. The main librarian probably didn't find it important enough to fix. She referred to the books as "Satan's handbooks" and would shake her head at anyone who even got too close to the section. Jade and I loved to go there often, mostly to make the librarian mad. But there were also some fascinating reads.

My fingers trailed along the spines of the books, the bumpy texture immediately calming me. The answers had to be somewhere in these books. They *needed* to be.

"Where do we even start?" Leya asked, straining her neck to look up at the top shelf. Her pink glittery shirt contrasted with all the horror going on. But it gave me this spark of hope that there was still light to be found in the darkness.

Nirah rippled under my skin in a laugh. All she'd ever known was darkness and would do everything in her power to keep me from the light.

"I'll show you, Nirah," I said under my breath, my thumb rubbing the side of my dahlia ring. "We can put a stop to this."

"What?" Leya asked, turning her head toward me.

Wrapping my hand around one of the books, I took it from the shelf and tossed it to her. "I remember there being some folklore in this one. See if there's anything on Birch Lake."

She took it and headed to a table where Dad and Sheriff Hayes sat, deep in history books. They thought they'd find something in there, but I didn't think what happened at Birch Lake would want to be shared in the history books.

I continued down the aisle, skimming all the titles. As I neared the end of the aisle, Nirah heated, swirling around in an excited dance. It intensified when I got to the end. Once I crossed to the other side, she simmered down, so I went back to where I'd been before, only to have her bounce around, sending off waves of heat.

Raising my arm, I waited to see her reaction. She backed off just a tad. So, I crouched low until she was practically doing cartwheels inside me. None of the titles looked all that interesting.

I was about to stand back up when something glinted in the very back corner of the bottom shelf. Moving some books to the side, I peered behind them, seeing a red hardbound book shoved against the back of the shelf. It glowed just barely like a light reflected off it, but the light above me was out.

Nirah flared, the pain so intense that my left arm shot out toward the book, knocking into it and turning it onto its side. Licking my dry lips, I watched my skin turn orange, glowing from the heat inside. Nirah wanted that book. She craved it.

With trembling fingers, I pulled it out, brushing off a thin layer of dust on the surface. In bright, gold lettering, it read: *Lucifer's Reign*. Nirah purred inside, and while the rational side of me wanted to toss the book far away, my glowing hand gripped it tight like it never wanted to let go.

I checked down the aisle to see if anyone noticed all the light coming from my little corner of the library, but no one was there. I could hear them whispering at the table, distracted by their books.

My gaze went back to the book. The heat from my hand transferred to it, the red cover slightly ablaze with light. No way I was taking this book to the table with everyone else. Dad and the sheriff would freak out.

I was freaking out.

Sitting down with my back against the shelf, I set the glowing book on my legs and took a deep breath. It was just a book. It couldn't hurt me.

Right?

I mean, it was glowing. That certainly didn't bode well.

"You have to open it to read it." Reed was suddenly in front of me, resting his now red ghostly figure against the bookshelf.

At the sight of him, I jumped, the book flying from my lap and thumping on the floor.

"Everything okay over there?" Dad asked from around the corner.

"Yeah, totally." Too bad my voice cracked when I said that. I cleared my throat and retrieved the book from the ground. "Just dropped a book. Everything is fine."

Reed winked at me in a major exaggeration. "Totally." His sugary tone had a slight condescending edge to it.

"Why are you red?" I asked.

He looked down at his figure. "What are you talking about?"

"You're always dull and gray. Now, you're red."

He cocked his head to the side. "Me? Dull and gray?"

Sitting back down, I placed the book in my lap again and kept my voice low. "What do you want, Reed?"

He floated down until he sat next to me, his feet crossed at his ankles. He licked his thumb and then wiped his boot. Everything was red to me, so I had no idea what he saw.

He held up his wrist, showing me his watch. "My father gave this to me on my sixteenth birthday."

"Congratulations?" Why was he telling me this? I didn't care about his presents over the years.

Reed's lips twitched in amusement. "It belonged to my ancestor. Albert Harrison? You saw his coffin the night you killed me."

I held up a finger. "You didn't need to remind me." Another finger went up. "And, technically, it was Delilah that pulled the trigger. Not me."

Reed moved to grab my hand, but his hand went right

through it. He let out a small hiss, mad he couldn't touch me. "It was still your hand, doll. She just gave you a little boost." He shook his wrist at me. "Anyway, good ol' great-grandpappy got it during a poker game."

"Someone bet their watch?"

Reed chuckled, light and airy. "Oh, no. Grandpappy got in a fight, killed a man, and stole his watch."

I scooted away from Reed, even though he was already dead. "Sounds like a nice guy."

"Before the man died, though," Reed went on, his tilted head staring at his watch, "he whispered something." He stopped talking, going back to cleaning off his boots.

"Are you going to tell me the rest?" I asked.

His head quirked toward me like he just remembered I was there. "Oh, yes. He said, 'Be ready, for soon we rise.' No one ever knew what he meant, but from the whisperings I've been hearing over here, I think it's connected with what's happening down at Birch Lake."

I placed my hands on top of the book. "That was, like, a hundred and fifty years ago. I wouldn't really consider that 'soon.'"

Reed shrugged. "Time is different on this side. For them, it is soon." He pointed to the book. "Whatcha reading?"

I held it up so he could read the title.

"Oh." Reed drummed his fingertips together. "*Lucifer's Reign*. Sounds marvelous. Want to read it out loud to me?"

"No, Reed, I really don't." I sighed. "But I think the answers might be in here."

"Then, what are you waiting for?" He cooed the words like he was speaking to a child. He reached out, his finger trying to poke the tip of my nose. "Is someone scared?"

If I could touch him, I'd whack him in the face with the book.

"I'm not scared. More terrified of how much Nirah likes it."

"Oh, sweet Nirah," Reed said. "How is our friend doing? Liking her new living arrangement?"

I gripped the book, wanting to swing it, just to get the aggression out of me. "Have you found out anything or not? I don't have time for your games."

Reed pouted. "Someone is grouchy. Well, if you must know, the answers will be in that book. You probably won't like them, though."

"I don't like any of this," I mumbled.

Out of nowhere, a high-pitched squeal came from the other end of the aisle, making my hairs stand on end.

CHAPTER 25

Both Reed and I whipped in the direction of the scream. Marcel stood there, one hand on top of his head, the other pointing at us, hyperventilating.

"Marcel, calm dow…" Leya trailed off when she saw Reed and me sitting on the floor, her scream putting Marcel's to shame.

When the sheriff ran over and spotted us, I worried he'd scream, too, but thankfully, he just let out a "Whoa!" and jumped back.

Reed stood, brushing off his jeans and then straightening his flannel jacket. "How lovely to see you all again." He smiled over his shoulder at me as I stood up beside him. "I do love a nice greeting."

"They screamed," I said.

Reed smiled, a glint in his eyes. "And they were so high caliber. Really, the top of their game."

Leya's head jerked back. "Reed? Why are you red? At first, I thought you were like a demon or something."

Reed shrugged. "Not sure."

"What now?" Dad groaned, coming to stand next to the sheriff. "Why are you *here*?"

Reed motioned to the shelves. "This is a *public* library."

"Pretty sure when they say *public*," I said, holding the book close to my chest, "they are referring to people who are *alive*."

"There's a ghost!" Marcel's voice trembled, his shaking finger still seeking us out.

Leya tried to push his arm down, but Marcel held it stiff. She shrugged apologetically at Reed. At least her initial scare had worn off. But she had seen him before. The first time was always the hardest.

Reed clasped his hands behind his back. "Just wanted to check in on our special Tessa here. See how things are going."

"But. But. But." Marcel took a huge gulp of air. "You're, you're *dead*."

Reed glanced down at his red figure. "Yes, I know. Thank you for pointing out the obvious." He looked at me, his tips turned to the side, his voice low. "Never quite bright, that one." He dramatically sighed. "Well, now onto business. Tessa has the book you'll need. You'll find all the answers right in there."

Leya crept down the aisle, staying close to the shelf opposite where Reed stood. "What book?" She gave us a strained smile, trying to appear calm, but her trembling body shook the shelf.

I held it up for them, surprised to see it still glowing. I thought maybe it would stop with more witnesses. Or, maybe they couldn't see it. Just me. "*Lucifer's Reign*."

"Sounds like those bad CW shows you watch," Dad grumbled.

"Why is it glowing?" Marcel asked, not holding back his fear. "The book is glowing. You all can see that, right?" He glanced at the sheriff, his arm still outstretched and pointing down the aisle. "You can see the glowing, right? Right?" His gaze wandered back to the book. "It's *glowing.*" He swallowed. "And, there's a ghost."

Marcel swayed where he stood, and I worried for a second that he would pass out. Dad immediately steadied him, keeping him upright.

"Maybe I'll take him back to the table," Dad said, steering Marcel away from the aisle.

Sheriff Hayes cracked a small smile. "I think that's a good idea."

Marcel's arm didn't lower as they disappeared around the corner. "Glowing. Ghost."

Leya waved out her hand. "I'm sure he'll be fine. I mean, he might be traumatized for the rest of this life, but he'll be fine." She awkwardly waved at Reed as she saddled up next to me, gripping tightly on my arm. "Hi, Reed. You're here. Again. All ghostly and stuff. It's nice. It's totally fine and normal."

Her long, manicured nails dug into my skin. I tried to yank my arm away, but she held me tight. I guess I'd just have to live with permanent indentations in my skin from her nails.

Sheriff Hayes slowly came down the aisle, stopping a good five feet from Reed. His hand rested on the grip of his gun at his waist. A lot of good that would do him. Reed was already dead.

Reed moved his hands so they were clasped in front of him. "Well, now that we're all here, we should talk about our game plan."

The sheriff quirked his thick eyebrow. "*Our* game plan?"

"You don't seriously think you can do this all on your own, now do you?" Reed nodded his head down the aisle. "Seeing how that young man just acted, I'm thinking the majority of you won't be able to handle something this powerful." He winked at me. "Thank goodness we have Tessa. With our powers combined—"

I held up a palm. "Whoa, there. I'm so not working with you."

At the same time, Leya had said, "She's so not working with you."

"Come now," Reed said. "Can't we just let bygones be bygones? I tried to kill Tessa. She killed me. What's done is done."

Dead or alive, no matter what that man said, I'd never trust him. He could be serious, but he wasn't someone I'd want to work with anyway. He wouldn't do anything unless he was getting something out of it himself. It could all be a trap, too. He could be working with Andras, which I wouldn't put past Reed. I think the only thing that would hold him back would be the fact that Reed couldn't be in charge, and he loved control. Would he relinquish it, even to someone as powerful as a demon?

Sheriff Hayes nodded at the book. "What's it say in there?"

"I haven't read it yet." I was still nervous about opening it.

"No matter," Reed said, waving a hand. "You can read it later. Now, Tessa, could you be a doll and take me to see my brothers?"

I arched an eyebrow at him. "Just go yourself."

He squirmed where he floated, his face scrunched in discomfort.

I held back my smile. "You can't manifest unless *I'm* there." I tsked. "Such a shame."

Reed growled, low and throaty, that clashed with his usual sugary-coated tone. "I'm trying to help you here, even after everything you've done to me." He motioned to his ghostly figure. "The least you can do is offer me the courtesy of seeing my baby brothers."

"You haven't really helped us." I waved the book at him. "I'd already found this book when you came. All the information you've given me is vague."

Reed came close, towering over me, but I stood my ground, not letting him intimidate me. His chest puffed out. "If you want *her* out of you, I suggest you be kind. Otherwise, I'll make sure she stays there forever."

Nirah swirled through my blood, having the time of her life. She was more than content in my body.

Reed tilted his head to the side, held out his hand toward Leya, and moved his fingers toward each other like he was squeezing something. "Or, I can resort to this. Though, I'd rather not."

Leya's hand went to her throat, her open mouth seeking air in vain. He was cutting off her airflow.

Sheriff Hayes immediately tightened his grip on his gun, but then loosened, probably realizing it wouldn't do any good in this situation.

"Reed, stop," I hissed.

"Not until you promise to take me to my brothers," Reed said, head still tilted, his vacant eyes on me.

I held out my hands. "Fine, just stop."

Leya grabbed her throat, losing oxygen.

"And you apologize," Reed cooed.

My gaze shot to Leya, who was seconds away from passing out. I hated apologizing to Reed, but I'd do anything to save my best friend. I looked at Reed. "I'm sorry, Reed, for being rude. We'll go see your brothers." It took everything in me to keep my tone steady, my gaze firmly on him, my feet rooted on the ground. I wanted to go to Leya and help her, but there was nothing I could physically do.

Reed's hand popped open, and he shook out his fingers. "Now, that wasn't so hard, was it?"

Leya gasped, inhaling a ton of air and dropping to her

knees. Her glare cut to Reed, practically slicing him in two. "You're lucky you're already dead, creep." Her voice was raspy and dry.

Reed grinned at her. "And to think, you could have just joined me."

Leya scoffed, then cleared her throat. "Ha! I'll be going to heaven, a place you'll never see."

Reed shrugged. "Not really my preference of company anyway. They're so...dull there. Really, no fun at all."

"Keep on telling yourself that, buddy," Leya mumbled.

"And trailing me everywhere I go is fun?" I asked him. Reed lifted his arm, ready to strangle Leya again, so I quickly went on. "I'm assuming your brothers will be at home? It's not like they have a life." Oh, Nirah. She kept making me speak my mind instead of biting my tongue. I needed to play nice with Reed.

Reed's mouth twitched, but he didn't comment. Instead, he just nodded.

Tessa! Corrine's voice echoed around the aisle.

"Corrine?"

In front of me, Corrine's transparent figure flickered into view for just a second before disappearing. I reached out, wishing for her to come back. How had she appeared? Was it because she was near Reed?

"Corrine!" Leya's eyes lit up in hope.

I turned to her. "Did you see her, too?"

"*See* her?" Leya's hand went to her mouth. "I just heard you say her name and thought you'd heard her. Is she here?"

I shook my head. "Not anymore."

Reed's gaze was contemplative. "You saw her? How interesting." He looked over his shoulder at something I couldn't see and hissed. Actually opened his mouth and hissed like a cat.

Corrine's form appeared again, this time full of static like there was something interfering. She opened her mouth, and the growly hiss she threw at Reed made me smile.

Corrine turned to me, the annoyance in her eyes replaced with fear. Her entire figure was a dull red, just like Reed's. "Tessa, we need your help! You have to save us!"

Reed flicked his fingers like he was shooing her away. "Not now, ladybug."

She vanished, her angry shouts at Reed cutting off.

He turned his attention back to me. "See you at my brother's house." He disappeared, leaving no trace of him in the aisle.

"Corrine?" I asked, though I already knew I wouldn't hear anything. She could only speak when Reed manifested.

I'd forgotten to ask about what he was trying to tell me in the woods. Were there others with him besides Corrine? Why was she even there? And how had I seen her?

Leya rose to her feet. "You seriously can't be thinking of going over to the Harrison's place." She rubbed her throat like it was sore.

I shook my head at her, afraid of Reed being able to hear me. I would go over there. Eventually. He didn't give me a timeline, which was his oversight, not mine.

Leya came to my side. "How did Corrine look?"

"Her figure was red, like Reed's." My voice dropped. "She looked terrified, Leya."

"We have to save her." Leya tapped her fingers against her folded arms. "But how?"

I marched past the sheriff and Leya, heading down the aisle and plopping the book on the table. Marcel jumped in his seat and then straightened his glasses.

"Is *he* gone?" Marcel asked in a shaky voice.

"For now." I sat down in the chair across from him.

Leya took a seat on the other side of me while Dad and Sheriff Hayes stood near the table, Dad leaning against a bookshelf with his arms folded, the sheriff glancing around like he was waiting for Reed to reappear.

With a prayer of courage, I opened the book, only to be hit right in the chest by a gush of wind, sending me and my chair flying backward a good few feet.

Both Marcel and Leya hopped up from their seats, their scared eyes darting between me and the book.

The pages of the book turned with a flutter, stopping on a page towards the end. Rubbing my chest, I scooted the chair back to the table and glanced at the page.

Two images took up the pages. On the left, Andras stood tall, bare chest puffed out, holding a gold scepter and wearing a gold crown that dripped with blood. His loin cloth whipped behind him with the wind. He was on a tall mountain, lava oozing down the sides. Men, women, and children kneeled around him, their arms flat against the mountainside, in the deepest bow possible. Other bodies perished in the lava, decaying hands and screaming heads protruding from it. Below the image was the caption: *Andras' Rise to Power*.

"Well, that looks inviting," Leya mumbled next to me. She'd retaken her seat and scooted in close to me. "Who wouldn't want to live there?"

With a tight smile, my eyes wandered to the other page. It was a continuation of the previous image—what lay at the base of the mountain.

There was a large lake surrounded by birch and willow trees. I'd seen it enough times to know it was Birch Lake, right here in Willow Marsh. Men, women, and children surrounded the perimeter of the lake, their gaunt faces and tired bodies close to withering away. Their backs were hunched, their empty gazes on the boiling lake.

In the center of the lake was a small island, just like the one Graham had taken me to. A lady floated a few feet off the ground, her arms held out and her entire being glowing.

Leya gasped. "She looks just like you, Tessa."

She did. She had thick, dark hair pulled back with a green scarf. She wore a flowy baby blue dress, the bottom billowing out and moving with the breeze.

I picked up the book and pulled it closer, examining the girl's hand. On her right pointer finger was a ring in the shape of a dahlia. My eyes immediately sought out the family ring on my hand, noticing that they were one and the same.

"No way in hell," Dad said, pointing at the picture. He'd moved away from the bookshelf at some point, joining us at the table. I'd been too focused to notice. His finger moved to the caption.

A pure and selfless sacrifice, cleansing the world of Andras' powers.

"Kind of a poor choice of words, Daddy dearest," Reed suddenly said. I yelped and looked up to see him sitting on the edge of the table, legs crossed, fingers drumming along his knee to an imaginary beat. "But unless you want to send this town and your daughter to hell, then this is the only way." His beady eyes sought out mine. "Tessa must sacrifice herself."

CHAPTER 26

Dad reached over me and slammed the book closed. "This is nonsense. Tessa is not *sacrificing* herself."

"Of course she's not!" Leya had her hands in fists like she wanted to punch something. Probably Reed.

Marcel scooted away from Reed, inching himself around the table and closer to me. He swallowed, doing his best to look at me and not Reed. "You're supposed to sacrifice yourself?"

I wanted to pause the conversation, not wanting to talk about me sacrificing myself. I mean, it was completely ridiculous and out of the question. Not to mention totally cliché. "Reed, why is Corrine with you?"

"Is that really important—" Reed began.

"Yes!" I took a few deep, calming breaths. "Enough with your games. What is going on over there, Reed? You were in color, then gray, and now you're red. Corrine keeps asking for help. Who else is there?"

Reed swung his head back and forth, humming a twangy melody while he was thinking. He finally rolled his eyes.

"Okay. Fine. Let's just say it's crowded over here, okay? Lots of people."

"What people?" Sheriff Hayes asked.

Marcel licked his lips. "Are we just going to skip over the sacrificing bit? Seems like really important, right?"

"Why won't you tell me?" I was losing my patience with Reed.

"I'll take that as a yes," Marcel mumbled.

"I'm still trying to piece everything together," Reed said, annoyance in his tone, "but what we can gather is that everyone who has died in Willow Marsh since that fateful night back in the sixteen hundreds has been stuck here in The Gray."

I sat back, taking that in. Everyone? Like, *everyone?*

"How is that even possible?" Leya looked from me to Reed, to me, and back to Reed.

Reed waved his hand nonchalantly. "There are so many theories. I can hardly keep track."

"Chloe." I swallowed. "Reed, has Chloe Heathrow shown up there?"

He lifted a shoulder in a shrug. "Not that I know about, but I'm also not entirely sure who that is."

I clenched my jaw and took a few breaths, trying to stay calm. "She's Duncan's nine-year-old daughter."

"The answer is still no." Reed glanced over his shoulder at something on his end before turning back to us, a slight terror in his eyes. "Things are changing. Andras is separating everyone and putting together his army."

Army?

Reed clapped his hands, the fear dwindling in his eyes. "Now, back to sacrifice."

Dad held up a hand. "This is just a legend. It's not real."

"Oh, but it is." Reed leaned toward us, causing Marcel and Leya to shirk back. "And it's going to happen whether you like it or not." He rubbed the bottom of his beard. "Tessa is the only one with the power to stop Andras and get everyone out of The Gray. It's that simple."

I stared at the ring on my finger. "Killing myself doesn't sound *simple*, Reed. It sounds stupid."

"Definitely stupid," Leya put in.

"Besides, it just says 'a pure and selfless sacrifice.' Not I have to sacrifice *myself*." I stared at the blood dripping from the wrists of the girl in the picture and my insides tightened.

"I think we can all read between the lines." When I just glared at him, Reed threw out his arms. "Listen, it's up to you. Do you want Willow Marsh to disappear forever, killing the stubborn residents that refuse to leave, and giving Andras free reign of the land? Which will, in turn, give Lucifer himself a chance to pop in every and then for a quick vacay? Or, do you want to stop Andras and save lives?"

"Well, when you put it like that," I mumbled.

Leya put her hand on my arm. "It still sounds stupid. We have no idea if this will work."

Reed pointed at the book. "That was made years ago. Before you were born, Tessa. They saw this coming. They've told you how to stop it. I'm really not sure what more you need."

"A way for us to do it without Tessa dying," Marcel said.

"Agreed," Leya said.

Dad scoffed. "How do we know we can trust whoever wrote this anyway? For all we know, you could have put it together, Reed."

Sheriff Hayes kinked his head. "You really think Reed is capable of *that*?" He pointed at the book.

Reed frowned. "Well, that's just not nice."

But the sheriff did have a point. It didn't seem up Reed's alley. Leaning forward, I reached for the book to check for the author. When I saw the name, I dropped the book like I'd been scalded.

"No way," I said, so quiet I barely heard it myself. "Someone could have put her name there. It doesn't mean *she* was the one to actually write this."

"Who?" Dad asked, leaning over to check out the book. His mouth formed into an 'O'.

Marcel adjusted his glasses, trying to get a better look at the spine. "Tessa Isaacson?" He chuckled. "We're supposed to believe that Tessa wrote this? I think she would know if she wrote a book."

Reed clucked his tongue. "Not Tessa Isaacson. It's Tessa Isaacson Walker."

"My great-great-grandmother," I said.

Marcel's eyes went wide.

A thought rushed to me. "Is *she* with you, Reed? Is my great-great grandma there?"

"Everyone, dearie." Reed whistled a tragic tune, his eyes dancing in delight.

Had she been stuck in The Gray all this time? If time was different, maybe it hadn't seemed like that long to her. I hoped not.

"Can I talk to her?" She could answer so many questions.

Reed shook his head. "Afraid she's been locked in Andras' dungeon for quite some time now. Quite stubborn, I hear. Won't listen to a thing he says." He quirked an eyebrow. "A family trait, I believe."

Dad snatched up the book, flipping through the pages. His hardened face softened with each turn of the page. "I thought this was a pro-Lucifer book. But it's not." His finger skimmed across a page as he read to himself. "She knew this was coming. She's trying to warn us."

Leya put her hand on my arm. "Why would Tessa's great-

great-grandmother want Tessa to kill herself? That seems a little extreme, don't you think?"

"She doesn't *want* it," Reed said in his honey tone. "She just knows it's necessary. She's showing you your options, but you get to choose, Tessa doll." He tilted his head. "What will it be?"

Dad threw down the book on the table, the thud echoing in the quiet library. "Enough! This is ridiculous. We're listening to a dead man tell my daughter to kill herself. I will *not* let this happen! I don't care what some book says. We have no proof it's real or that Tessa Walker wrote it herself. It was probably some sick nut job." His eyes went to Reed. "So, I guess Reed could have written it after all."

If the mood weren't so gloomy, I would have laughed.

Sheriff Hayes sighed, scratching at his stubble. "Everyone needs to calm down. Nothing is decided right now. Maybe we should talk to Mrs. Morales after the meeting and see what she thinks."

"I think that's a good idea." I pushed back from the table and stood, wanting out of the library and into fresh air.

I grabbed the book and moved toward the front door, but Reed floated in front of me, stopping me in my path.

"We're going to see my brothers. Remember our agreement?" Reed straightened his flannel jacket and rolled out his neck. "I've been *dying* to see them. I hope they're doing well."

"This is more important, Reed," I said, waving the book at him. "We need to stop this attack. Then we can see your brothers."

Reed's jaw clenched, and his sweet tone turned sour. "We see them *now,* Tessa." His eyes flicked behind me. "Remember what I did to your friend. I can do it again to her. To your father. To everyone you love."

"Why, Reed?" I asked. "Why do you need to see your

brothers so bad? Why is that more important than stopping Andras and getting you out of The Gray?"

Reed had to be stalling. If he was working with Andras, then that was what he'd do. He'd stall for him, giving him more time to get his army in position.

The wheels turned in Reed's head as he thought. He kept opening his mouth and then closing it. He had no solid reason as to why we needed to go see Lars and Ace. I liked to keep my interactions with them at a minimum, so Reed wasn't going to get his way.

He'd hurt my friends if I said no. But Reed could only manifest where *I* was. I glanced over my shoulder at Dad. "Is your car still out on Main Street in front of your office?"

Dad nodded, a confused look on his face. "Yeah."

I rushed to him, keeping my voice low and talking fast. "Take the book, and everyone else here, to the meeting. Reed can only follow me."

Understanding passed over Dad's eyes. He pulled out his keys and set them in my palm. "Be safe, Tessa."

I hugged him tightly, then kissed him on the cheek. He answered with a kiss on my forehead.

"What's..." Leya started, but I ran out of the library before she could finish.

I booked it down Main Street, heading to my dad's car. When I was a few feet away, I pressed the unlock button on the key fob. The front and back lights flashed as I approached, the doors now unlocked. I jumped into the driver's seat and slammed the door.

Seconds later, Reed was sitting in the passenger seat. "I'm impressed. You're a clever little girl."

"Haven't we already established that?" I pressed the push start button, and the car came to life, the engine quiet.

Reed tried to put on his seatbelt but remembered he was just a ghost. "Habit." He draped his arm across the center of the car, leaning his palm against my headrest. "Shall we see what Lars and Ace are up to?"

Putting the car in drive, I checked over my shoulder before I pulled away from the curb. "We're going to find Graham."

Reed chuckled. "Oh, doll. He's not answering you. Can't you take a hint?"

"Shut it, Reed."

He just smiled and whistled along with the song on the radio, thankfully keeping quiet the rest of the ride to Graham's house.

Graham's truck was parked in its spot along the curb, but Barbie's car wasn't in the driveway.

I pulled up behind the truck and got out, jogging over to the front door. I rang the doorbell and knocked on the door. No answer.

I tried his phone again, but it went to voicemail.

"You're coming across as desperate, Tessa." Reed was suddenly at my side. "No guy likes desperate."

Ignoring him, I went around the side of the house and peered inside Graham's bedroom window. Empty.

Then I checked the back, looking through the sliding glass door. The house was completely still. Lifeless.

Goosebumps broke out along my arms.

Where were Graham and Barbie?

My phone rang, causing me to jump. I quickly went to answer it, not bothering to see who was calling.

"Graham?"

"Uh, no." Sheriff Hayes. "Sorry." He sighed. "Another kid has gone missing."

I held my trembling arms against me. "Who?"

He paused a few beats before he spoke. "Nash Jenson."

CHAPTER 27

The drive to the Jenson residence was a blur. Reed was bouncing in his seat, talking about how exciting this whole ordeal was getting while I was busy trying to quell the unease stirring inside me.

Nash. Gone.

His big smile, blond curly hair, and bright blue eyes flashed through my mind.

We had to find him. To save him.

When I asked Reed, he said no one had entered The Gray in a while, so Andras had to be holding Chloe and Nash somewhere in Willow Marsh. But where?

The Jenson's street was dark, all the neighbors probably headed for the meeting. When I got to their household, it was lit up like a beacon in the night. They had all the indoor and outdoor lights on. I was surprised to see there weren't as many cars outside of the house like there had been at Chloe Heathrow's.

Lola, her husband, and Jade were on the lawn, all screaming at Sheriff Hayes when I ran onto the driveway.

Jade turned and saw me. "Tessa! Please tell the sheriff that they need to get everyone out there searching for Nash. Forget the stupid meeting." She turned back to the sheriff. "Send out a text like Mayor Morgan did."

Sheriff Hayes rested his hand on his hip. "You all need to calm down—"

"Calm down?" Mr. Jenson roared. "Our son is *missing*. There's blood in his room. On his wall." His eyes welled up with tears. "He's dead, isn't he?"

Lola shook her head frantically. "We can't think that way. We need to be positive."

"I have all my deputies out there," Sheriff Hayes said, "scouring the area for any signs of Chloe and Nash. We will search every inch of this town, I promise."

Jade got right up in my face, causing me to shrink back. "You need to figure this whole thing out, now. No more games. No more stupid séances. End this, Tessa."

Nirah flared to life, zipping through all my limbs like she wanted a way to reach Jade. Probably to strangle Jade, knowing Nirah.

"Why do you think only *I* have the power to do that?" I asked, anger creeping into my tone.

Jade threw her arm out behind her, motioning toward the house. "They used Nash's blood to draw a dahlia on the wall." She grabbed my hand, squeezing it tight. "Just like your ring, Tessa."

I tried to yank my hand away, but she held too tight of a grip. "This isn't my fault, Jade."

She scoffed. "None of this started until you moved here." She let go of my hand, pushing me back. "You've ruined everything." Her jaw clenched. "Fix it, now."

Nirah's anger caused my hand to twitch, and it took everything in me to not strangle Jade.

I needed more time. I needed to talk to Mrs. Morales and do more research. I moved toward the house, but Jade grabbed my arm, yanking me back.

"Let go, Jade," I snarled. "I want to see Nash's bedroom."

Nirah vibrated in a chuckle, but that rage was all me this time. Jade's tantrum wasn't going to bring Nash home.

A war raged behind her eyes like she wasn't sure if she should help me or hate me.

I kept my voice low. "If you want me to figure out what's going on, I need to go inside."

She swallowed, tears trickling down her cheeks. She finally let go of me. "Fine." She spun around and stormed into the house.

I hurried after her, leaving the sheriff to talk with Lola and Mr. Jenson. I stopped short of Nash's bedroom door, wanting to brace myself before I stepped inside.

My heart clenched at seeing Nash's room. It felt like a hand was physically wrapping around my heart and squeezing the life out of me.

I guess I should have known other kids would be taken and known that Nash would be on that list, but I secretly hoped I'd been wrong about this whole thing.

What about the other kids in town? Like Livvy, the sheriff's daughter.

I needed to focus on what was in front of me.

I scanned the room, noticing that it was smothered in everything Paw Patrol. The bedding, posters on the wall, toys strewn about like he'd been playing with them moments ago.

A Paw Patrol tent sat in the corner of the room. I went to it, kneeling in front. Nash had stuffed animals of all the characters tucked into a makeshift bed.

If I thought my heart was tight before, it was in a vice now. I had to choke back tears. Crying wouldn't save Nash. Action would.

As I was standing, my hand turned orange, lightly shining.

A small ball of fire flickered above my palm before it disappeared. What was that?

"What does that mean?" Jade pointed at the wall, so much anger radiating off her. She hadn't seen what had happened with my hand, which was probably a good thing.

"I don't know, Jade." I took a step closer to the dahlia, examining the blood. It seemed ... off. A weird, gooey texture that didn't seem human. "He's still alive."

Jade stormed over and grabbed my arm. "Where is he?"

I tried to shake her off, but her grip was too tight. "I don't know. I just know he's not dead."

Jade choked back a sob. "How can you possibly know that?"

I relaxed, trying to soften my gaze. "According to Reed, they haven't shown up in The Gray." I went to the closed window, only to see it was locked. "Do you know how they came in?"

Jade sniffed, wiping her nose on her arm. "No. There were no signs of a break-in. I just happened to peek my head in when I got home and saw that his bed was empty." She nodded her head toward the wall. "Then I saw that."

Had Andras not shown up as a wolf? If he hadn't, who took Nash, and how?

I sat down on his bed. I needed to tell Jade about Corrine before she found out from someone else.

"Jade, I saw Corrine."

Jade's eyes went wide. "What?"

I patted the seat next to me on the bed. After a few seconds, she finally huffed and sat down. I turned to face her, my back to the dahlia on the wall.

"She's stuck where Reed is." I blew out a shaky breath. "I saw her for a brief second when I was talking to Reed. Corrine was shouting for help."

Jade snatched the stuffed Paw Patrol dog near the pillow

and held it close to her chest. I'd never seen her so vulnerable. So broken down and defeated.

"How?" Jade's voice was barely a whisper.

"I don't know."

Jade's red-rimmed eyes snapped to mine. "You keep saying that. You have to know *something*, Tessa."

I placed my hand on her arm. She tried to yank it away, but I held firm. "Jade, I'm going to do everything in my power to find Nash and save Corrine. I'll stop this, no matter what."

I swallowed, blinking back tears. I would stop it.

Even if that meant sacrificing myself.

CHAPTER 28

Even though the sheriff had pushed the meeting back another half hour, everyone in town was already jammed inside waiting impatiently when we got there.

I really hoped Graham got all the texts from the sheriff and would show up. He might be ignoring me, but he couldn't ignore what was happening in our town.

Dad and Mayor Morgan were on either side of Sheriff Hayes on a raised platform. I took in the three men, noting their differences. Sheriff Hayes looked worn down and tired. I knew this whole thing was difficult for him, with so many unknowns that he couldn't control. Demons and the supernatural weren't something he'd been trained for. He didn't even believe in them until recently. Even then, I knew he struggled. It was a lot to wrap your head around.

Mayor Morgan was a smug and sweaty mess. He'd taken off his blazer, revealing his sweat-soaked white button-down shirt. The air conditioner had been cranked up high, but with so many bodies, it didn't make much difference. It didn't stop him from smirking like he was the most important man in the room. There was a fine line between cocky and confident, and Mayor Morgan teetered so far over the edge of the cocky side that there was no pulling him back over.

Dad surprised me. He wore a determination I hadn't seen on him in a while. At that moment, I knew he'd do everything in his power to stop the demise of our town.

So much chatter filled the air, all the residents buzzing with confusion and fear. Nirah giddily slithered through me, like she was feeding off everyone's fear. She nudged my limbs, wanting me to move closer to the crowd. I really didn't need her interference right now.

I wished I could communicate with her like I could Delilah, just so I could tell her to calm down.

I paused. Had I ever tried to communicate with her?

Nirah? I thought.

Nirah zoomed up to my throat, circling around, her excitement tingling my neck.

Uh, can you do me a solid and calm down? I need to stay focused right now.

Nirah slumped to the bottom of my neck, her disappointment obvious. So she could understand me. She surprised me and slinked her way over to my shoulder, coming to rest there.

I searched the room, hoping to see Graham or Barbie, but neither were there. Another scan told me Mrs. Morales wasn't here as well. Where were they?

Sheriff Hayes held up a hand. "Can I get everyone's attention, please?"

The room slowly quieted, a few mumbles rolling over the crowd, until it went still, the only sound of everyone's anticipation.

Sheriff Hayes lowered his hand. "As most of you probably already know, Chloe Heathrow and Nash Jenson have gone missing."

The murmurs rose, rippling around the room.

Lola stepped forward. "Why aren't we looking for them? We should be out there searching for them, not here talking about it."

"She's right." Duncan took a shaky breath. "We need to find our children. We need to bring them home." His voice hitched on the last word. His wife, Steph, broke out into a sob. Duncan put his arm around her and held her close.

Shouts broke out, all those agreeing with Lola and Duncan making their stance known.

Mayor Morgan wiped at his forehead with a soggy handkerchief. "We will find them. With everyone's efforts, I think it can be done." His voice boomed around the room. "We will not let some sick monster take our children from us."

A few residents clapped in agreement.

Inside, Nirah stirred, nudging my skin. I had this overwhelming need to take my scarf and strangle the mayor with it.

Stop, Nirah, I sent to her. *We aren't going to kill him.*

She shook, clearly upset. I wasn't sure why, but she had an unnerving hatred for the mayor. I could practically feel it oozing out of her.

Sheriff Hayes shot Mayor Morgan a dark look.

The mayor just lifted his chin, so much defiance in his eyes. "We can't just stand here and do nothing, Coop! The residents deserve answers. They deserve action."

The cheering amplified. Jade was the loudest, her shouts heard over everyone else.

Leya and I exchanged a weary glance. If the residents knew what we were really dealing with, would they still be cheering? Would they be willing to face a demon?

Sheriff Hayes put his thumb and index finger in his mouth and whistled loudly.

The room went quiet.

Sheriff Hayes set his hand on his hip, right above his gun. "I understand your concerns. However, this is something we've never seen before. We can't walk blindly into it. We need to be deliberate and smart with every choice we make."

"Maybe it's time we call in reinforcements," Willy Heathrow, Sr., said. "Have you reached out to the FBI?"

I bit back a laugh. The FBI would have no idea what to do. Unless there was a Demon Analysis Unit.

"Ha!" Cromwell used his cane to push people out of his way so he could come up front. "Law enforcement can't stop a demon!"

Lola moved toward him. "This isn't the time for your nonsense, Cromwell. My child is missing!"

I stole a glance at Jade. Apparently, she hadn't said anything to her mom about seeing Reed, which was understandable. It was something you had to witness.

"It's not nonsense!" Cromwell shook his finger vigorously. "Andras is coming back. He will take all the children in this town and kill them unless we do something." He looked at the sheriff, his wild eyes pleading. "I think the best course of action would be to evacuate the town until this is over."

Lola snorted a strained laugh. "You're crazy."

"I'm not crazy!" Cromwell turned to me. "Tessa knows the truth, right?"

All eyes landed on me.

"Oh, boy," Leya whispered next to me. "Want me to create a distraction so you can make a run for it?"

Nirah purred on my shoulder, almost in a chuckle. Thank goodness she was inside me. If everyone could see her, I had a feeling she'd be putting on quite the show.

I looked at the sheriff, not sure what to say. The supernatural wasn't something you could casually talk about. It would be better to handle Andras discreetly. The town didn't need to know what was really happening. They just needed to know that it would be handled.

The sheriff slightly shook his head, telling me not to say anything. He cleared his throat. "Listen, I know this is all confusing. The thing we need to remember is that we are up against something evil, and it needs to be stopped." He paused, standing tall. "We all need to be vigilant right now. Keep your eyes and ears open. Make sure you keep your homes locked." His eyes wandered to his daughter, Livvy, who stood between her mom and Blake. "Keep your children close. Be cautious. Report anything suspicious. This town has been through a lot, but we've always pulled through."

That seemed to calm the crowd a little.

Mayor Morgan took off his cowboy hat and held it at his side. Sweat beaded on the top of his balding head. "That's all fine and well, Sheriff, but something needs to be done. I'm calling for any residents that want to help, to join me in searching the woods. We need to amp up security around the perimeter of the town. Anyone with guns is urged to volunteer."

"Miller," Sheriff Hayes said in a warning tone, "you do not have the authority to organize that. My deputies and I will handle the situation."

"Coop," Mayor Morgan started.

"Enough!" Sheriff Hayes roared. "I did not call this meeting to gather troops. I wanted to urge all the residents to stay on high alert, stay home when they can, and, if possible, maybe leave town for a bit. I promise you this will be solved, but with the proper authority."

"Promises, promises." Lars' deadpan voice came from near the entrance, sending my hairs on end.

CHAPTER 29

The crowd parted, Lars and Ace sauntering toward the front. Ace winked at a lady, and she blushed a deep red, splotchy on her neck and cheeks.

"Sorry we're late," Ace said, his hand resting above his snake belt buckle.

Lars tilted his head to the side, running his fingers through his greasy hair, showing off his green ring with spiders etched all the way around. "We had other matters to attend to."

He sounded so much like Reed. With Reed dead, did Lars feel the need to take his role as the eldest Harrison and leader of the pack? I wouldn't want any of them in charge, but if I *had* to choose between Lars and Ace, I'd choose Ace.

Nirah heated on my shoulder before snaking up to my eyes. She slid back and forth between each socket like she wanted the best vantage point. She finally snapped into multiple pieces, slithering to different places in my body.

Simmering steam heated inside, waiting to be released. I didn't want to glow in front of the town. Cromwell had already cast suspicion in my direction. The residents could take it the wrong way like everything happening was *my* fault.

But wasn't it my fault? Nirah was inside me, and I couldn't control her. Closing my eyes, I steadied my breath.

Control. Steady. Calm.

I peeled one eye open, glancing at my skin. Normal. But the pressure was on the valve, ready to crank the heat to boil.

"Correct me if I'm wrong," Lars said, his hauntingly beautiful eyes on me, "but I believe all of this started when the Isaacson family moved to Willow Marsh."

Murmurs rose once again as everyone's gazes swept between my dad and me.

"I'm thinking we should ask them to leave." Lars moved toward me. "I believe you've outstayed your welcome."

Cromwell pointed at me. "She's the only one who can stop this!"

Maura Fowler, the owner of Willow Marsh Inn, stepped forward, sneering at Lars. "She found out the truth about the deaths of Delilah Morgan, Greg Dixon, and the Barnett family, and finally put a stop to Reed Harrison, something none of us have been able to do! If anything, she's been cleaning up the town." She turned toward the mayor. "You should be grateful she found your daughter's killer."

Lots of people cheered and shouted at that, a mix of agreeing and disagreeing.

The sheriff opened his mouth to speak right as the entire building began to shake. It was a quiet rumble at first, barely vibrating the chairs and our feet, but enough to capture everyone's attention. We all stood with our arms held out, trying to brace ourselves before the true quake reared its face.

Suddenly the floor jolted, rippling in a wave across the room. Floorboards shifted and cracked. Residents lost their footing and crashed to the ground. I held tightly onto Leya, trying to stay on my feet.

Dad, Sheriff Hayes, and Mayor Morgan tried to escort people out of the building, but there was too much chaos to make much progress.

People were stepping on fallen bodies, fighting their way to the exit, clawing likes savages. In the back corner of the room, I saw a red outline floating in the air, the person watching over everyone in amusement.

Reed.

He caught me staring, winking at me before his focus went to the chandeliers hanging from the ceiling, making me look there too. They swayed back and forth, almost in a hypnotizing motion. I couldn't peel my gaze away from it.

I watched it swing, the lights blurring together until all I could see was a yellow haze. My feet flipped out from beneath me, and my world went black.

❧

The forest surrounded me as I ran, pushing willow branches out of my way. They scraped across my skin, stinging me, but I didn't care. I knew I couldn't stop. I had to keep moving and trying to get away from...away from what?

Rustles of leaves sounded behind me as I continued to run. All my muscles were on fire, burning me to a crisp and cramping under my sweaty skin, but I couldn't stop. Had to keep moving. Had to.

A shrill cackle echoed through the woods, attacking my nerves until goosebumps erupted all over me. Nausea fought for control of my stomach, wanting me to stop.

Teeessssaaaa. My name was distorted in the wind, high-pitched and screeching. *Darling Tessa.* It taunted me, basking in my terror.

My muscles seized, bringing me to a stop. My legs felt like lead as I tried to lift them, trying to move myself forward.

Black, fuzzy vines broke out from the ground in a quiet movement, slithering up my legs and holding me in place. They continued up my torso and arms, the icy fuzz searing my skin. The vines suctioned to me, pulsing with my heartbeat, moving up and down against my skin like it was trying to suck the life right out of me.

The vines laced through my lips, stitching them closed, and I was *really* getting tired of them doing that.

Tessa. They sang my name this time, a lilting, dreadful tune.

My knees tried to buckle, but the vines held my body upright.

Suddenly a vampire finch, with its beady black eyes and orange beak, appeared at my side, biting at the vines, trying to free me. But the vines just opened and wrapped around the bird, squeezing until the bird's head drooped, its life gone.

My life was seconds away from the same fate. The vines sucked at me, all my energy draining until I went limp, the vines holding me up like a puppet.

Everything went red. Oranges and yellows swirled with the red, taking up my vision. I couldn't see anyone, but I could *feel* them. A dark presence wiped the happiness from anything that went near it.

Tears pooled in my eyes until they escaped, falling in a river down the vines wrapped around my face. Sorrow embraced me, cleaving to my very soul. I wanted to writhe, to twist away from the darkness, but the vines kept me in place. The evil entity suddenly consumed the air around me, shutting everything else off.

It's almost time, the dark voice grated, vibrating my eardrums. *Be ready, Tessa. For soon, we rise.*

CHAPTER 30

I jolted awake, flinging myself upright so hard I almost lost my balance and fell off the couch. The couch. I was on the couch in my family room, slick with sweat. It covered my skin, clinging to my clothes and hair.

The only light came from a small candle flickering on the coffee table. Dad was passed out in my abuelo's chair, his jaw hanging wide, his snores echoing around the room. Leya was curled up on the loveseat, smiling in her sleep, probably dreaming about happy things like puppies and rainbows.

Water. I needed water. Swinging my legs off the side of the couch, I clutched the cushions, trying to control my dizziness.

"Not so fast," the deep voice said from behind me.

I whipped around, one hand flying to my chest, the other shooting out in front of me as if to stop someone from advancing on me.

Sheriff Hayes quirked his thin lips in a smile. "What do you need? I'll get it for you."

Taking deep breaths, I waited until my heart found a

normal rhythm and some moisture had worked its way back into my mouth. "Water."

With a nod, the sheriff disappeared into the kitchen. He came back, holding a glass of water in one hand and a bottle of water in the other.

"Have a prefe—" the sheriff started, but I snatched both from his hands.

I downed the glass first, then switched to the opened water bottle while holding out the glass so the sheriff could take it back into his hand.

He eyed the couch next to me, then his gaze slid to my clothes clinging to my wet body, and he took a seat on the arm of the couch instead, probably not wanting to sit in my sweat.

After setting the empty water bottle on the coffee table, I sat back on the couch, my hands clasped over my stomach. "What happened?"

Sheriff Hayes kept his voice low since Dad and Leya were still asleep. "Part way during the earthquake, you passed out." He arched a thick eyebrow. "I could have sworn you glowed orange right before you did."

"It wouldn't surprise me."

Sheriff Hayes rubbed at the scruff on the side of his face. "The quake stopped not long after."

"Any injuries?" Everyone had been shoving to get out.

"Not that we know about."

What about Graham and Barbie? And Mrs. Morales? Were they okay? I reached forward, snatching my cell from the coffee table, wanting to call Graham, but my phone was dead.

I slowly worked my way onto my feet and shuffled to the kitchen, where we had some cords set up for charging on the countertop. Every step took more effort than it should have. My muscles were still clutched tight like they were clinging to all the humanity left inside me. I'd hoped the water would help loosen them.

After plugging in the phone, I leaned rested my head on the counter, closing my eyes tight. *Control. Steady. Calm.* I would get through this. I could get through anything.

Graham would be fine. He would be.

"Need another water?" Sheriff Hayes asked.

I opened my eyes to find him leaning against the counter between the sink and the fridge.

"Dr Pepper?" I asked.

Sheriff Hayes grabbed two bottles from the fridge, handing one to me and keeping the other for himself. "So, you're a bottle snob?"

I twisted the lid off. "I hate the taste of the can. It taints the pureness of DP."

He took a swig, slightly shaking his head in amusement.

I turned so my back was against the counter and held the cold bottle against my neck, hoping to cool down. My blood still simmered. Nirah hummed to life, heating her path as she traveled through my body like she was enjoying a water park.

I couldn't wait for the day when I didn't have something occupying me.

"That earthquake sure moved things along, though," the sheriff said. "The evacuation has started."

"Shouldn't you be out there patrolling or something?" I asked.

He moved his thumb and index finger across his eyebrows, starting from the bridge of his nose and working his way to his temples. Then he rubbed his temples for a couple of seconds. "I have my deputies out there. Some people left right away; some went home to pack up a few things. Helped spread out the crowd."

"Are a lot of people staying?" I asked.

"Just the stubborn ones." Sheriff Hayes took a long drink,

then looked at the bottle like he wished it was something a lot stronger than soda.

I grunted a laugh. "Just the people we want protecting us."

"At least we know they'd do anything to fight for this town."

"True." I pushed the bottle against my cheek, where a part of Nirah was hanging out. "So, what now?"

The sheriff finished off his soda and then tossed the bottle in the recycling bin near the back door, making it from where he stood. "We still can't get ahold of Esme Morales. I can't believe I'm going to suggest this, but we should probably talk to Lloyd Cromwell."

I glanced at the clock hanging on the wall. It was a little after ten. "Is it too late to go now?" I needed a distraction from thinking about Graham.

"Not for Lloyd. He'll be more than happy to talk to us."

"I should probably see if Dad and Leya want to come. We need all hands on deck."

I pushed away from the counter, but the sheriff's grim voice stopped me.

"Tessa." He took a deep breath. His jaw pulled tight, his eyes still on the floor. "Remi told me what happened the night of Corrine's murder."

I really didn't want to talk about this with the sheriff. His son had basically tried to rape me. Blake knew I didn't have full control of my body, and Delilah was in me.

"Sheriff, it's not like that. I..." What could I say? Did I dare tell him the truth? Maybe he'd want to know what his son had done.

Sheriff Hayes finally met my eyes. "I talked with Blake. He told me what happened." There was an anger in his eyes I'd never seen before. Was he mad at me? It wasn't like I was going to his son for comfort sex after losing a friend.

I was still at a loss for words. I wriggled, uncomfortable.

Even Nirah retreated behind my heart like she didn't want to be part of this conversation.

"He told me about...Delilah." His voice cracked on the last word.

"Wait, Blake told you the *truth?* Like, what really happened?"

The sheriff nodded. "Trust me when I say I had a lot of words with that boy. What he did to you was unacceptable. I have no idea what he was thinking."

I folded my arms close to my chest. "Thanks, Sheriff. I'm not sure if I can ever forgive him."

"I don't blame you. He's been grounded ever since I found out, but he still finds ways to sneak out of the house. I might need to get a GPS chip put in him." Amusement touched his eyes, but there was a truth lingering behind it. "He's never been the same since his mom died." He looked at me. "How did you stay so stable after losing your mom?"

I bit back a laugh. "I don't think having séances, letting ghosts into our realm, being possessed by a spirit to the point I kill a man isn't what I'd consider 'stable.'"

"True, but you still seem to have a decent head on your shoulders."

But I didn't for a long time. I still had to repeat my mantra on at least a daily basis. I still had to see Rita to keep myself sane. I was a work in progress, and I had a feeling it would be like that my whole life.

Leya shimmied into the kitchen. "Is this where the party's at?"

"I'll be out in the car." With a heavy sigh, Sheriff Hayes left the kitchen, brushing past Leya.

Leya frowned after him. "Was it my sweet moves that scared him away?"

"I think it was the fact that he's taking us to see Lloyd Cromwell."

Leya blanched. "Okay, so Jade told me all about him the other night, and the guy is off his rocker. Apparently, there's a good chance he's a serial killer. Totally gives off that vibe."

"He's not a serial killer, Leya." I plucked my clothes away from my skin. "I'm going to rinse off really quick and change into new clothes. Let the sheriff know I won't be more than five minutes. Tops."

I really hoped we'd find the answer soon, but I wasn't holding my breath. And whatever we did find? No way it was going to be easy.

CHAPTER 31

Two ravens perched on the gutter attached to Lloyd Cromwell's roof. Their beady eyes watched as we stepped out of the police cruiser and moved toward the front door.

Leya linked her arm through mine, her eyes fixated on the birds. "Hey, Sheriff? On a scale of one to ten, like, how illegal is it to kill a bird?"

Both ravens croaked as they scooted down the gutter, closer to us.

Amusement touched Sheriff Hayes' tone. "Ten."

We all stepped onto the porch, almost in unison.

Leya twirled a few of her long braids in her hand. "Ten being, don't do it, or ten being, yeah, sure, no big deal?"

Dad shook his head. "No killing birds. That's one step closer to becoming a Harrison."

I shivered at the thought.

Leya huffed. "Yeah, fine. They're just totally creepy, and I'm about ninety-eight percent sure those ones aren't real of-this-earth ravens."

No one moved to knock on the door. We just huddled on

the porch, not making eye contact with each other. Guess none of us were that eager to hear what Cromwell had to say. I worried about how awful it would be.

Leya finally gave in and knocked, quickly clinging to me when she scooted back. "Please don't be a serial killer." She mumbled under her breath. "Please don't be a serial killer."

We waited in eerie silence as the seconds ticked by. Was he home? Had he heard the knock? Had he heard Leya's mutterings and gotten spooked?

After a minute, Dad leaned forward to knock again when the door whooshed open.

Lloyd Cromwell was hunched in the shadows of his entry-way, the darkness masking his face. A humid chill flew out the door, surrounding us. He must have had the A/C cranked way high.

Leya's hold on my arm tightened.

"It's about time," Cromwell said in a gruff voice. He stepped back, making room for us to enter his home.

I glanced at the sheriff. "You first."

He smirked before stepping over the threshold. Dad followed, but not before gently squeezing my arm, letting me know it was okay. We were safe. Even if Cromwell turned out to be a serial killer, it was four against one. Sheriff Hayes had a gun, plus a taser and mace. Besides, Cromwell couldn't even stand on his own.

The inside of Cromwell's home was freezing. Coming from the humid summer heat outside, the cold shocked me.

"It's like one of those ice bars in here." Leya glanced around the front room as she rubbed her bare arms. "Without cool sculptures or anything."

Cromwell's tone was matter-of-fact. "The cold keeps away the demons."

Leya forced a smile. "Right. Those pesky demons. Always loving the heat. It's like, chill already, you know?"

Cromwell's eyes narrowed, his bushy white eyebrows becoming one. "If you're not going to take this seriously, I'm going to have to ask you to leave."

I hurried to chime in before Leya could say anything else sarcastic. "We are taking it seriously. It's just demons are a lot to process when you grew up thinking they didn't exist."

Leya held up a hand. "It stops there, though, right? Because if you start throwing vampires at me, I'm out."

Cromwell let out a weird grunt that I wasn't sure if it was a laugh or annoyance. "No vampires. Just shapeshifting demons and witches."

Dad tilted his head ever-so-slightly, his breath hitching up. "Witches?"

"Local coven. I'm guessing that's where Esme Morales has run off to." Cromwell moved toward the hallway, using his cane as a support. "Everything I have is in here." He disappeared around the corner, leaving us alone in the foyer.

Dad ran his hand down his face. "A coven. That's great. Just great."

Leya pointed a manicured nail at him. "Hey, you want to run this town."

"That was before I knew about demons and witches." Dad looked at the sheriff. "Is it too late for me to back out?"

Sheriff Hayes clapped Dad on the shoulder. "This is exactly why we need you, Alec." He took off down the hall.

With a long sigh, Dad followed him. Leya and I were quick at his heels.

At the end of the hall was a massive room. Metal shelves filled one half. The other half had a large, waist-high, rectangular table with papers and books scattered all over. An expensive-looking projector sat in the middle of the table.

"This place is huge." I stopped in front of the wall behind the table. Pictures and notes were taped all over, with strings of yarn in various colors connecting them.

Leya bounced beside me, clinking her nails together. "I've always wanted to do one of these. They look so cool in the movies."

"Everything used to be in the garage," Cromwell said from behind us. We turned around to find him sitting in a tall chair at the head of the table. He'd hooked his cane on the edge of the table. "But I quickly ran out of room. Plus, I needed a more climate-controlled area. So I tore down the wall between the master and the guest room and converted this into my work area."

Leya and I joined them at the table, standing opposite my dad and the sheriff.

"Uh, where do you sleep?" Leya asked, glancing around the room.

"Couch in the front room." Cromwell rolled on his chair off to the side, then pressed a couple of buttons on a controller in his hand. The lights in the room dimmed as the projector came to life.

"This guy is no joke," Leya whispered next to me.

"Have you all heard about the Legend of Birch Lake?" Cromwell asked as an image of the lake appeared on the wall, the version of Andras we'd seen in the book standing in the middle of the lake.

"Yeah," I said.

"Did you read *Lucifer's Reign?*" Cromwell asked.

"We skimmed it." I had to push out the image of the girl sacrificing herself from my head.

Cromwell pressed a button on his remote, and a big, fat FALSE stamp whooshed onto the screen over the image of the lake. "Forget everything you learned. I'm going to tell you the truth."

"Wait, the legend is fake?" Leya shimmied next to me, rubbing her hands up and down her arms, probably dancing to raise her temperature. It was *freezing* in the room.

Cromwell shook his head. "It's real. It's just been changed over the years that the real truth behind it all got lost. I want to start you off fresh."

A large, gold figure popped up on the wall, practically covering the entire area. Its shape was tall and muscular, hands and feet both massive. He wore a simple gold loincloth that blended in with the rest of him. The shape of his head was wide, coming to thick points on either side, almost like ears, but not quite. Similar to what we saw in *Lucifer's Reign*, yet so different. And exactly like the vision I'd seen.

"Meet the real Andras." Cromwell set his hands in his lap. "He followed Lucifer for years, doing his bidding with no questions asked. After a time, Andras grew tired of being a puppet. He wanted somewhere he could reign and be the one in charge. He shifted into a wolf and went on the run and into hiding."

The slide changed, showing a massive black wolf with gold eyes.

"I've seen that wolf."

Cromwell nodded. "Not surprising. He's been stalking this town for months now."

Sheriff Hayes leaned forward. "Did you say *months?*"

"He's been keeping an eye on everyone," Cromwell continued, "learning everyone's patterns and behaviors." The slide changed again, and the gold Andras came back, only this time, there was a raven perched on his shoulder. "Andras searched everywhere for a place to build his army and begin his reign. He finally settled on below Birch Lake."

"Why here?" Dad asked.

"Willow Marsh is a powerful epicenter for magic." Cromwell kept saying things in a way like we should have already known it. "The barrier between his realm and ours is thin here."

"This seems like what we already know," Sheriff Hayes said.

Cromwell grunted and then coughed. "You only know a small sliver of it. That malarky about a girl sacrificing herself, slitting her wrists and bleeding out, is laughable."

Across the table, Dad let out a very audible breath of relief. We shared a smile, knowing we felt the same way.

I leaned my hip against the table. "Why hasn't he already taken over?"

"He quickly learned that he could only manifest as a wolf in our realm," Cromwell said. "As terrifying as a wolf is, it can't run a country full of humans." He changed the slide, and a beautiful, angelic woman came on the screen. "He also didn't know about her."

The woman had long, black hair that flowed down to her waist. She wore a pale blue gown made of silk, with pink dahlias embroidered all over. She wore a simple bronze crown, the design similar to the band of my ring. She looked like an older version of me.

"This is Thezanna." Cromwell stared in awe at the screen. "Goddess of justice, wisdom, and rebirth."

Dad rubbed his jaw. "That's an interesting combo."

Cromwell looked over his shoulder at my dad. "She's an interesting creature. She's been known to drown herself during the spring equinox and then come back to life, symbolizing the end of one season and the rebirth of another."

"So, she does sacrifice herself." Leya's teeth were clattering together, thanks to the cold. "Just by drowning."

Cromwell nodded. "Yes, but then she's reborn."

Dad and I shared a wary look. Drowning and being reborn didn't sound much better than slitting my wrists and bleeding out.

Cromwell tossed his remote on the table. "Let me just

boil everything down really quick. I think that will be easiest." He waited for all of us to nod before he continued. "Andras wants to reign on the earth, but he can't unless he's human. To become human, he needs the purest of souls to cleanse himself, almost a rebirth of himself."

"Children," I muttered.

Cromwell frowned. "Unfortunately, yes. He tried that back in the sixteen hundreds, but Thezanna intervened. She was too late to save the children, as they had already drowned, but she got there just in time to stop Andras from receiving their souls. In a pure and selfless sacrifice, Thezanna drowned herself in the lake, transferring the children's souls to heaven and removing their bodies from the lake." He coughed into the crook of his elbow. "Andras was *not* happy about that."

The slide switched to a circle of ladies hovering above the water of the lake. Their hands were clasped, their heads tilted toward the sky.

"What Thezanna didn't know was that a local coven of witches had figured out Andras' plan and wanted to stop him as well. They placed a spell over the lake, trapping Andras from ever getting through. Thezanna was still in the lake, inches from death, when they cast the spell, shattering her immortal soul. She was eventually reborn but was mortal." Cromwell's focus flickered over to me.

Everyone followed his gaze.

Sheriff Hayes leaned his palms on the table. "Are you saying that Tessa is Thezanna reborn?"

This was so weird. I couldn't be. Right?

"Her great-great-grandma, Tessa Isaacson Walker, was the first," Cromwell said. "Once she passed, she was reborn again in Tessa."

Leya gasped. "Tessa is a goddess?"

"A mortal version," Cromwell said. "It's why she's so powerful and strong, but not—"

"Full goddess power level," Leya interjected. She rubbed my arm. "Sorry, Tessa. You'll always be a goddess to me, though."

A small smile found its way to my face as I lightly shoved her arm.

"If the witches cast the spell, how has Andras been able to come now?" There was intrigue in Sheriff Hayes' tone. He was way more invested in this than I thought he'd be.

Cromwell motioned to me. "When Tessa destroyed the box during her battle with Reed and Ellington down in the crypt, she unknowingly shattered that spell."

My hand went to my throat. "This really is my fault."

"It was bound to happen at some point," Cromwell said.

Leya clasped her hands on top of her head. "Okay, but I still have like a million questions."

"Hopefully, we can provide some answers." At a lady's angelic voice, the five of us turned toward the door, only to find four women, one of them Mrs. Morales.

CHAPTER 32

I ran to Mrs. Morales, giving her a tight hug. At least one missing person was now accounted for. That just left Graham and Barbie.

"Where have you been?" I pulled back so I could see her. "We've been trying to contact you."

Mrs. Morales softly smiled. "Sorry, my dear. I was doing research about your ring and remembered something Nyx and I once talked about and—"

"Who's Nyx?" I asked.

Mrs. Morales motioned to one of the women.

My jaw dropped. I'd met her before, outside of the sheriff's station. She'd given me back my ring that I'd supposedly dropped.

"This is Nyx," Mrs. Morales said. "Leader of a local coven."

Nyx gave me a knowing smile, slightly nodding her head.

Mrs. Morales motioned to a short lady with shoulder-length black hair, her skin unbelievably pale. "This is Allegra." Her hand swept toward the last woman. "And this is Sheba."

She was beautiful, tall, and lean, her skin even darker than Leya's.

"I was hoping you'd come." Cromwell slid off his chair, grabbed his cane, and then worked his way over to the ladies. "We have so much to do, and I hardly know where to start."

Nyx cupped her hands over Cromwell's hand that he had extended. "Sorry we couldn't get here sooner, Crom. We've been so busy getting ready."

"Ready for what?" Leya asked.

Nyx smiled at her. "The battle, of course." She let go of Cromwell's hand and practically floated over to me, her moves so graceful. She put her hand under my chin and turned my head side to side. "You look just like Thezanna." Her thumb stroked my chin. "You aren't quite ready, but we'll get you there."

Nyx glided to the head of the table, standing next to Cromwell, who had taken a seat in his tall chair again.

"While I'd love to do the formalities," Nyx said, smiling softly at everyone, "we really have a lot to attend to and not much time."

"Andras is way ahead of schedule." Sheba's voice was the total opposite of Nyx's smooth, calming tone. There was grit to her gravelly voice like she'd seen so much in her lifetime, though she couldn't have been much older than her mid-thirties.

Sheba had taken a spot between Dad and Sheriff Hayes, while Allegra had come to my side, standing incredibly close. She smelled like roses and sweet fruit.

"He has a lot more help this time around," Allegra said, leaning her head on my shoulder like we were long-lost friends.

Leya's eyes narrowed in on Allegra. Leya quickly snatched my hand, intertwining our fingers like this was a competition of who was my closer friend.

I squeezed Leya's hand, and I could feel some of the tension in her body melt away.

"In three moons' time," Nyx said, turning all attention to her, "Andras will attempt to break the barrier at Birch Lake. Instead of summoning all the children to the lake like he did before, he's going to use the ones he kidnapped so they can't get away this time."

My heart sank, thinking of Chloe and Nash.

"Using their pure souls, he'll cross over to our side, beginning his reign on earth." Nyx looked at me. "But we're going to send Tessa to stop him before he can."

Dad looked between Nyx and me. "Where are you sending Tessa?"

Allegra stroked my hair. "She must finish what Thezanna started."

I took a step away from her. "Uh, Thezanna tried to drown herself."

"And she would have succeeded if my predecessors hadn't messed things up." Nyx floated toward me. "Tessa, back then, Thezanna and the local coven weren't aware of each other. We know each other now, and I believe we can work together this time to stop Andras for good."

I opened my mouth, but Nyx continued. "I know this is difficult to process—"

"Difficult seems like an understatement," Leya murmured.

"But this time we *can* win." Nyx glanced around at everyone, her gaze finally settling on Mrs. Morales. "We have the right help."

Mrs. Morales smiled at me. "Sweet girl, with your mother's heritage, your father's heritage, plus Thezanna, you are more powerful than we could hope for. We believe once you get into Andras' realm, memories from Thezanna will trickle back in. And she knows him better than anyone else."

"How?" I asked.

Nyx took a deep breath. "Thezanna and Andras were once allies."

Leya gasped.

"Lovers," Allegra whispered in my ear.

"Didn't need to know that part," I muttered.

Nirah heated inside me, slinking all over like she was worked up.

"Why would a goddess and a demon work together?" It made no sense.

Nyx went back to the head of the table, setting her palms on it. "Thezanna was once a demon herself. She and Andras were thick as thieves. But something inside Thezanna changed. Over the years, the hate and malice she held shifted to love and acceptance."

"It was a long process." Sheba ran a lanky finger across her collarbone. "Thousands of years in the making."

Allegra twirled next to me. "But Thezanna turned herself around."

"Andras was unaware of the change," Nyx continued. "Thezanna worked behind Andras' back with the help of some other gods and goddesses, gathering her strength. To change sides, she sacrificed herself over and over for those who were struggling and needing aide until she felt she'd paid her penance. When she fully shifted sides, she chose to be the goddess of justice, wisdom, and rebirth."

"Justice as a symbol of how we must all pay the price for our sins," Sheba said, running a hand over her shaved head.

Allegra swayed side to side. "Wisdom because with knowledge, our minds may be opened and changed."

"And rebirth to show we can all be reborn, no matter our past mistakes." Nyx smiled softly at me, and I couldn't help but think of my mom and brother, their deaths on my hands.

Sheriff Hayes cleared his throat. "As lovely as this all is, I'd like to know your plan."

Nyx turned her golden eyes toward him. "There should be a relic that holds the symbols of Thezanna: a gavel, a book, and a fur-covered snake."

Leya held up a hand and waited for Nyx to nod before she spoke. "Uh, why a fur-covered snake? That's rebirth?"

"Snakes do shed their skin," Dad said. "But why the fur?"

Nyx motioned to me. "Because of Nirah."

At her name, my skin began to glow.

CHAPTER 33

Dad, Cromwell, and Sheriff Hayes' eyes practically bulged out of their sockets. Allegra clapped her hands and jumped like I was putting on a show.

I stared at my outstretched arms, watching as my skin became brighter wherever Nirah traveled. She loved this introduction.

"Nirah never left Thezanna's side all those years." Nyx motioned for Cromwell to change the slide, and up came a picture of a red-fur snake-like creature with round, beady eyes and sharp fangs. "She's as loyal as they come."

I shook my arms, hoping to get Nirah to subside, but she continued to travel my body almost like she was in a parade, knowing everyone was watching.

"Wait." Leya licked her lips. "Nirah is Thezanna's pet? Not Andras'?"

Sheba smirked. "I bet some days she seems evil, other days friendly?"

I slowly nodded. That described her perfectly.

"Nirah wasn't too sure about the change from demoness to goddess," Nyx said. "But she stayed loyal to Thezanna."

Allegra leaned her head on my shoulder. "Doesn't mean she got rid of all her evil, though. She can still be a little punk sometimes."

Nirah zoomed up to my neck, going around and around.

That would explain why she held me back at the lake. She'd been helping me. It also explained why she loved the snake on Ace's belt buckle and constantly wanted to strangle people.

Nirah finally calmed, my skin going back to its normal color.

"I've checked the list of relics." Cromwell coughed into the crook of his elbow. "There's nothing with those symbols."

Sheriff Hayes arched a bushy eyebrow. "How have you seen the list? We haven't released it to the public."

Cromwell harrumphed but didn't say anything.

Nyx stood gracefully, her presence demanding attention. "It must be there. We need to go back to the crypt and do another search."

Dad stared at the image of Nirah on the screen. "Let's say we find it. Then what?"

Nyx gestured to me. "We'll send Tessa into Andras' realm, have her trap him in the relic, and then come back up."

I put a hand to my throat. "But I have to drown myself to get into his realm, correct?"

Sheba nodded curtly. "You need to crossover. But we have protections in place."

"What *protections*?" Dad's voice was tight. No way he was liking any of this.

I wasn't liking any of this.

"Our coven will surround the island in the lake." Nyx motioned to Mrs. Morales, who pulled a beaded necklace out of her bag.

"We've been working on these." Mrs. Morales laid the necklace on the table. "We'll each be wearing one."

Dad reached across the table and snatched it up. "You're going to protect my daughter with a *necklace?*"

"It has spells in place." Mrs. Morales tone was that of a scolding parent.

Dad quickly dropped the necklace and wiped his hand off on his shirt like he'd gotten some of the spell on him.

"Protection spells." Allegra stroked my neck. "Tessa will be wearing one, too."

"Plus, with her mother's ring," Nyx said. "We'll never lose her."

I stared at the ring on my finger. "What do you mean?"

Nyx held out a graceful hand. "Not only is it enchanted with its own spells, it has a location beacon in it. Think of it as a GPS tracker."

"How—" I cut off, remembering when she'd handed me my ring outside the sheriff's station, claiming that it had fallen off. I couldn't help but be impressed. I tugged on the ring, but nothing happened. "Is that why the ring is suctioned to me? I can't get it off."

Mrs. Morales gently smiled. "Yes. It's what I originally thought when you first asked me about it, but I wanted to make sure before I said anything."

"Is there a reason it won't come off, though?" I asked.

"We can't have you losing it," Nyx calmly said.

I glanced between Mrs. Morales and Nyx. "But when this is all over, it will come off again, right?"

Nyx simply shrugged. "Time will tell. Now, we must get to work."

Dad slammed a hand down on the table. "I'm sorry, but this is a lot for a father to take in. You want my daughter to kill herself, and thanks to some stupid spells, she'll come back to life? I'm just supposed to trust you on that?"

Nyx glided over and stood between my dad and the sheriff, placing her hands on their shoulders. "I know this is diffi-cult, but I promise you, Tessa will be okay."

Both men seemed to relax under her touch, almost like she bewitched them.

Nyx lowered her hands. "We'll start by finding the relic."

Mrs. Morales scooped up the necklace and set it back in her bag. "Sheba, Allegra, and I will work with the rest of the coven to create the necklaces."

Nyx strolled over to me. "Once we find the relic, we'll work on teaching you some spells to get you ready to face Andras."

The sheriff's phone rang, so he stepped out of the room to answer it.

I pressed a shaking hand to my stomach. "Whatever you did to my dad and the sheriff, can you do that to me? I'm really freaking out."

Nyx placed her finger under my chin. "We need you sharp and focused. You'll be fine, Tessa. And you'll have Nirah with you. She should manifest once you cross over."

"Like, not be inside me anymore?"

"Yes." She took my hands in hers, turning them so they were palm up. She glanced at the scar on my right hand between my thumb and forefinger and then the scar on my left palm. "The nice thing about Nirah? She has healing powers."

At her name, Nirah snapped into two and raced to both hands, warming them from the inside. The scars on me faded until they were gone.

Leya gasped over my shoulder, making me jump. She smiled sheepishly. "Sorry, that was just really cool."

I stared at my hands in shock. "Wait, Nirah had the ability to do this the whole time she's been in me?" I couldn't hold back the annoyance in my tone, thinking of how these scars had caused me so much misery. Not to mention the burn rash Graham and I received at the lake.

Nirah danced around inside me, almost in a teasing nature.

Allegra patted my arm. "Remember when I said she could be a punk?"

I lowered my hands. "So, if she can heal my hands, she could possibly..."

Sheba suddenly appeared at my said and placed her hand over my heart. "Heal this as well."

The sheriff came back into the room, a distraught look on his face. "It's my daughter." He briefly closed his eyes. "Livvy is missing."

CHAPTER 34

Sheriff Hayes handed over the key to the crypt and left without another word. I couldn't imagine what he was going through.

After swift goodbyes, Mrs. Morales, Sheba, and Allegra left to work on the necklaces.

Nyx looked up at the ravens on the roof. "Ladies, please follow us." She motioned to my dad's car. "Alec, will you please escort us to the crypt?"

Dad hurried over to the passenger side door and held it open for Nyx. "Of course."

Leya eyed me. "Uh, what is happening?"

I shook my head in disbelief. "She really did bewitch him."

"Girls, let's go!" Dad barked, rushing around to the driver's side.

We scrambled to get inside.

"Those are your ravens?" I clicked my seatbelt into place.

Nyx smiled over her shoulder at me. "I've been having them keep an eye on you."

Leya leaned forward and tapped the headrest. "Well, FYI, it came across as creepy."

I thought back to the bird that had lured me toward the lake with its music. It took everything in Nirah to hold me back and not enter the water. "Was it one of your ravens that tried to get me to enter the lake?"

Nyx placed her hand on the side of Dad's seat and shifted so she should see me better. Her eyebrows were furrowed in deep thought. "That wasn't one of mine."

Leya drummed her nails along the seat between us. "How many creepy, supernatural ravens does this place have?"

I thought back to the image of Andras. "On the slide, there was a picture of Andras with a raven on his shoulder. Could it be the same one?"

"Clever girl." Nyx's lips twitched in mild amusement. "That would make sense. Eribell is one to hang in the shadows. For someone so memorable, she's so easily forgotten."

"Is Eribell a shapeshifter, too?" Was she just another person to add to the list of those working against me?

Nyx nodded. "Yes. You'll know her the second you see her when you're down there."

Dad shifted uncomfortably in the driver's seat. He looked through the rearview mirror, locking eyes with me for a moment.

Down there. When I was dead.

I stroked my ring, trying to summon every ounce of courage I could. It had to work.

When we got to the city building, I called Graham. No answer. So I texted.

"Where could he be?" I asked Leya as we waited in the lobby for the elevator.

"Who? Graham?" Leya shrugged. "Working long hours? You did say his boss hated him."

I glanced over at my dad. "What did you say to him at the lake? He's been ignoring me ever since then."

Dad smirked as the elevator doors pinged open. "Just a little guy talk."

"Uh huh." I slid into the elevator next him. "You traumatized him."

When Leya and Nyx were both in the elevator, I inserted the key that would take us down below, deep into the crypt.

We rode in silence as the elevator music played, a light jazz melody.

Reed's red form suddenly flickered into view right before me, looking terrified. He clawed at his eyes and screamed, reminding me of when I was stuck in the elevator with him. Ellington had somehow made Reed's eyes bleed, causing Reed to claw at his face, leaving him with permanent scars.

Leya grabbed my arm, screaming along with Reed.

"Enough with the theatrics." Nyx's smooth voice cut through the elevator.

Reed lowered his hands and stopped screaming, a frown forming on his face. "Mood killer."

Leya let out a loud breath, still clinging to my arm.

I narrowed my eyes at him. "You were faking?"

Reed swept out his arms. "Reenacting." He ran his fingers along his scars. "Truly a turning point in my life."

Dad ran his hand down his face. "I'm so over all of this."

"Amen." Leya held up her hand for Dad to high-five, but he just shook his head.

Reed tried to high-five her for Dad, but his ghostly hand just passed right on through. He tsked. "Boo. This being dead thing sucks." He leaned to the side, tilting his head. "You still need to solve my problem, dearest Tessa. *I'm so over* The Gray. And our little ladybug won't stop yelling and whining about it."

Corrine. I had to save her somehow while I was down there. Though, I had no idea how to go about that.

The elevator doors finally opened, and we stepped into the cold passageway. Leya and I pulled out our phones and turned on the flashlights to see where we were going.

"Nyx," I said as we walked, "a lot of people are stuck down there with Andras. If I stop him—"

"*When* you stop him," Nyx cut in.

"Right. *When* I stop him, can we help everyone stuck in The Gray? Like, get them on a train to heaven or something?"

How did one go about doing that? If I did have some of Thezanna in me and her goddess powers, maybe I could conjure something up.

Nyx was quiet for a moment as we trudged in a single-file line through the dark passageway. At least I had my family with me this time around. Last time I had to trek this alone with so much uncertainty and fear in my heart.

The uncertainty and fear were still here, though, weighing me down. This all seemed so impossible.

"I believe so," Nyx finally said, her voice echoing off the rock walls. "It's a very delicate matter. Since they're stuck in an in-between realm, we should be able to transfer them on. The tricky part will be making sure their destination is heaven. They're already so close to hell."

I reached back, taking Leya's hand in mine. There had to be a way to save Corrine and the others. They didn't deserve an eternity in hell.

CHAPTER 35

Walking into the crypt sent a shiver coursing through me, and not just because of the cold.

This crypt was where I shot and killed Reed. It was where I ended Ellington and destroyed the box linking the living and the dead.

It was also the last time I'd spoken to Amá.

Reed's red ghostly figure appeared next to me, his arm out like he was trying to rest it on my shoulder. "Should we reenact the tragedy that unfolded here months ago? We know my acting skills are magnifique, but yours, I'm not so sure."

Leya raised her hand. "Oh! Can I play Tessa?"

"No reenactments." Dad scanned the crypt with his eyes, really soaking everything in.

Leya pouted. "But I wanted a chance to kill Reed."

Reed chuckled, though it was distorted. "Isn't it so great that we can joke about my death like this?" The darkness in his eyes showed he was just as mad to be dead now as he was when it happened.

Leya shrunk back under his intense glare.

Nyx picked up a gold candelabra, running a finger along it. "This belonged to my ancestor."

"How do you know?" I asked, coming up to her.

She smiled softly. "I can feel it." With a deep breath, she glanced around the crypt. "Search everything for those symbols. We have no idea where they will be or how big they will be."

Reed floated until he was sitting on top of Albert Harrison's casket. He swung his legs like he was trying to bang the soles against the coffin. "Have I told you about the one time my good ol' great-grandpappy—"

I rounded on him. "No one cares about your great-grandpappy, Reed. Enough with the trips down memory lane."

He rolled up the cuffs of his flannel jacket. "I'd be careful if I were you, dear Tessa, for you'll be with me soon, within arms' reach."

My stomach rolled, thinking about my upcoming death. I quickly shook the thought from my head. If I dwelled on it, I'd go insane and get absolutely nothing done.

So, I turned my attention to scavenging the crypt. We searched high and low, checking every nook and cranny of the place.

"It has to be somewhere." Dad paused in the middle of the crypt, defeat weighing on him.

Leya picked up a blue soldiers' hat and gently put it on her head. "Unless it's at the Hayes' house."

I really didn't want to go over there and chance coming across Blake. Plus, they were dealing with the disappearance of Livvy.

Reed hopped down from the casket. "There is one place you *haven't* searched yet." His grin turned lopsided. "Well, three places." His head nodded toward the three caskets.

Leya scrunched her face in disgust. "You want us to open

the caskets? The one with the bones and souls of really old dead dudes?"

Nyx ran a finger along Walker's casket. "Their souls aren't here. Just their bones."

Leya took off the hat and used it to block her mouth so only I could see and mouthed, *The souls are* totally *there.*

Reed popped up next to her. "Only one way to find out."

Leya shrieked, jumping into the air. Then she swatted at Reed's figure with the hat, her frustration growing with every swing that swooshed right through him.

Dad reached down and grabbed a rusty crowbar from the floor. He looked at Nyx. "Is there a way to cast a spell on the caskets, so the guys won't know we're interfering with their corpses? With everything going on, I really don't want to have to add 'worry about the three ticked-off ghosts stalking me.'"

Nyx set her palms on top of the casket. "I assure you, nothing bad will happen." She closed her eyes, her lips barely moving as she mumbled something practically inaudible.

Dad leaned toward me. "I was kidding about the spell."

I patted his arm. "Another layer of protection won't hurt."

When Nyx lowered her hands, Dad inserted the crowbar and lifted back the lid of Joseph Walker's casket. It took all four of us to take it fully off and lean it against the wall. Reed just watched the entire time in amusement.

I stared at the remains of my great-great-grandfather.

"Is it strange that I'm getting used to bizarre things happening around me?" Leya asked. "Because this is freaking weird, but also a day in the life, ya know?"

Nyx reached into the casket and gently took one of Joseph's hands in hers. There, on the bone of the right ring finger, was a shiny gold ring. No rust or anything.

"Okay, how is everything preserved so well?" Leya touched one of the buttons on Joseph's vest. She grimaced. "Except for poor Joseph." She looked at his skeletal head. "I'm thinking he had brown hair? Kind of thick and wavy. Maybe a little curl at the nape of his neck."

Dad just stared at her, his head tilted slightly to the side.

Reed sidled up next to him, forming the same stance. "She's an odd one, no?"

Dad scooted away from Reed, muttering something incoherent under his breath.

Nyx slid off the ring and examined it. "There. Etched into the ring. A gavel, a book, and a fur-covered snake." She reached across the casket, handing me the ring.

I took the cold metal between my thumb and pointer finger, and everything exploded into a blur of colors. I stumbled back, hitting the casket behind me before I fell to my knees.

My fingers could not drop the ring, no matter how hard I tried. It was almost like they were glued to it. My vision went in and out a few times before I was cloaked in darkness. Silence fell around me as I struggled to grasp for air.

Suddenly images overtook my vision, brief flashes of a life that wasn't mine. There were so many rushing through that I couldn't pin any of them down. They kept coming, flying through my mind like an endless reel of slides. Every now and then, I thought I saw Thezanna, Andras, and Nirah, but they fluttered so quickly, like my mind was downloading millions of moments in mere seconds.

Finally, the images stopped until static filled my vision.

Then Andras appeared, a smile so evil and distorted that dread clawed its way inside me. It spread, ripping happiness and life from me in an instant.

The last thing I saw before I passed out was his grin growing, and his sharply pointed teeth dripping with blood.

You're ready, Tessa. Ready to rise.

CHAPTER 36

When I woke, I was lying in my bed at home, tucked into the covers tight like a mummy. My eyelids drooped as I noticed the morning light shining through my window. My throat was dry and scratchy, in desperate need of some water.

I wet my lips, trying to work moisture back into my mouth.

The house was quiet, like I was the only one home.

"Dad?" I managed to croak out. I coughed, regaining my voice. "Leya?"

I turned my head, seeing a piece of paper on the pillow next to me. It took a lot of effort, but I managed to wriggle myself free from the confines of my covers.

The light in the room suddenly came on, and Reed stood at the foot of the bed. "Enjoy your rest?"

I slowly sat up, too groggy to make a snide remark about him watching me sleep. "Where is everyone?"

"Getting ready for Death Day." Reed clasped his hands together and squealed. "I'm so looking forward to it."

"Can we please not call it that?" I picked up the piece of paper and read it.

Tessa! If you're reading this, you're alive and that makes me soooooo happy. I wanted to stay by your side but Nyx wouldn't shut up about all the work that needed to be done. She dragged your father and me out of the house to do prep stuff or whatever. Call me when you wake up! We'll rush home. If Nyx lets us. She's reading this as I write and says that it won't happen. Oh, and she says to rest and drink the smoothie that's on the nightstand. Don't let the bubbles scare you. Also, we weren't sure what to do with the ring since you obviously had an allergic reaction to it, and we didn't want you to lose it, so we put it on a chain, wrapped it in some leather we found, and put it around your neck. I miss you already. Call me!

*   All the squishy hugs and kisses,*

*   Leya*

I glanced down to see a dark leather pouch attached to a gold chain around my neck. Then I turned to see a glass full of blood-red liquid on the nightstand. I had no doubt Nyx's concoction would help, but as I stared down into the glass, bubbles formed and popped, not helping the situation at all.

"Is this what we're drinking for Death Day?" Reed grimaced. "I think I'll pass."

I glared at him. "One, stop calling it 'Death Day.' And two, you can't drink anything anyway. You're dead."

Reed matched my glare. "I'll stop calling it 'Death Day' when you stop bringing up the fact that I'm dead."

"'Death Day' it is," I muttered.

Closing my eyes, I took a sip of the drink. The taste of fresh strawberries exploded in my mouth, the bubbles continuing to pop as the liquid slid down my throat.

I smacked my lips and stared at the glass. "This is delicious and so extremely bizarre that I don't know how to process it fully." Fizzles erupted in my throat, going all the way down to my stomach like a million Pop Rocks had been released inside. "And we're past bizarre."

My phone buzzed on my nightstand. It was probably Leya calling to see if I was awake yet.

Reed looked down at the screen. "That's Ace's number."

"Ace? Why would he be calling me?"

"Answer, and you'll find out."

"Really not in the mood to talk to creepy brother number two." I took another sip of the drink, the strawberry flavor just as strong.

Within seconds of the phone stopping, it started ringing again.

"He won't stop until you answer. He's persistent, my kid brother."

I really didn't want to talk to another Harrison, but I knew Reed was right. Might as well get it over with.

With a snarl, I snatched my phone and answered it. "What?" The edge in my tone was strong.

Ace chuckled on the other end. "Lovely to talk to you, too, Tessa."

"Put it on speaker phone," Reed said.

Ace inhaled sharply. "Was that my brother?"

"You can hear him?" I stared incredulously at Reed.

Reed tried to poke my nose but thank goodness he couldn't touch me. "How many times have we gone over how powerful you are? You make me stronger. You make everything around you stronger. It's awe-inspiring, really."

"Reed?" Ace's voice held a hope that made him, for the moment, seem human. Not the monsters I saw the entire Harrison family as, thanks to their emotionless eyes.

I lowered the phone and pressed the speaker button. "What do you want, Ace?"

"Hello, brother," Reed purred.

"Brother!" Ace mumbled something in the background, probably to Lars. Then his voice came back. "Tessa, we need you over here. Right away."

"Can it wait?" I asked.

"I'm afraid not." Ace's tone was smooth like his brother's. "If you want your boyfriend to remain alive, then I'd get over here as soon as possible. Lars is in *quite* the mood."

"What are you talking about?" I asked.

"You remember your boyfriend, yes?" Ace asked. "Graham Dixon?"

I rolled my eyes. "I know who my boyfriend is."

"Good." Ace paused. "Well, you see, he's tied up in the basement, and Lars—"

I quickly ended the call and jumped out of bed. Lars had Graham. Which meant Graham was alive. For now. I couldn't trust Lars to keep him that way.

I wondered if it had something to do with the memory card. Had Graham stolen it from Lars? Why would he do that?

I expected to feel lightheaded and dizzy, but there was a newfound strength buzzing inside me. Whether it was adrenaline or the smoothie, I wasn't sure, but I'd take it.

I hurried down the stairs and out of the house.

"Why would my brothers have your boyfriend?" Reed asked, casually sitting in the passenger seat as I sped toward his house.

Thank goodness a lot of the streets were deserted. It kept everything nice and clear for me.

"I'm thinking it has something to do with the footage of you killing Delilah." I yanked on the steering wheel, turning the car to the right, the tires squealing on the asphalt, the car shaking until it righted itself on the road and we continued down the street, only blocks away from the Harrison household.

"Oh, yes." Reed set his hand on my headrest. "Lovely day. The weather was absolutely perfect for a hike." He stared longingly out the window. "It feels like a lifetime ago. I miss those days."

"The days where you murdered innocent people?"

Reed laughed like I said the most hilarious thing. "Those would be the ones. It's just so thrilling when they don't see it coming." He looked over at me. "You know, I almost had Lars do it. He was ready to take command. Sometimes, though, I can be selfish. Shocking, I know."

I tore my gaze from the street so I could look at him. He was being serious. I wanted to respond, but no words would form. For a fraction of a second, I felt relief that Reed was no longer alive. The man was capable of the worst.

An image of strangling Reed popped into my mind—all Nirah's doing. I shoved it down, no matter how tempting it was.

"You're going to miss the turn, doll," Reed said, pointing at the street that would take me straight to his house.

Slamming on the brakes, I turned the wheel, skidding yet again, and probably ruining my tires.

We came to a stop outside the Harrison house, and I threw the car into park. I didn't bother shutting the driver's side door. I ran up the porch steps and lifted my hand to knock right as Ace opened the door.

Ace swept out his arm, motioning for me to go in. "Welcome, Tessa. Always a pleasure to see you." He looked past me, but I was alone. His shoulders drooped. "I was hoping to see my brother."

"I'm right here." Reed popped up behind Ace, grinning like the Cheshire cat.

Ace spun on his boots, his eyes lighting up when they took in his brother. He moved to hug him but just went through Reed's transparent form.

Reed shook himself out. "Feels kind of weird when that happens. Like a small tingling."

Ace frowned at his arms, but his smile quickly came back. "It is good to see you, brother."

"Feeling is mutual, brother."

I rolled my eyes. "Will you please stop talking like you're Loki and Thor? Even Loki's a better guy than either of you."

Reed rubbed at his beard. "I highly doubt that."

Ace opened his mouth, but I cut him off. "Where's Graham?"

As if answering my question, Graham's distorted cry came from the belly of the house.

Ace looked sheepishly at me. "Like I said on the phone, Lars is in quite the mood. He's made Graham his plaything, and I worry Graham won't last much longer."

Reed folded his arms and nodded like this was completely normal. "That last guy he had, oof. Poor soul. I was almost relieved when Lars finally killed him." He grinned at me. "Almost."

"Lars doesn't have the same wiring as us." Ace motioned between him and Reed. "He's almost like a robot. Doesn't know when to stop or when enough is enough. He just keeps going until he gets bored."

"And he doesn't get bored easily," Reed said.

My jaw dropped in horror. These *monsters* were insane. I swallowed, looking at Ace. "Take me to them."

Ace finally shut the front door and then led us down the hall. He looked over his shoulder at me. "You'll have to forgive the mess downstairs. Life has been a little crazy since Reed went and got himself killed."

Reed popped his head over my shoulder. "And who's fault is that?" His wide, emotionless eyes stared at me, and I shrunk away.

Both Reed and Ace broke out in a cackle that made me clutch at the ring on my finger. *Amá, save me, please.*

Ace's laugh faded out as he opened the door. He grinned at me. "Ladies first." Then he winked.

My hand curled into a fist, and I wanted so badly to punch the guy. So, I did. Right in the gut. Nirah purred in excitement.

Ace groaned and held his hand against his stomach. "A feminist, I see."

I popped up on my tiptoes so I could look him in the eye, grateful he was bending a little at the waist. "It's more of an 'I don't like creepy men winking at me' kind of thing." I tilted my chin and quickly descended the stairs.

CHAPTER 37

Halfway down the stairs, my limbs seized. My vision turned to static, and I found myself clutching to the railing for support.

Tessa. The male voice was distorted.

Andras' face entered my vision but was gone just as quickly, bringing me back to reality.

Squeaky barking came closer as Fluffsies turned the corner and ran up the stairs, jumping when she got to me, making it up to my waist. Her white tail flipped back and forth in excitement.

Fluffsies *hated* me. But maybe I was one light in the darkness. I bent down and scooped her into my arms.

"Hey, girl." I kissed the side of her head. "Where's Graham?"

Fluffsies barked and licked my cheek.

"Do we have company?" Lars' empty voice came from around the corner. He slunk into view, and his thin white shirt was spotted with blood. His doll-like eyes took me in, showing no emotion. "Hello there. What may I do for you?"

"You can give me my boyfriend," I said with a growl.

Fluffsies growled in my arms, making me flinch. I almost lifted her away from me, but then I noticed she was growling at Lars, not me. That was a first.

"Tt...Tessa?" Graham's quiet, scratchy voice squeezed at my heart.

Holding Fluffsies close, I hurried down the stairs and around the corner, sliding to a stop on the smooth cement ground when I took in the scene.

Graham was kneeling on the ground, blood, cuts, and bruises covering his face, arms, and bare torso. His wrists were tied up with rope that hung from the ceiling, keeping his arms suspended in the air.

Barbie was curled into the very back corner, her curly blonde hair a matted red mess. She shook violently, her weak cries heartbreaking. I couldn't tell if the blood was hers or someone else's.

I moved toward them, but Lars put a palm on my forehead and shoved me back.

"They're mine," Lars said. "And it will remain that way until I get the information I want."

I wanted to run to Graham. To cut the ropes that bound him and take him into my arms. Tears welled in my eyes, and I fought to keep them there.

"What do you want?" I asked through clenched teeth.

"Something they took from me." Lars flexed his hand, and it was then that I noticed a piece of spiked metal was wrapped around his fist, wet with blood. My stomach churned, knowing he'd used it on Graham. Maybe even Barbie.

Nirah nudged me, and for the first time, I was tempted to follow through on her strangling wish. "If it's the memory card, you can have it."

Graham tried to lift his head, but he didn't have the energy. His voice came out weak. "No, Tessa. Don't."

I tried to move forward again, but Lars shoved me in the chest this time. Fluffsies bit at his arm, barely missing.

"Why, Graham?" I asked. "You don't need it."

Barbie muttered something from her corner, but it was too quiet to make out the words.

"What?" I asked.

"Speak up," Lars said, cool and monotone.

Barbie lifted her head, her stained red bangs falling over her swollen eyes. The long gash on her head told me the blood was definitely hers. "They can't get away with it."

I motioned to Reed's ghostly figure. Barbie opened her mouth wide open, but the scream that came out was dry and shallow. I waited until she settled before I spoke. "Greg's killer is dead. Justice is served."

"No!" Barbie shrieked, and Fluffsies squirmed in my arms. "Lars and Ace were accomplices! They should be in jail."

They'd never cared before. Why now? What had suddenly changed that would make them break into the Harrison home, steal something, and go toe-to-toe with killers?

Fluffsies squirmed again. I went to put her down when I noticed she had blood in her fur. My gaze snapped to Lars. "Please tell me you didn't hurt the dog." She was innocent in all of this.

Lars' head kinked to the side. "Of course not. I'm not a monster."

Graham spat some blood onto the floor. "Right."

"I'll give you the memory card," I said. "Just let them go."

"Tessa," Graham forced out. "No."

Lars walked toward Graham, his body tilted to the side, his haunting eyes unblinking. "I'll let them go when I have the card."

"Let me speak to Graham," I said. "Then I'll go get your card."

"No." Lars whistled, sauntering in tilted circles around Graham.

"Sorry, girl," I whispered into Fluffsies' fur. I set her down, and she immediately ran to Barbie.

I forced myself to go to Lars, blocking his path and stopping him in his tracks. "I just want a minute. I think that's fair."

Lars studied me for a moment, his blinking slow and spaced out. If it were anyone else, I'd think they were on something. But Lars always looked this way. Tripped out.

He finally bent at the middle, leaning close to me. "One. Minute." With a flash of a tight smile, he waltzed toward his brothers, and the three of them huddled together, speaking in hushed tones.

I dropped to my knees and took Graham's face in my hands, lifting his head so he could see me. For once, he wasn't blinking rapidly.

"Tessa," he whispered. "Please don't give them the card."

"Did you steal it from their house?" I asked.

He blinked slowly, his way of saying, "yes."

"Why? Why would you do that?"

He licked his dry lips, then grimaced, probably tasting his blood. "Mom wanted it. She's been hell-bent on getting it back."

"How did she even know it was here?"

His gaze fell to the floor. "She's been spending some time with Ace."

Gross.

"She saw the combo to the safe and told me to get it." He looked at me. "I know you hate her, but she's my mom. She's done a lot for me."

"I don't *hate* her." She'd kind of grown on me once I got to know her better. She was annoying and manipulative, but she'd do anything for her sons. I once thought she treated Graham horribly, but it was all a ruse on her end.

As a kid, Graham accidentally hurt his father, and Barbie had to finish the job. She'd done it to save Graham, knowing his father would kill him if he got better, but blamed it fully on Graham so she wouldn't get in trouble. They wouldn't convict a kid.

"Time's a ticking," Reed said in a singsong voice.

I rubbed my thumb along Graham's cheek, avoiding a long gash. "Where did you put it?"

"No, Tessa," Graham whispered.

"I have a backup," I whispered. "And Sheriff Hayes has the footage and he's opening an investigation. They won't get away with it."

Graham took a deep, shaky breath. "It's at the Willow Marsh Inn. Room five."

I gently kissed his lips and then stood, turning to look at the brothers. "I can take you to the card."

Ace grinned. "Great. I'll take Tessa there, and we'll be back before you know it."

That meant Lars would stay with Barbie and Graham. No way I was letting that happen.

"I'll show Lars where it is," I said, keeping my chin lifted high. "Reed can tag along if he wants."

Reed rubbed his hands together. "Oh, goody. A field trip across Willow Marsh. It must be my lucky day."

Ace stared at me, something close to hurt in his eyes. Was he sad I chose Lars over him?

"I don't mind," Ace said, finding his smile once again, but it was strained.

I glanced over my shoulder at Graham and Barbie. "Why don't we all go?" I turned back to the Harrisons. "It's not like they're going anywhere. That way, you brothers can have some time together." And I wouldn't be alone with Lars

Harrison. But I would be alone with all of them. I had to hold onto the hope that Lars would be less likely to do something drastic with his brothers at his side.

Lars nodded, mulling it over. He rubbed at his long chin, his spider ring moving with the motion. "Yes, that sounds good." His vacant eyes stared at me, unblinking. "Just give me a minute to tie up the whore."

I flinched at his word choice. Barbie wasn't my favorite person, but she wasn't a whore.

"Now, brother," Ace said in a scolding tone. "That's no way to talk about my *lover*."

I dry heaved, pressing a fist to my mouth. Why did everyone keep using that word while referring to creepy people?

Barbie tried to fight Lars as he tied her up, but she was too weak. Lars whistled the entire time, not batting an eye at her attempts to hit him. When he finished, he dusted off his hands. "Shall we go then?"

He strolled past all of us and up the stairs, not waiting for a reply. I shot a quick look at Graham before I turned to follow Lars, only to have my limbs seized again. This time, I fell to my knees as static filled my vision.

Tessa? Andras. *Where are you, Tessa?*

I pressed my palms to my eyes, wishing the static away. Cries overtook my hearing. Children and adults, all wailing, begging for help.

Tessa! Corrine.

Tessa! Nash.

Tessa! So many distressed voices.

Come home, Tessa, Andras said. *Come home, Thezanna.*

In a split second, it all stopped. My vision came back, and I found myself sprawled on the floor of the Harrison's basement.

"Tessa?" Graham's worried voice came from somewhere behind me.

I'd heard Nash. Did that mean he was there? In The Gray? Dead?

Ace took my arm and helped me to my feet.

"Does this have anything to do with Death Day?" Reed asked, his curious eyes filled with awe.

Ace looked at him. "Death Day?"

Reed tapped his fingers together. "Oh, brother, do we have the story for you."

"Tessa?" Graham begged.

I needed out of the house. I needed to get the stupid memory card so I could get on with my mission. I didn't have time for the stupid Harrison brothers.

I glanced over my shoulder at Graham. "We'll be right back."

I ran up the stairs, Reed and Ace close at my heels.

I hoped I didn't regret my choice, being alone with all the Harrisons. Besides Graham and Barbie, no one knew where I was. I went to pull my phone out of my pocket, only to realize I'd left it in my car.

"Can we take my truck?" Reed asked.

His jacked-up truck was parked in front of the house, all shiny and clean. Lars and Ace must have been taking good care of it.

"As you wish, brother." Ace opened the passenger door and motioned for me to slide in.

"You can follow me in my car," I said, trying to keep my voice steady. I eyed the single bench. "Four people is a tight squeeze."

Reed laughed. "I'm dead. I won't take up any room."

"You're coming with us," Lars said, his sharp tone closing the conversation.

"Then I'll just get my things, and we'll be on our way." I

turned toward my car, but Lars wrapped his hand around my arm, squeezing so tight I flinched.

Lars' face was inches from mine. "You don't need anything." He tapped my head with the tip of a knife. "Just your brain." He shoved me toward the truck. "I'm driving."

Reed floated over to Lars and tried to elbow him. "Mind if I sit in your lap?" He chuckled. "I kid. I kid."

Lars actually cracked the smallest of smiles before he wiped it away. He walked his crooked walk to the truck and got into the driver's seat. Reed perched himself in the bed, standing so he could peer over the top of the truck. He shook his head out like he could feel the wind in his hair.

Ace still held the door open for me. "I would call you 'my lady,' but I don't want to get punched in the stomach again." He started to wink but quickly stopped himself.

Clenching my fists, I climbed into the truck, taking the seat in the middle. Ace slid in beside me, his arm resting behind me on the bench. I shrunk into myself as much as I could, not wanting to touch either brother.

Lars sat like a typical guy, taking up more room than he needed. I scooted a little closer to Ace.

Ace brushed his lips against my ear. "I won't let anything happen to you, sugar. Just behave, and Lars won't lay a hand on you."

I pushed my hand into my stomach, praying I wouldn't throw up.

I was trapped inside Reed Harrison's truck with Lars and Ace on either side of me.

CHAPTER 38

The sheriff already had a copy of the footage, and I had a backup on my laptop, which left the copy that was now at Willow Marsh Inn.

It was where I'd first found it. Greg had been staying in room five before he died, and he'd hidden a box in there, full of keepsakes and a camera with a recording of the event that led to his death.

Greg had to have known it was coming. Graham had never said anything like Greg had said goodbye to him or his mom. Maybe Greg didn't want to worry them. Or maybe he really thought he could survive the Harrison brothers. Not many people did. Like poor Delilah.

There were random moments where I missed her sultry voice clogging up my brain. She was annoying, but when she was there, I was never alone. Looking back now, she had some pretty funny commentary, too. I just hadn't appreciated it at the time.

She'd be going off right now if she were with me. She'd be filling me with all her thoughts and feelings about the Harrisons, none of which were kind. It was nice to have someone to share those moments with. No one exactly knew what I had gone through. Except her.

But she'd crossed over to the other side finally. She'd been given the closure she needed with Reed's death.

Nirah nudged me, and I wished I could communicate with her like I could Delilah. I had so many questions for her.

I wasn't sure why it surprised me, but Lars was a decent driver. Though the streets were empty, he never went above the speed limit, stopped at all the stop signs and lights, and used his blinkers and mirrors like it was a normal drive on a nice summer day.

With the way my heart raced and the sweat forming all over me, it was anything but. I rubbed at the back of my neck, wiping away the sweat. My tank top clung to me, but I didn't want to air it out and draw attention to myself.

Country music drifted from the speakers as Lars' fingers drummed along the steering wheel, and he mouthed the words. Ace moved with the song next to me, his fingers creating the beat on his leg.

Ace grinned when he saw me staring at him. "Love this song. Ever seen Willie Nelson in person?"

"Can't say that I have." I wanted to scoot away from him, but it would put me closer to Lars. Maybe I should have ridden in the bed of the truck with Reed.

As if he'd heard me, his head suddenly popped up between Lars and me, making me lean into Ace.

"Can we listen to Dwight Yoakam? I miss his music." Reed's full form floated in until he sat between Lars and me. Even though he was just a ghost, I pushed myself farther away from him, practically sitting on Ace's lap.

Ace apparently appreciated the gesture because his finger trailed up and down my arm. I slapped his hand away, making him chuckle, his chest moving up and down against my back. I stared at the open window, tempted to throw myself out.

Lars wasn't going too fast. I'd probably survive the fall with just a few minor injuries.

Thankfully, the Willow Marsh Inn came into view, saving me from having to pick between the jump and more time with the Harrisons.

The truck pulled into the gravel parking lot, stopping in front of room five. None of the brothers moved to get out.

"I'm sure there's a key up front," I said, reaching over Ace to open the door. I climbed over him and out of the truck, shaking myself off like I could rid my body of their taint.

Ace slunk out next to me, brushing back the hair from my ponytail that clung to my sweaty skin. I went to swat him again, but he stepped back, stuffing his hands in his pockets and grinning madly.

"I do love hanging out with you," he said through his smile.

"That makes one of us," I grumbled under my breath. I hurried to the front office, letting out a breath of relief when I found it unlocked. The Fowlers must have been one of the residents to flee.

The bronze room keys hung from hooks on the wall behind the desk. I scurried around, grabbed the key, and ran back outside, wanting to get this over with.

The three of them were hanging outside of room five, chatting away. Reed's red form moved up and down in the air, like he'd found a new thing he could do with his ghostly self. Ace seemed to be enjoying the show, trying to mimic his brother by jumping up and down.

I looked over my shoulder, wondering how far I could make it before they caught me. Not far. Not with their truck and me just on foot, no matter how fast a runner I was.

"Oh, Tessa doll," Reed sang. "I hope you're not getting any ideas."

Briefly closing my eyes, I said a quick prayer and turned around, forcing myself to walk down the path to room five.

I didn't meet any of their eyes as I put the key into the lock and turned it.

Nirah stirred behind my heart, heating and expanding, breaking into multiple pieces and searing me from the inside. I clutched at the top of my tank as I fell to my knees, the heat overbearing.

"Tessa?" Ace's sweet voice sounded far away.

"Doll?" Reed said from behind me.

Nirah poked at my bones and skin, pushing with all her might. Pain exploded inside as my skin glowed orange, lighting up everything around me.

"Would you look at that," Lars said with awe. "It's so beautiful."

I bent over, pressing my hand into the ground, trying to keep myself from completely falling over. Someone's arm draped around my back, probably Ace. I was in too much pain to shake him off.

Below me, the ground began to tremble.

Thezanna. Andras' raspy voice boomed all around me. *Come home, Thezanna.*

I wasn't sure exactly what was about to happen, but I knew it wouldn't be good. I tried to speak, tried to tell Ace and the others to move back, but the words were lodged in my fiery throat.

Nirah moved frantically through me like she wasn't sure exactly what to do.

I forced my arm behind me, trying to get Ace's attention.

"What is it, Tessa?" he asked, bending close to me.

Don't fight it, Thezanna. Come home, my love. Come now.

The rumbling grew, cracks forming in the ground. The gravel bounced around, flying high into the air, smacking into the awning above us and the truck behind us. I could hear each *whack* like it was amplified.

"I believe you should all move back," Reed said, all calm and smooth.

Ace's arm wrapped around my torso and scooped me into the air, yanking me away from the inn.

Out of the corner of my eye, I could see Lars moving toward the driver's seat of the truck, but Ace yelled over all the noise. "There isn't time!"

He sprinted away from the inn, holding me in his arms like a baby, the pain inside me on the brink of making me pass out.

I pushed my hands against my ears and looked up just in time to see the Willow Marsh Inn get swallowed up by the earth, the truck falling down in with it. Ace was far enough away, but Lars' slow pace kept him barely ahead of the falling earth. He was almost jogging, like nothing crazy was going on behind him and was seconds away from his demise.

Ace held me in the middle of the road, shouting at his brother to run faster. As soon as Lars reached the start of the asphalt, the earth stopped shaking, the pain inside me retreating.

"Put me down," I growled.

Ace did as told, his gaze focused on the huge hole that was once the inn. I straightened, tugging down the bottom of my tank top and shorts, watching the cloud of dust float into the air.

Lars bent over, leaning his hands on his knees, and panting like he'd just run a marathon.

Reed appeared next to us, frowning. "There goes my truck."

I glanced over at him. "Look on the bright side. At least the memory card is in a place no one will ever find it." I shrugged. "Except maybe Satan. But who knows how good he is with technology?"

Ace's chuckle started softly until it expanded and hogged the air around us. Reed soon joined in. Lars was too busy trying to catch his breath to do anything.

I'd just wanted to ease the tension eating away at me.

I'd almost been reunited with Andras without anything to protect me.

CHAPTER 39

My body trembled as I stared at the gigantic hole in the earth.

You can't escape, Thezanna. Andras' voice bounced inside my head. *We* will *be reunited.*

I glanced over at the Harrison brothers, who were in a deep discussion. They had no vehicle. I'd just witnessed the fact that Lars was completely out of shape. He was still bent over with his hands on his knees, trying to gather his breath.

Ace had his cowboy boots on, which weren't made for running. I looked down at my Nike Pegasus'. They were made for running, and I was a runner.

So I ran.

I took off, sprinting in the direction of the Harrison household and leaving the disturbing brothers in the dust.

My blood buzzed with energy, pushing harder and faster than I'd ever gone before. I had a feeling Andras would keep trying to swallow me up until I was with him once again. I just had to make sure I got there on my own accord, with all the safety spells and measures in place.

Maybe it was something in the smoothie Nyx had made

me, but I felt on cloud nine. I felt invincible. I knew the feeling wouldn't last forever, but I hoped it would be enough to get me through the next little bit.

When I rounded the corner and saw the Harrison's house, relief flooded over me, something I never thought I'd feel looking at the Harrison's. But it would be a while until they showed up. I had a chance to free Barbie and Graham and get off the property before the sleaze bags got back.

I sprinted to my car, yanked the door open, and searched frantically for my phone. I needed to call Dad or Leya and let them know where I was.

"It probably fell on the ground," Reed said from over my shoulder, making me jump in surprise. "You were driving quite carelessly."

I guess I couldn't escape the dead Harrison. He was tethered to me, not his brothers.

Hissing, I searched under the passenger side seat and found my phone under there. I brushed it off and immediately called Dad, noticing I had a few missed calls.

He answered right away. "Why aren't you answering your phone?"

"I didn't have it with me." I hurried toward the house. "Is everything okay?"

"Are you okay?" Dad asked. "Nyx had some weird vision of you being swallowed into the earth."

"I'm fine." I stepped over the threshold and into the Harrison home. "The Willow Marsh Inn is gone, though. The sheriff might want to send a unit over there or something." Since there was now a huge hole in the earth.

Dad sucked in a sharp breath. "What? Why were you over there? Why aren't you in bed?"

"It's a long story. I'll call you back soon." I stopped at the foot of the stairs. "I have Graham and Barbie. I'll explain everything when I see you. Love you, Dad."

"I love you, too, Tessa," Dad said. "Just hurry up. Nyx has me really worried."

I ended the call and ran down the stairs, heading straight for Graham.

"Tessa." Graham's voice was so quiet and full of pain. His arms were in the air, being held up by ropes.

I frantically searched the basement until I found a huge knife. It easily sliced through the ropes, filling me with relief at Graham's release but horror that the Harrison's had a knife that sharp.

I bent over to help Graham, but he shook his head.

"My mom."

Right. Barbie. I quickly cut off the zip ties that bound her hands and feet. She took me by surprise and threw her arms around my neck.

"Thank you," she whispered. "Thank you."

I rubbed her back. "Of course."

She held onto me for a while, and I let her. She sobbed against my shoulder, her small body rocking.

My boyfriend's mother finally liked me—and so did her dog, who was licking my arms and face—but soon, it wouldn't matter. I'd be dead.

It was weird how calm I felt. Like my fate had already been sealed. Like this was my destiny. Why I'd had come to Willow Marsh in the first place.

Amá said I belonged here. Was this why? Was I their savior? I shook the thought from my head. I was no savior. But if I could help against the war with Andras, I would.

"Tessa," Graham's pained voice came from the side of me.

Barbie reluctantly let me go, and I wrapped my arms around Graham, holding him close. His normal pine scent was drenched in blood and sweat. What had Lars done to him? I pulled back to look at him when I heard footsteps upstairs.

They couldn't have been back so soon.

"Wait right here," I said to Graham and Barbie before I headed up the stairs.

Both Lars and Ace were in the kitchen. Ace opened the fridge and grabbed a pitcher with a pink liquid inside. Lars leaned against the side of the island while Reed sat on the counter, swinging his legs like a child.

Ace poured a glass and then slid it across the counter toward me. "Strawberry lemonade." He winked at me and then pulled back. "Whoops. Didn't mean that." He put the pitcher back in the fridge. "Gonna have to get used to not winking. I just can't help it when I'm around pretty girls."

"Uh, maybe just remind yourself that I'm a teenager and completely illegal." I stared at the glass. No way I was drinking something offered to me by a Harrison.

"Ma's recipe." Ace took the stool beside me, holding his own glass of lemonade.

I looked between him and Lars. "How did you get back here so fast?"

"A friend happened to be driving by and gave us a ride." Ace took a long drink of his lemonade.

"You have a friend?" I couldn't hide the shock in my voice.

Ace completely ignored me. "So, what now?"

Reed grinned at me, pulling his lips tight. "Well, Tessa doll is in for a *fun* evening, that's for sure."

Lars cocked his head. "What do you mean?"

Reed held his hands out in front of him, his red figure pulsing. "Are you ready for this, brothers? You better brace yourself."

Ace put his hands on top of the island. "I'm braced."

Lars turned his cocked head to his oldest brother, a tiny resemblance of intrigue in his eyes. "Always braced."

"Everything going on in Willow Marsh is about to be put

to a stop." Reed almost sang the words. "Thanks to dear Tessa here."

Ace turned to me. "How, Tessa? How will you save Willow Marsh?"

I stared at the glass in front of me, not wanting to speak. While I had accepted my fate, their enthusiasm was weirding me out.

"It's Death Day!" Reed hopped down from the counter, throwing his arms wide. "She's going to..." He jumped with a flourish, his floating form landing on top of the island. "Sacrifice herself!"

"What?" Graham's tight voice behind me made me jump from my stool and whip around.

CHAPTER 40

Graham stood in the doorway leading to the basement, a wide-eyed Barbie next to him, Fluff-sies cradled in her arms. Both Graham and Barbie looked like something straight out of a horror film with the ripped clothes, Graham's missing shirt, blood, cuts, and bruises all over them.

Fluffsies licked at the blood in Barbie's hair.

Reed appeared beside me, moving back and forth on his feet like he was itching to tell the story. "There's this book called Lucifer's Reign."

"My favorite," Lars said in his flat tone. "I've probably checked it out of the library a hundred times over the years." He slunk into view, his leaning form taking up a lot of space. "Page one-thirty-eight, yes? Is this the one we're referring to?" His lackadaisical eyes traveled my body. "Yes, yes. You do look just like her. Amazing, really."

"Right?" Reed said with way too much glee. "Astounding, the similarity."

Ace hopped up from his stool, resting his arm on my shoulder. "What book is this? I haven't read it."

"Maybe you should read more often, little brother," Reed said.

Ace winked at Barbie. "I have other things to occupy my time."

Barbie blushed and stared at the floor. Her usual arrogant self perturbed me, but I preferred it over this cowering version. It was like her backbone had completely disappeared. What had they done to her?

Graham's eyes narrowed in on Ace's arm on my shoulder, so I shrunk away from him, putting a noticeable space between us. Ace frowned at the emptiness, not noticing the hatred radiating from Graham.

I moved toward Graham, but he took a step away from me, moving closer to the front door.

"What does he mean by sacrificing yourself?" Graham asked in a hushed tone.

I stepped toward him, but with every step I took, he took two back. I finally stopped. "It's kind of hard to explain."

Reed popped up, making me jump a little. "Not really, doll. It's quite simple. Graham, you've really missed so much. Tessa is actually a goddess reborn, and she's going to drown herself so she can enter The Gray." He gazed adoringly down at me like I was his prized puppy. "Our girl will stop Andras and remove me from this hellhole. How marvelous is that?"

Graham stared at me in confused silence.

"It sounds so stupid when you say it out loud." I licked my lips. "But he's right. There's this goddess, Thezanna, she tried to drown herself to save the children in this town years ago, but this coven showed up, and her soul got shattered, and—"

Graham whipped around and limped out of the house, most of his weight on his right leg.

I ran after him, easily catching up to him. I stopped him on the porch. "Graham, please, just wait. This isn't even important right now. We should get you and your mom to a hospital."

"Don't change the subject." Graham wiped at some dried blood on his arm, grimacing in the process. "Go back to everything you and Reed just said. It's crazy."

"I know. But you need to meet Nyx and talk with Mrs. Morales. They can make more sense of this." I reached toward him, but he shrunk back. "I know this is a lot to take in. I wasn't expecting Reed to just throw everything on you like this. Let's get you to a hospital, and I can explain everything later, I promise."

We stood in silence for a bit, and he stared at me, his blinking out of control.

When he finally spoke, anger clung to his tone. "You're going to drown yourself?"

"Well, yes, but there will be spells in place, and—"

"You've accepted this." His tone was matter-of-fact. "I know you, Tessa, and I know that look. You're really going to sacrifice yourself, aren't you?" His voice raised. "Who cares ww...what anyone else thinks!"

"That's not fair," I said, hating the whine in my voice.

"Not fair?" He scoffed, pushing past me and down the porch steps. "Unbelievable."

I scrambled after him. "If I have a chance to save everyone in this town, shouldn't I take it?"

"You're not a goddess, Tessa," he growled. "You're just a girl. I think all this stupid séance stuff has gotten to your head."

I pulled back, stung by his words. "I know I'm not a goddess. But I saw the book. Nyx and Mrs. Morales confirmed it. Andras is coming, Graham, whether you like it or not."

He ran his hand over his head. "Can you hear yourself?

Andras is coming. That's insane. Demons don't just pop-up places." He threw out his arms. "Demons don't exist."

Nirah wiggled inside, making me shift uncomfortably.

"There are just some natural disasters going on," Graham said, "and you can't just stop them."

"Natural disasters?" I moved until I was right in front of him. "How is the lake boiling and lightning bugs exploding a *natural disaster*? You were there! You saw it. And I just watched an entire inn get swallowed up by the earth. Nash is missing, along with other kids. Don't tell me I'm crazy. There is stuff going on that we can't control. It's going to keep happening whether we like it or not. And if I have a chance to stop it, I can't in good conscience just sit back and do nothing!"

Tears fell from his eyes as he threw his arms around me, pulling me into him. He grunted from the pain but held strong. "I can't lose you, Tessa. I just can't."

I hugged him tight. "It's not like I want this, Graham. Fate has never been kind to me. I don't think I was meant to last long on this earth."

He pulled back, putting his hand on my cheeks, his tears flowing freely down his battered face. "Don't say that. Please don't say that." He leaned his forehead against mine. "I love you, Tessa."

"I love you, too," I whispered. "But that doesn't change my path."

His hands shook against my cheeks. "Why? Why is all of this happening?"

"I don't know," I said, my own tears now falling. "I really wish I knew."

His lips crashed against mine, and even though they tasted slightly of blood, I didn't care. I kissed him back, wanting to savor every moment I had left with him. Our tears landed on our lips, adding sorrow to the hungry and loving kiss.

Below us, the earth trembled in a way that said something was coming. Something bigger than us, bigger than Willow Marsh.

Fat raindrops fell from the sky. Graham and I peeled our lips apart and stared up, letting the rain fall against our skin.

Nirah came alive, heating my skin until it glowed. Graham stared at my skin like he wished it wasn't happening. It proved I was right about all the unnatural stuff.

Around us, lightning bugs appeared, dancing in a controlled frenzy, swirling with the breeze that was starting to pick up. Thunder roared overhead, followed by lightning rippling through the sky.

"That was weird," Graham muttered.

It was. Lightning always came first.

My phone rang out from my pocket, so I put it on speaker phone. "Hello?"

"Tessa, it's Nyx. I'm afraid the timeline has been pushed up. Andras has grown impatient. Meet us at the lake."

The line went dead before I could say anything.

Suddenly, the ground swayed, moving back and forth in a slow motion, almost like it was rocking us to sleep. All the lightning bugs swarmed together, taking off toward the lake.

My ponytail twirled in the breeze, the air growing colder to the point goosebumps broke out onto my arms. Graham held me close to his chest, trying to keep us steady.

A swirl of wind licked my ears, bringing with it a raspy voice, deep with a hunger that shook me to the core. *It's time.*

I looked at Graham, trying to see if he noticed the voice, but he made no indication that he had.

You can't stop it, Thezanna, the voice whispered. *Not even the Lord Himself could stop my power. My time to reign has come. Together, we will rise. Not against one another, but together.*

We will rise.

CHAPTER 41

I hurried to my car, got into the driver's seat, and started the engine, hoping Graham and Barbie would follow. The ground continued to tremble, the thick raindrops sounding like bullets against the car.

It brought me back to the night of the crash. The night I had killed my mom and little brother. They had entrusted me with their lives, and I'd stolen them. Could I drive in the rain? Could I drive safely in this weather?

The passenger door slammed closed, catching my attention. Graham sat in the passenger seat, grimacing in pain. He rubbed at his temple and closed his eyes.

Aside from the other day with Jade and Nash, I hadn't driven with anyone in the car with me since the crash. I'd been too terrified. I glanced at the road, trying to see through the rain. I turned the windshield wipers on full blast, but it hardly helped.

A bark behind me made me glance in the rearview mirror. Barbie and Fluffsies had climbed into the back seat as I hoped but now there were two more lives in my hands.

When I drove Jade and Nash, the weather was nice. The drive wasn't too far. This storm was a whole other beast.

Both the back doors opened and in slunk Lars and Ace, forcing Barbie into the middle seat. She held Fluffsies close to her, trying to make herself as small as possible.

Ace flung a shirt at Graham. "Thought you might need this."

Graham held up the shirt. It had a huge deer with the words *Buck Off* below it. He glanced at his bare chest covered in blood and sighed before gingerly pulling it on.

"This isn't a taxi," I said, glaring in the rearview mirror at Lars.

He kept his vacant eyes out the window. "Our brother's truck has been eaten."

"You have your own vehicles," I said.

Lars finally made eye contact with me through the mirror. "We're all going to the same place. Carpooling is a reasonable, economy-saving option."

I wanted to make some snide remark, but the panic of driving and being responsible for five other lives set in.

I couldn't do it.

Control. Steady. Calm.

Graham's hand landed on my arm, making me turn my attention to him. Through all the cuts and bruises, his eyes were soft, blinking at a normal rate. He kept his voice low. "You can do this, Tessa."

"What's the holdup?" Ace asked, leaning forward and making Barbie shrink back.

"Ss...stay out of this," Graham growled at him.

Ace smiled in return, not sitting back. His head and chest were between our two seats, hovering over the center console.

Just like the Harrison brothers loved to do, I put my palm

on his forehead and shoved him back, making Ace cackle with glee.

"Tessa," Graham said, so sweet and tender it softened my heart. Shutting out everything around me, I focused only on him. "You're going to be fine. I promise. Just drive slowly. I'll be an extra pair of eyes for you. We'll get through this. Together."

"Together." I leaned across the console and kissed him gently on the lips.

"As lovely as this moment is," Ace said, leaning forward so his face was back next to ours, "we really should be going. Got a town to save."

I checked to make sure I was buckled in—and everyone else in the car—and slowly pulled out of the Harrisons driveway, the windshield wipers on as high as they could go.

I positioned the car to turn right.

"Where are you going?" Graham asked. "The lake is to the left."

I stared at him incredulously. "Um, the hospital. You and your mom need stitches, along with who knows what else."

Graham shook his head. "That can wait."

My gaze went to the blood soaking through the borrowed shirt he wore. "Pretty sure it can't."

"I'm not leaving your side, Tessa, so deal with it. My mom and I will be fine."

I caught Barbie's gaze through the rearview mirror. She nodded. "Graham is right. This is far bigger than us living with scars. We'll be fine." When I didn't move, she went on. "The sheriff will be there, right? I'm sure he has a first aid kit in his car. We can do a temporary fix for now."

Arguing with them was just a waste of time. With a sigh, I turned left, heading toward the lake.

The rain, wind, and thunder were almost deafening. A few

times, Barbie said something from the back seat, but I couldn't hear her over all the noise. Both my hands were gripped tightly around the wheel, and I was hunched forward like an old person.

I kept the odometer under twenty the entire ride. Through my rearview mirror, I saw Ace roll his eyes a few times, annoyed with how slow I was going. A couple of times, he leaned over and tried to kiss Barbie on the cheek or neck, but she'd cower away. It only made Ace laugh.

As I neared our turnoff for the road that would lead us to the lake, I slowed down, squinting my eyes to see if anyone was coming from the other direction.

Graham leaned toward me, his arm resting on the console. "It's clear."

I turned the wheel, lifting my foot off the brakes, when a powerful wind smacked into the driver's side of the car, sending the car hydroplaning across the wet asphalt. We swirled in circles, the wind jerking us around, tires squealing, and Barbie screaming so loud this time I could hear it over all the noise.

I couldn't remember my training. I'd done so much research after the crash, learning how to drive in rough conditions. Did I let go of the wheel and let the car come to a stop? Did I try to right it? Foot on the brakes? Off? Let Jesus take the wheel?

Then it all clicked into place. Letting my foot off the break, I shifted the car into neutral and then turned the wheel in the direction of the skid. As the car began to slow, I gently tapped the brakes a few times, trying to help the process.

A few moments later, the car came to a complete stop on the side of the road.

My hands gripped the steering wheel tight as my heart pounded through my chest. I quickly checked everyone in the car, noticing that they were fine. A little freaked out, but fine.

Ace clapped his hands. "Nicely done."

"But really, we *must* go." Reed suddenly appeared between Graham and me, his head and torso sticking out from the center console. He clasped his hands together and sang the next words. *"It's Death Day!"*

With a growl, I put the car into drive and headed down the road leading to the lake. A few cars were already there, so I pulled up next to them. There didn't appear to be anyone inside any of them.

The rain crashed down hard, turning into hail.

"Where are they?" Graham asked in a low voice.

"Good question." I squinted, trying to see through the windshield wipers and hail. There was an orange glow radiating on the shore of the lake. "Maybe there?"

I pulled out my phone and called Leya.

"Are you here?" Leya asked. It was difficult to hear her over the pelting of hail against the car.

"Yes," I said. "Where are you guys?"

"Just walk toward the orange ball of light," Leya said. "You'll find us."

I looked over at Graham, and he just shrugged. With a deep breath, I opened my door and ran out into the storm, heading straight for the glow. I kept my eyes trained there, trying to ignore the wind and hail attacking me.

When I was a few feet from the light, I stepped through an invisible barrier.

A bunch of people were all standing under an invisible tent. Dad, Leya, Jade, and Marcel stood off to one side. Sheriff Hayes, his wife Remi, and his son Blake were next to them, huddled close together. Rita and Mrs. Morales stood with Nyx and her coven.

"Totally cool, right?" Leya grinned. "I think I'm taking

Nyx everywhere I go from now on. I mean, it's a portable, climate-controlled, sound-reducing tent."

"It's a spell." Nyx trained her eyes on me. "Has Andras tried to contact you?"

The rain smacked the top of the invisible roof and then cascaded down the sides, no water entering the area where everyone stood.

Graham stepped in next to me, jumping in surprise when he saw everyone.

Leya gasped, her hands flying to her chin. "Graham! What happened to you?" She scrunched her face. "And why are you wearing that shirt?"

Graham threw a glare at the Harrison brothers that made my skin crawl. "Long story."

Lars, Ace, and Barbie—with Fluffsies in tow—entered the tent. Barbie held the same amount of shock Graham had when he first stepped through, but Lars and Ace had no reaction.

Leya flinched as she took in Barbie's bloody state. The sheriff eyed me, but I shook my head. We'd have time for an explanation later.

Sheriff Hayes moved toward his car. "I'll get the first aid kit. Be right back."

"What are *they* doing here?" Jade asked, her eyes narrowed on the Harrison brothers.

"They're here, squirrel," Reed said, suddenly appearing next to Jade, "to make sure none of you try any funny business. I told Tessa I'd help down in The Gray, but only if she gets me out of here."

Jade folded her arms. "Can we please go back to the part where you called me 'squirrel?'"

Reed cackled. "Well, Tessa is doll, and Corrine is ladybug, so I thought I'd give you one as well."

Leya huffed. "I'm not sure whether to be relieved or

offended that I haven't made the nickname list."

Reed popped up next to her. "Definitely offended."

Mrs. Morales stepped close to Reed. "Do you give all your victims nicknames?"

Reed shook his head. "No. It's just that she's dressed in black, has red hair, and keeps coming back to bother me no matter how many times I flick her away."

All the color drained from Mrs. Morales' face. "Corrine is with you?"

Reed glanced at me before turning his attention back to her. "Yes. Didn't Tessa tell you?"

Mrs. Morales clasped her hands together, her eyes filled with hope, surprising me. I thought she'd be angry.

I swallowed. "I wasn't sure how to tell you this, but Corrine is stuck in The Gray with Reed. And possibly others."

Mrs. Morales made the sign of the cross. "I knew it. I had this feeling she was stuck somewhere. This is good news."

Good news? How was Corrine being stuck in The Gray good news?

"Others?" Graham asked.

"Can we get past this, please?" Reed meandered to the center of the invisible tent. "Corrine, Greg, Trenton, Nash, yada yada yada, are all here. We have more important issues at hand."

Barbie fell to her knees, clutching Fluffsies close to her chest. "Greg is there?"

Graham bent forward, resting his hands on his knees for support. I gently placed my hand on his back. He'd been missing so long that I forgot he didn't know much.

Jade fell to the ground as well. "Nash is dead?"

Leya kneeled next to her, holding Jade as she wept.

Sheriff Hayes had just stepped back into the tent in time

to hear the news. He glanced at his horror-stricken wife and son before he turned to back to Reed. "Is Livvy there, too?"

Reed's eyes went wide in horror, looking at something we couldn't see. "Tessa, *hurry.*" He flickered out of view.

Nyx held out her hand toward me. "Come, Tessa. It's time."

CHAPTER 42

Nyx tried to get everyone aside from her coven and Mrs. Morales to stay on shore, but they all insisted on coming. She didn't mask her annoyance.

We piled into the sheriff's boat and traveled to the island in the center of the lake. The water was choppy thanks to the storm, but Nyx had cast a spell over the boat, protecting us from the wind and rain.

Graham and Leya clung to me as if they never wanted to let go. Dad stood nearby, wearing a level of fear I'd never seen on him. Whatever calm Nyx had weaved into him before had now worn off.

I knew they were all terrified, but I could have really used some positive vibes. Some hope.

So, I thought about Amá and Felix. They always held unwavering faith in me. They'd tell me I could accomplish anything. They'd both moved on to the other side, but they were always a part of me. I carried them in my heart and soul.

As we neared the island, the sheriff slowed the boat and pulled up right next to the edge of the land. Nyx and Sheba had to practically pry Leya and Graham from my grasp. They wouldn't let go.

"If you don't let go," Sheba said in her low, gravelly voice, "I'm going to gag you, tie you both to the boat, and send you back to shore." The fierceness in her eyes let us know she wasn't bluffing.

Graham and Leya finally released me, but they stayed close to my side.

Jade took my hands in hers and squeezed them tight. "Find Nash. Please, Tessa."

I didn't know what to say. If he was really there, he was dead. There was no coming back from that.

Except, I was coming back.

I turned to Nyx. "Is there a way to bring the others back with me? Do we have more necklaces that I can give them?"

Nyx shook her head. "I'm afraid it doesn't work like that."

Jade shoved her hard in the chest. "You're bringing Tessa back! Bring Nash back!"

Nyx didn't so much as flinch. She held her ground.

Blake inserted himself between them. "And Livvy!"

Nyx remained calm, her voice even. "They don't have Tessa's powers. They don't have the goddess of rebirth inside them. I'm sorry, but nothing can be done."

Taking me by the arm, Nyx yanked me away from the others. Mrs. Morales came with us and placed a snug black beaded necklace around my neck.

Tears formed in my eyes. "Are Nash, Chloe, and Livvy really dead? Is there nothing we can do?"

Nyx looked over her shoulder to make sure the others were out of earshot, then spoke low. "There's a possibility, but I didn't want to get their hopes up. It all depends on how dead they are."

"How dead they are? Are there different levels of death I should know about?"

Mrs. Morales shook her head. "Not really." She took a deep breath. "It's difficult to explain, but with our epicenter of magic, the seal broken between here and The Gray, and Andras' power all combined, it wouldn't take much for him to bring their bodies and souls to his side."

"When you get there," Nyx said, "if the children's bodies and souls are still connected, there's a chance to bring them back. If they've already been split, it's too late."

Hope bloomed in my chest. Maybe Andras hadn't separated their bodies and souls quite yet. But I wouldn't know until I got down there.

I ran my fingers over some of the beads. "This is actually going to do something, right? It's not just for decoration?"

Mrs. Morales softly smiled. "Its magic will help make it difficult for Andras to touch you."

Nyx took my hand in hers, running her finger over my family ring. "This will let me know where you are at all times." She glanced at the leather pouch against my chest. It held the gold ring Joseph Walker had been wearing. "When the time is right, slip the ring on your finger. It's imperative that you make sure no one is touching Andras when you do it."

"Why?"

"Anyone bound to him will be trapped in the ring with him."

"That sucks," I mumbled, then I realized I'd said it out loud. Not a very heroic thing to say.

But Nyx just grinned and said, "that it does."

I swallowed, looking out over the lake as I slipped off my Chuck Taylor's. Nirah stirred inside, zipping through my body until she wrapped in circles around my left leg, almost like she was getting a good grip on me.

"How are we going to do this?" My voice came out in

barely a whisper. The overwhelming realization of what was about to happen slammed into me. I was about to die.

Nyx cupped a steady hand over my shoulder. "I'm going to give you a little serum that will knock you out for a bit. We'll place you in the water, and Nirah can hold you underneath."

Mrs. Morales smiled softly. "Allegra had originally brought up tying a weight to your ankle to keep you underwater, but we liked the idea of having the option to abort if something goes wrong."

"*Will* something go wrong?" I thought about how Thezanna's immortal soul had been shattered into multiple pieces. If my mortal body shattered, there was no coming back from that.

"It's best to be prepared for any scenario." Nyx steered me toward the water until it was lapping on my bare feet. "When you wake, you should be in The Gray. It won't take long for Andras to find you." She set both her hands on my shoulders. "Tessa, it's important to remember that Andras will do everything in his power to sway you to his side. You'll be bombarded with Thezanna's memories, including the good ones she had with him. Though they are now enemies, they were once allies. You cannot let him persuade you. You must fight, Tessa, with everything you have in you." She held up my hand that had the dahlia ring. "Remember that you're Tessa Isaacson. Daughter of Alec and Ariela. Sister of Felix. They are you, and you are them."

I looked over my shoulder at Dad, Graham, and Leya. They all anxiously watched on. I could feel the battle inside each of them from where I stood. They wanted to come to me. Protect me. Stop this all from happening.

But they knew they couldn't.

Andras wouldn't stop until he got what he wanted.

The ground shook, starting small and growing to the point that it became difficult to keep balanced.

"It's time, Tessa." Nyx's voice cut through all the noise around me like my eardrum was a speaker. "Once your mission is done, a portal will open. Make sure you get you and the others through it before it closes."

"Okay." I moved toward my family and friends. "Let me say goodbye—"

Nyx stopped me in my tracks and shoved a small vial between my lips, the cool liquid going down my throat. She took a step back from me. "I'm sorry, Tessa. But it's better this way."

With a sharp tug, Nirah yanked me into the lake, pulling my body under the water, and closing off my gateway to air.

I didn't have time to panic before the serum took hold, and everything faded to black.

CHAPTER 43

Two things attacked me at once: the smell of rotting flesh and the hum of "Thriller" by Michael Jackson.

My eyes slowly opened, taking in the murky gray surroundings. Reed's pallid face suddenly came into view, hovering over me as I lay on the hard ground. He barely had coloring to him, like he'd been desaturated.

Reed flashed his crooked smile, still humming the song.

"You've officially ruined Michael Jackson for me." I moved to sit up.

Reed's hand landed on my arm, trying to help.

I could *feel* him. His touch. His skin.

On instinct, I scrambled back, wanting far, far away from him.

Reed frowned. "You're going to ruin your pretty dress."

I glanced down to see the flowy baby blue dress Thezanna had worn in all the drawings of her. It fit me perfectly, hugging my curves before billowing out at the waist.

Reed pointed to my chest. "What's in the pouch? A lucky potion?"

My hand went to the leather pouch wrapped around the

ring hanging from a chain around my neck. "Hopefully, a way to end this."

I quickly got to my feet, the rotting smell and endless gray overcoming my senses once again.

I covered my nose with my hand. "What is that smell?"

Reed flicked out his arms. "Dead people, doll. They are all over The Gray. Everywhere I turn, poof! A dead person."

I pointed at him. "You're talking like you're not part of the problem."

"Well, I'm not."

Keeping my hand over my nose, I took a shaky step, trying to gain my bearings. Everything felt...off.

"What do you mean?"

Reed came forward and rested his arm on my shoulder. "My soul and body are still united, so I haven't rotted yet."

I slinked away from him, finally just giving up and lowering my hand. It did nothing to dull the putrid smell.

I held out my hand in front of me, moving my fingers. I could feel nothing. No air. It wasn't hot or cold. It took me a moment to realize I wasn't even breathing. I didn't have to. Though my body did the motion out of habit.

The feeling of nothingness was the absolute worst.

Turning in circles, I glanced over the vast, desolate land-scape of broken, rotting trees. We were alone.

I looked over my shoulder at Reed. "I thought you said there were lots of people here."

Reed simply stuffed his hands in his pockets and shrugged. He teetered to the side. "They don't hang around in the open all day, doll."

"Where's Corrine?"

Reed stayed leaning to the side. "Occupied."

I went to stand directly in front of him. "I'm done with vague answers, Reed. I died to get here."

"So did I!" When I didn't return his smile, he rolled his

eyes. "Okay, fine. She disappeared a little while ago. Haven't seen her since."

What did that mean? Had her soul and body been separated? Had she rotted like the others?

"When someone rots, what happens to them?"

Reed's eyes lit up. "So glad you asked. Their skin pretty much deteriorates until they're basically bone. It's disgusting and fascinating, and I really wish you could see the process."

Tessa! Corrine's panicked voice bounced around in my head. *Help!*

I spun in circles, trying to find her, but aside from Reed, there wasn't a soul in sight.

"Are you okay?" Reed asked.

I narrowed my eyes at him. "You didn't hear that?"

"Hear what?"

Sighing, I picked a direction and started walking. Maybe I'd get a spidey sense or something when I got close.

Reed soundlessly appeared at my side, matching my stride. "My, my, Tessa. Hearing voices is how the deterioration begins. That took you no time at all."

Ignoring him, I trudged on, desperately scanning the area for answers.

We'd been walking for what seemed like five minutes when something tickled my leg. I glanced down to see a furry red snake, at least a few yards long.

With a yelp, I jumped back, my hand flying to my chest in shock.

Big, black beady eyes blinked up at me as a smile spread across its thin lips. It suddenly zipped up my leg, wrapping in circles around my body until the head settled on my shoulder.

"Nirah?"

She purred against my skin. *Welcome home.*

I started at the voice in my head, making Nirah vibrate in a chuckle.

You're so similar to Thezanna, yet so different.

Uh, thanks? I didn't know what else to say to that.

A series of memories seized my vision, flying through at a rapid speed. I fell to my knees, my palms on the dry ground, my stomach coiling into knots. So many sounds and images flipped through at once, just like it had when I first put on the ring. But I wasn't wearing the ring.

Nyx had said I'd receive all Thezanna's memories. She'd existed for so many years that there had to be millions.

My stomach churned, and it took everything in me not to throw up. All the feelings she'd experienced flew through me: happiness, anger, love, rage, intrigue, lust, confusion, fear, forgiveness, sorrow, torment, glee, and so many more.

So. Many. More.

When it finally stopped, I gasped, my fingers curling into my palms. Nirah slithered around me on the ground, laughter in her large eyes.

"So glad you find this amusing." I slowly stood, my legs trembling.

Nirah worked her way up my body and draped herself around my neck like a feather boa. An immediate calm settled inside, a feeling of peace I hadn't felt in the longest time. I wasn't sure if it was Nirah or the part of Thezanna in me. Maybe both.

I had a newfound strength, and for the first time, I didn't doubt my ability to end Andras' reign.

I kept my sight trained on the land before me but spoke to Reed. "Take me to him."

Reed chuckled, the sound distorted and strained. "That's not how it works. When the time is right, he'll find you."

No way I was going to sit around and wait for Andras to find me. I didn't want to stay in The Gray longer than I had to. The sooner I trapped Andras, the sooner I could save

Corrine, Nash, and the others and get back to the land of the living.

A high-pitch screech came from behind me. I spun around to see a swarm of tilted bodies running toward us. They were in various states of decay, all the way from a lot of skin to just bone.

"Those would be the decayed." Reed grabbed my arm. "Time to run, Tessa dear."

I let him yank me away before I finally gained my bearings and took off, leaving Reed in the dust.

He screamed behind me, calling my name, but I just ran with Nirah still draped around my shoulders. Without the need to breathe and without the need to worry about my body getting tired, I zoomed through the rotting trees like an Olympic athlete. Aside from the whole being dead thing, I could get used to this. The absolute freedom was exhilarating.

The moment quickly vanished when I entered a clearing. Aside from the dry, cracked dirt beneath my feet, there was nothing for as far as I could see.

I stopped a few yards in, taking a moment to look back from where I came.

Reed's blurry form zipped through the trees, going in and out of view.

We should leave him, Nirah said. *He's a burden.*

It's not like I want him here, I responded.

The screeching had died down, telling me the decayed were not nearly as fast as us. A small advantage. I had no idea what they'd do if they caught us, and I really didn't want to find out.

Tessa! Corrine's voice boomed inside my head. *Run! It's a tr* — Her voice cut off sharply.

The ground shook beneath me, the cracks in the hard-packed dirt growing. I stepped backward with my arms spread, trying to keep my balance as the shaking grew.

Black, fuzzy vines sprang from the cracks, zipping up and wrapping around my legs, rooting me to the ground. Nirah jumped on them, using her sharp teeth to rip them. Each part she tore just made it multiply and get more aggressive.

The vines had wrapped around my torso and made their way to my head.

"Nirah, st—" A branch shredded into thin strips and weaved its way through the skin around my lips, sewing my mouth shut.

Andras could cut off my ability to speak, but not to communicate with her.

Nirah, stop! You're making it worse!

With a vibration of annoyance, she quit biting at the vines. She curled on top of my head, her warmth breaking through my skin and calming me a little.

Reed finally made it to the clearing. When he saw me, his eyes went wide. He surprised me by letting out a roar and pouncing on me, trying to yank the vines away from my body.

I shook my head, willing him to stop. He was too focused on his task at hand to notice, though. I couldn't believe the sheer determination in his blue-gray eyes. For once, they held an emotion close to concern. Worry. For me.

Moments later, he froze, his confused gaze settling on my eyes as a new set of fuzzy black vines strapped him into place and sewed his mouth shut.

Darkness clouded around us, a thick black fog that cut off sight of anything near us. It had gone completely silent, rattling me to the core.

Something felt very, very wrong, but I wasn't sure what. By the fear growing in Reed's eyes, I knew it was bad. The man hardly feared a thing.

Nirah perked up, slinking around Reed and me in endless loops.

He's here, Nirah said. *Andras is here.* She bared her fangs. *So is his welcoming committee.*

Welcoming committee? That didn't sound inviting at all.

Screeches broke through the fog, and the next thing I knew, the decayed were upon us, clawing their way through the vines.

CHAPTER 44

Decaying hands flew at my face, trying to break through the rotted vines. Their screeches were agonizing, piercing my eardrums with vicious force.

Nirah snapped at them, but they completely ignored her, their focus on my flesh.

A pair of brown eyes met mine, and I knew them instantly.

Greg. Graham's brother.

His body was mid-decay, the life and soul in his eyes completely gone. He ripped and clawed at me with a hunger that made me shiver.

It wasn't Greg. It was just his body. I needed to remember that.

But if his soul was no longer a part of him, where was it? Had it moved on or was it trapped somewhere else? I closed my eyes, hoping and praying that it was in heaven.

Reed still seemed to have his soul. I mean, it wasn't the greatest soul to begin with, but it was still intact. Wait. Did that mean he could return with me? But he'd died before I broke the barrier, hadn't he?

"Thezanna." Andras' voice broke through all the screaming, but he was nowhere in sight. "You're finally home." He laughed, all grit. "I've waited so long for this."

I wanted to speak, to tell him this was the worst way to welcome someone home, but my mouth was still sewn shut. Could I communicate with him like I did Nirah?

A memory came to me. One of Thezanna and Andras using telepathy when they were apart or when they didn't want their subjects to hear them.

Andras, release me.

"But you used to love to play." Andras broke out in a distorted chuckle, causing my skin to crawl.

Other memories burned through my mind, and yes, Thezanna once had a very interesting view of "playing." I shook the thoughts from my head, hoping to never see them again.

I was not Thezanna. I was Tessa. Tessa Isaacson.

Daughter of Alec and Ariela. Sister of Felix.

Decaying Greg clacked his teeth together, snapping at my face, his jagged fingernails getting uncomfortably close to my skin. The vines created the only barrier, but once that fell, I'd become victim to the decayed.

Enough, Andras. I tried to keep my tone as calm as possible. *We need to talk.*

Andras tsked. "I forgot how boring you've become."

Decaying Greg and the others were suddenly yanked away by an invisible thread. They were sent flying through the black fog, swirling it around in a mist.

The vines finally loosened, sliding down around me until they were out of sight. I felt around my mouth, grateful to feel my smooth skin. No permanent damage.

Reed made a strangled noise. He was still bound by the vines.

"Release him, Andras," I said with all the command I could gather.

Andras' voice shook the entire area. "No."

The wall of black fog fell, revealing a dark room. Those same fuzzy black vines were moving along the floor and walls in a continuous state of motion, hungry for more victims.

Distant wailing echoed around the chamber, cries of despair and torment, like the walls were telling stories of tragedies that had unfolded in this room. I knew I could dredge up those memories from Thezanna's past, but they were things I *never* wanted to see.

Two gigantic red thrones sat on one end of the room, a series of corroded stairs leading to them. Andras sat calmly in one of them, resting his arm to the side. His shiny, gold skin made it seem like he was sparkling. The thick points on either side of his head were basically like horn implants. Though he was sitting, his massive frame told me he was extremely tall and wide.

Had Thezanna once been that massive?

No. Nirah settled in around my shoulders. *She was bigger than you but so tiny compared to Andras.* She purred. *Yet somehow commanded a presence more powerful than Andras. Just like you, Tessa.*

I appreciated her words but wasn't sure if I believed them. Andras certainly had a draw that pulled everyone in the room toward him.

A small whimper finally tore my gaze from him. Attached to his massive wrist was a black chain connecting to someone kneeling on the ground next to him. A thick ring was wrapped around her throat, shackled to the chain.

Corrine.

I moved toward her, but one of the vines on the ground

quickly wrapped around my ankle and held me in place. The vine burned my skin, searing it. With a hiss, Nirah zoomed down to my ankle and covered the vine, her healing powers combating the venom.

Every inch of me wanted to slip on the ring I'd found in Ellington's casket and trap Andras right here and now, but I couldn't get close enough, and even if I could, Corrine was tethered to him.

Andras knew about the ring. He knew of its power.

I somehow needed to get close enough to touch him and release Corrine.

But first, I needed to know where Nash, Chloe, and Livvy were, and if their souls were still intact.

I held my chin high. "Where are they, Andras?"

He sneered at me. "Who, my love?" He tugged on the chain, making Corrine lose her balance and fall over.

"The children. Where are they?"

"Oh, them." He snapped his large fingers, the sound echoing around the chamber.

Moments later, a lithe lady slinked into the room, her bare toes dragging across the ground as she waltzed. Her red skin shimmered with glitter. She had long, black hair, falling well past her waistline, and curling at the ends.

Nyx had mentioned I'd recognize her the moment I saw her. Eribell, the shapeshifting raven.

Tiny whimpers yanked my gaze away from her, releasing the trance she'd held on me. I hadn't noticed until now that I'd been in a trance. I needed to be wary of her and her powers.

Eribell held long pieces of rope in her hand, the ends tied around the wrists of three small children. Their limp bodies moved along the vined ground, going up and down with each protrusion they ran over.

Nash, Chloe, and Livvy.

I wanted to run to them, but the vines twisted around both my ankles, squeezing tight, almost making me fall forward. Nirah worked tirelessly at both sets of vines, trying to free me, but it was useless.

Reed struggled next to me, still held in place by the vines. His focus was on the kids, like he wanted to go to them and help, which took me by surprise. Death had changed this man so much.

Swallowing, I threw a sharpened gaze at Andras. "What have you done to them?"

"Who?" Andras stood, his massive form taking up so much room. "My feedlings?" He stomped down the stairs, dragging a stumbling Corrine along with him.

Corrine clung to the metal chain, trying to keep herself upright. From where I stood, it appeared her body and soul were still connected. She still had life in her eyes. The smallest bit of relief filled me.

"These precious souls are my salvation, Thezanna. They are the answer to everything we ever wanted." As he neared Nash, Andras scooped him off the ground. Nash looked like a tiny puppy in Andras' enormous arms. "There's one for each of us, Thezanna. You, me, and Eribell. We can rule the world."

I quickly shook my head. "You know I don't want that."

He smirked, revealing razor sharp teeth. "Tessa may not want it, but Thezanna surely does."

Inside me, something twisted. A darkness completely separate from what Nirah had been. Something I hadn't noticed before.

A piece of Thezanna. A piece still tainted by the years of being a demoness. It seized my heart, the anger in me slowly melting.

The walls and floor continuously moaned and wailed, like it was setting the ambiance.

Andras came to my side and his forked tongue flicked across his jagged teeth. Yeah, those features were definitely *not* in the pictures I'd seen of him. They added another layer to his creep factor.

Andras cradled Nash like a baby. Nash had one hand wrapped around Andras' large finger. His eyelids fluttered on a rapid repeat, but his chest was completely still.

Nash was dead.

Was that such a bad thing?

I squeezed my eyes shut, pushing out Thezanna's thoughts. Yes, it was bad. Very bad.

A chuckle crawled up my throat, and I had to clamp it down. Nyx had said Thezanna had switched sides, but maybe she'd been wrong. Maybe this was what Thezanna and Andras had planned all along. Maybe Thezanna was still a demoness after all.

But I, Tessa Isaacson, was not a demon.

CHAPTER 45

A moment of rebellion trickled through me. Andras was right in front of me, within arms' reach. I could trap him in the ring. Stop all this madness.

Nash's blond curls caught my attention. If I did that, Nash would be trapped in the ring with him. Then my gaze followed the chain connected to Corrine. So would she.

I couldn't condemn the two of them to hell like that. There had to be another way.

But we could rule the world. Together, Andras and I could be the king and queen of earth. We could reign with such power and force. Everyone would bow down to us. Worship us.

No.

I was Tessa Isaacson. Daughter of Alec and Ariela. Sister of Felix.

I was *not* a demon.

"Why are you fighting it, my love?" Andras' deep voice rumbled through me, vibrating my skin. "This is what we always wanted. Don't let the measly human girl mess with your mind."

Eribell sauntered into view, a mix of lust and rage in her eyes. Lust for Andras. Pure rage for me. For Thezanna. She gently placed a hand on his arm. "I told you she was a waste of time." Her voice was so melodic and dreamy. It captivated my entire being. "We don't need her, Andras. She's a traitor."

The fierceness in his eyes faltered as he turned to look at her. Her face sparkled, shining with pure beauty.

"*Together, as one*," she sang, each note flawless.

"Together," Andras repeated.

A warm hand wrapped around my leg. I looked down to see Corrine at my side, her eyes pleading for my attention. Andras and Eribell were focused on one another for the moment.

Corrine was desaturated the same as Reed like the color was draining from her. But her soul hadn't been separated from her body. Could I take her back with me as well?

She shook her head and mouthed my name. *Tessa.* Tears flowed down her blood-stained cheeks. It was then I noticed all the cuts and abrasions on her body. She'd been savagely beaten.

End this, Corrine mouthed. *Please.*

With a scream, Corrine flew black, thrown into the sky until the chain reached its length and yanked her back to the ground. She curled into a ball, clearly in pain.

"Stupid girl!" Andras roared.

A war brewed inside me. The human part of me that belonged to Tessa. All she wanted was to save Corrine, Nash, and the others and flee this place. Trap Andras, and maybe even Eribell, in the ring for eternity, stopping them once and for all.

The other part, the one belonging to Thezanna, was warring within itself. Almost all of her wanted exactly what Tessa wanted. Another part, just a small fraction, wanted to rule the world with Andras. Make Earth her kingdom and all the humans her subjects.

Though the part of Thezanna that wanted her life as a demoness once again was only a sliver of the power in my entity, it was such a formidable part. It would be tough to defeat.

But it had to be done.

"Tessa?" Nash's sweet voice contrasted with all the vileness in the room. His groggy eyes settled on me. "I wanna go home."

Andras and Eribell both roared with laughter, causing Nash to shrink in on himself.

Hearing his voice gave me newfound strength. He still had his soul. There was still hope.

I reached for him, but with one flick of the arm, Andras had me flying across the room. The vines had released their hold to make it possible. I landed with a hard thud on the ground, the fuzzy vines poking my back.

Nirah landed next to me, thrown like I had been. She hissed, her tongue flicking in Eribell's direction.

We need to kill them, Nirah sent to me. *One at a time. Let's start with Eribell.*

Because she's the easiest?

Nirah vibrated in a chuckle. *She'll be harder than Andras, with her siren ways and her hold on Andras. Unlike Andras, she doesn't have a soft spot for you or Thezanna. Trap her first.*

I took in Eribell, as she leaned against Andras, whispering things to him. Andras seemed caught in a stupor.

Eribell had no one linked to her since she'd dropped the rope on the ground. If I could just lure her away from the others, I could trap her in the ring.

I paused. Could the ring hold both of them? Or was it a first come, first serve sort of thing? If that were the case, I needed to get Andras first and deal with Eribell another way.

But Nyx had mentioned whoever was tethered to Andras would go in the ring as well, so it should hold more than one soul.

I'll distract the others, Nirah said. *You go for Eribell.*

Not yet, I thought. *It might be best to do both Andras and Eribell at the same time. Free Reed, Nirah,* I moved toward Andras and Eribell.

With a growl, Nirah slinked off toward Reed, clearly unhappy with her task.

Eribell flicked out a hand, stopping me in my tracks. "That's far enough, Tessa."

"Thezanna!" Andras roared. "She's Thezanna!"

Eribell softly smiled at him. "Thezanna is gone, love. This is just a weak human girl."

She was right. I was weak. Pathetic. Why had I even come down here? Did I really think I could stop a demon and a siren? I was just a dumb human. I knew nothing.

"Tessa." Nash's sweet voice snapped me back to reality.

Those thoughts. They'd been Eribell's doing.

Nirah was right. I needed Eribell gone first. She clouded the mind.

As Eribell gazed at Andras with a longing that made me dry-heave, I sprinted toward her. When I was only a couple of feet away, I flung myself, throwing my arms around her and bringing us both to the ground.

I'd definitely taken her by surprise, but she quickly composed herself, wrapping a warm hand around my throat and squeezing tight. I grabbed onto her wrists, trying to yank her off me, but she was strong.

"*Give up, Tessa,*" Eribell sang. "*You can't win this. Think of your mother and brother. You could be reunited with them.*"

How I longed to be with Amá and Felix again. To hear their laughter and hug them close. My hold on Eribell's wrists loosened.

Out of the corner of my eye, I saw Andras watching on, clearly amused.

"*Just let go,*" Eribell continued to sing. "*Release your spirit. Move on. There's nothing left for you here. Nothing left for you on earth.*"

Closing my eyes tight, I tried to drown out her voice and focus on my surroundings. She was choking me, but I couldn't be choked. I didn't need air. I was already dead. She wanted me to separate from my spirit. Was that a choice?

Everything was a choice, wasn't it?

I wasn't ready to die. I still had my dad. Graham. Leya. Jade. I had something to live for. To fight for.

Like Nash, Chloe, and Livvy. I could save them. I could stop Andras and Eribell from ruling the earth.

My energy drained, so fleeting. I felt so tired and done.

Snapping my eyes open, I looked into Eribell's eyes, realizing what she was doing. She wasn't choking me. She was sucking the life from me. Taking my soul.

Andras wouldn't stop her. Only I could, and I only knew one way how. With the minimal strength I had left, I wormed my hand toward my necklace and yanked at the pouch.

Eribell stopped singing, her focus going to the pouch. She let go of my throat, ripped the pouch from my necklace, and tossed it across the room.

The moment she let me go, my strength came pouring back. I quickly pushed her off me, then rammed my foot into her stomach, sending her flying away from me.

Andras and I both dove for the leather pouch, scrambling to get it. His massive hand was just inches from it. If Andras got the ring in his possession, it was all over.

His finger grazed the pouch just as a weird expression crossed his face. Annoyance. I glanced behind him to see a free Reed driving the sword through Andras' foot, anchoring him to the ground. Nirah zoomed up, wrapped her body around Andras' arm, and yanked it away from the pouch.

I quickly snatched it up and fumbled to get it open.

"*Foolish girl,*" Eribell sang, her tranquil voice coming closer.

As she drew near, I crawled away, trying to give myself some more time, putting me farther away from Andras than I wanted. I finally got the pouch open, yanked out the ring, and slipped it on my left pointer finger. Turning onto my back, I flung my arm out and took hold of Eribell's leg. I tried to reach for Andras, but Eribell's agonizing scream pierced so deep that I couldn't move. A blinding light filled the room, making me close my eyes.

Seconds later, her screams shut off.

I slowly opened my eyes to see that Eribell was gone.

A thunderous clap startled me. I scrambled to my feet and swung around to see Andras standing there, applauding.

"Well done, my love," he said with a chuckle.

Reed, Corrine, and Nirah all laid crumpled near his feet, none of them moving. The sword dangled from Andras' hand, looking more like a butter knife in his grip. He tossed it to the side, and it flung across the room, out of view.

As he continued to laugh, he snapped his fingers, and a few more restraining devices appeared in his hand. He bound Reed and Nirah to him, along with Nash, Chloe, and Livvy. Corrine was still tethered to him as well.

He had all of them in his power, and I had Eribell in my ring.

I glanced down at it. The ring had molded to my skin, just like my family ring had done. It faintly flickered black, almost like a pulse. Eribell's pulse.

Did this mean I couldn't trap Andras in it? Had I blown my one opportunity to stop him? Without the ring, how did I stop him? How did I put an end to a demon?

I couldn't kill him. I needed to end his existence somehow.

Tessa? Nirah's voice was groggy. She blinked her eyes open, glancing aimlessly around the room.

Are you okay? I kept my gaze on Andras, not wanting him to know I was communicating with her.

I'm fine, Nirah said. *What now?*

Good question. Know of anything else I could trap Andras in? A magic saucer or something?

Are you sure the ring won't work?

I'm not sure of anything anymore. I tore my gaze from Andras and glanced around the room. The vines continued to move across the floor and walls like they were searching for something to do. Wails traveled the chamber, not dying down.

Andras took a few steps toward me, dragging all the others with him. Nirah hissed in frustration, but none of the others made a sound.

Do they still have their souls? I asked her.

Yes, Nirah said. *They're just unconscious.*

Relief filled me. There was still a chance to save them. I just needed to unchain them, get them far away from Andras, and then somehow trap him in some object.

How could I possibly do any of that, and do it by myself?

But I wasn't by myself. I had Thezanna in me, right? Yeah, there was still a part of her that wanted to rule with Andras, but the other part felt the same way I did. If I could summon that part of Thezanna, maybe she'd know what to do. Maybe she had power that human me didn't possess.

"You're so quiet, my love," Andras said. "What are you thinking about?"

To summon Thezanna, I had to *be* Thezanna.

"You." I kept my voice as sure and steady as I could. I took a tentative step forward, putting a little more sway in my hips than usual.

Andras' eyes went to my waist, a sultry smile pulling at his lips. "Is that so?"

I tried not to shiver at the sight of his pointed teeth.

Briefly closing my eyes, I gathered memories in my mind, remembering the way Thezanna glided around a room. The way her silky voice drew Andras in, almost intoxicating him. She was his weakness.

"You traded me in, Andras," I said. "For her?"

Andras shook his head. "You left me, remember? I had to fill the void somehow."

"But with *her*?" I lifted my chin. "Eribell. The woman you knew I loathed down to my very core."

Andras swept toward me in two easy steps. Everyone tethered to him flung with the motion. "You know she meant nothing." He motioned to my hand. "Never the matter, anyway. She's gone forever."

I eyed my ring where Eribell was trapped. The black pulse had grown red in anger. I'd be angry, too, if I was trapped in a ring.

"But see, now we have a new problem on our hands." Andras reached out, his hand almost brushing my skin, when he recoiled. "Until you take off that ring, I cannot touch you."

It wasn't just the ring. The necklace Mrs. Morales had given me was supposed to make it difficult for him to touch me.

The ring was suctioned to me anyway. The only way it was coming off was to amputate my finger. No man was worth that.

"Looks like we are at an impasse." I stood tall, my shoulders squared, just like Thezanna would do. I gently set a hand on my hip. "You cannot take their souls, Andras. You cannot pass into the world of the living. I will not allow that to happen."

Inside, Thezanna's powers swirled to life. They started as

tiny specs but continued to grow with each passing second, setting my soul ablaze.

Andras leaned toward me, pure passion brewing in his eyes. "Oh, but I can, my love. I was hoping to persuade you, but I believe that time has long passed." He bent down, scooping all three kids into his arms, his gaze full of hunger. "Since I no longer have you and Eribell at my side, I will use all three souls for me." Greed flashed across his face. "Think of the power I could have. No mortal would be able to stop me."

"You're correct, Andras." My hands tingled in anticipation as my power grew. "No mortal could ever stop you."

He sneered, showing off his sharp teeth that glistened with saliva. "My time has finally come, Thezanna. I will rule the earth. Create my own kingdoms and riches."

Off to the side, Nirah slinked toward Andras, no longer bound to him. She'd somehow freed herself.

As Andras stared at the children with desire for their pure souls, I held open my palms, Thezanna's full power exploding inside me.

Nirah, I said, *get the children to safety.*

With a flick of my wrist, I shattered the chains connecting Andras to all his victims. I held my hand out in the sword's direction, willing it to come to me. A mere second later, the sword flew toward me, heading straight for my open palm.

"NO!" Andras dropped the children from his arms and flung himself toward the sword, catching it in his hand.

Nirah caught all three kids as they fell, coiling herself around them for their protection. She slithered away, taking them all with her. Reed wrapped an arm around Corrine and helped her stand. They hobbled in the direction Nirah had gone, leaving me alone with Andras.

Andras threw the sword to the ground, all his focus on

me. "You foolish child! There's nothing you can do to stop me. Your powers are *minuscule* compared to mine." He flung his arm toward Nirah and the others, scooped them up with his force, and threw them toward the wall. The black fuzzy vines slipped around each of them, holding them in place.

Everyone had awakened and was on full alert, their wide, terrified eyes on me. They were looking to me to save them. Because if I didn't stop Andras, their souls would be at Andras' mercy. And Andras had no mercy.

Andras held out his hand toward my throat, cupping the air in front of me. With an invisible force, he lifted me off the ground toward the ceiling. The black fuzzy vines squirmed in excitement, reaching down, eager to constrain me.

I tried to speak, but nothing came out. Whatever he was doing cut off my vocal cords. But I could still use telepathy, and the ability to do the same to him.

Reaching out my hand, I used *my* powers to lift Andras off the ground, so he was in the air, suspended like me.

We could do this for eternity, Andras, I sent to him.

He fought against my power, but with half of his strength keeping me suspended in the air, he didn't have enough to combat me. His power clawed at my skin, burning and twisting, trying to get me to break.

Enough, Andras, I sent. *How much longer do you want to drag this out?*

He sneered. *You'll get tired. You always do.*

A wave of memories slammed into me, flipping through my mind rapidly. Andras hurled them in my direction, reminding me of all the times Thezanna lost their arguments.

But she didn't always lose. So I threw some memories toward him, fighting back a smile when his face contorted, reliving each one.

I'd already spent too much time in The Gray. I needed to end this.

Andras was a fighter, not knowing when to back down. He let his anger get the best of him. I needed to make him so furious that he lost control.

You're pathetic, I sent to his mind. *You could never do anything on your own. You always needed me to hold your hand and guide you.*

Liar! Andras roared. *I lasted forever without you! I created my kingdom here. I turned all those who died into my puppets, controlling them at every turn. Soon, everyone will know my name.*

Yes, you'll go down as the demon that was defeated by a seventeen-year-old human.

Andras hurled me across the room, both of us releasing our grips on each other. His howl vibrated the room.

I slid to a stop right near the throne, so I scrambled around it, hiding while I could think.

Balls of fire were slung in my direction, sizzling the vines on impact. The vines shrunk in on themselves, hating the fire. A bunch wriggled out from the ground, trying to capture me. I kicked and stomped, wanting them away.

So far, I'd been able to do everything Andras could. Back at Jade's house, a small flame flickered over my palm, so I knew it could be done. I held out my hand, reaching deep inside until a ball of fire hovered above my skin.

Cool. "Man, I wish Graham and Leya could see this. They'd be freaking out."

I barely stuck my head around the throne, searching for Andras. He stood in the center of the room, growling and haphazardly throwing fireballs wherever he felt like it. This demon sure knew how to throw a tantrum.

While he was distracted, I hurled the fireball toward him, connecting with his torso. He glanced down in shock. It had done nothing to him. Well, except infuriate him.

When his eyes met mine, I saw a level of fury no one

should ever possess. That fury wanted to rule the world, and I would not let that happen.

Andras opened his mouth wide, and out came hundreds of lightning bugs, zipping toward me. I rolled to the side, barely missing them, but they changed direction, coming at me again.

As I scrambled to my feet, I threw fireballs at the lightning bugs and sprinted around the corner of the throne. I charged straight for Andras, tossing fireballs at him and behind me. When I was almost to him, I dove, extending my arm as far as possible.

My fingers grazed his foot as he sent a tornado of wind at me. It brushed my side, sending me spiraling in the opposite direction of him.

Vines climbed up from the ground, wrapping around my legs and arms and pinning me down. Andras grinned as he stomped toward me, balls of fire hovering above both his palms.

I couldn't move, no matter how hard I tried.

"Give in, my love," Andras bellowed. "It is over."

Among all the chaos, messy blond curls caught my attention. Nash's small body was pinned to the wall, being held by vines. He was biting at them, sheer determination in his eyes. Next to him, Chloe and Livvy looked terrified. Tears streamed down their cheeks as they sobbed.

Corrine's mouth had been sewn shut. Knowing her, she'd probably been trying to console the kids, and the vines wanted her to stop talking. Nirah fought against the vines, trying to go faster than they grew back. Her sharp fangs dug into them and ripped them apart.

Reed was on the other side, staring straight at me. He nodded, just once, firm and trusting. He believed I could defeat Andras. Reed, who once wanted me dead. Reed, who had killed so many without fear of the ramifications. Reed, who had never cared about another soul.

Until now.

He knew I had the ability to stop Andras. I'd stopped Ellington down in the crypt. I'd shattered the box using the power within me. Could I do the same to Andras?

Andras squatted, bending his head down to see me better. "Goodbye, my love. Too bad things ended as they did."

He put his hand right above the top of my head, the heat starting small and then growing. He was going to burn me alive.

"Once last kiss?" I asked.

Andras paused, putting his head close to mine. "Nice try, love. You know I cannot touch you."

I smiled. "I just needed you close."

In a flash, I produced a fireball, making the vines release my wrist. I quickly slapped my hand against the side of Andras' face. His agonizing scream penetrated deep into my bones.

My whole body burst with light, causing me to close my eyes. So many things were happening all at once. Eribell screeched within the ring, squirming as it tried to suck in Andras as well. The spell from my necklace burned Andras, his skin turning to ash in my hand.

Music drifted from the ring, switching from beautiful, to tragic, to disturbing as Eribell writhed and moaned. Andras' tormented cry set all my hair on end as one part of his body was slowly sucked into the ring, the other burning to a crisp.

Light, music, and smoke attacked the vines around us, causing them to retreat in confusion.

Suddenly, everything shut off, like a switch had been flipped. Haunted silence filled the chamber. I fell onto my back, all the energy inside me drained. My left pointer finger pulsed where the ring had forged itself with my skin. Swirls of black, red, and orange danced across the ring, a mixture of Eribell and a half-scorched Andras. Their anguish pulsed with my blood. I stroked my dahlia ring on my other hand, trying to summon some serenity, hoping to balance it out.

A soft hand touched my cheek. I turned to see Nash kneeling by my side, tears in his eyes.

"Can we go home, Tessa? I wanna go home." He wiped at the snot under his nose.

"You're free." I slowly sat up, taking in my surroundings.

The vines had cleared at least a ten-foot radius around me. Everyone had been released from the wall. Poor Livvy and Chloe stood huddled together, shaking, and terrified.

Nirah zoomed to my side, scanning my body like she was searching for injuries she could heal.

Corrine dropped to my side and hugged me close. "You did it."

I barely put my arms around her when our entire world began to shake.

CHAPTER 47

Corrine released me. "What's happening?"

The ground and walls began to crack, long, jagged lines forming all around us. Everything shook so viciously that it was difficult to stand.

"I believe, ladybug," Reed said, scooping a traumatized Chloe into his arms, "that The Gray is caving in on itself."

It is, Nirah said. *We must hurry.*

Chunks of dead fuzzy black vines fell from the ceiling, landing on the ground. I quickly picked up Nash, holding him close. He clung to me, his tiny fists wrapped around the material of my dress.

"We need to get out of here," I said.

"And how do we do that?" Reed asked, clumsily patting Chloe's back like he had no idea how to console a child. Add in the fact that though she was small for a nine-year-old, she was still passed the age of being held. But her arms wrapped around him tight like she never wanted to let go.

"Nyx said a gateway would open when my task was complete." I scanned the room, but there wasn't anything that looked remotely like a gateway.

Corrine hugged Livvy close to her, rubbing her back. "Maybe your task isn't complete."

"I trapped Andras," I said, holding up my hand that held the ring. "That was my task." I stumbled where I stood, the ground still shaking.

"What about the souls?" Corrine asked.

Oh, yes, the souls, Nirah said.

"The souls?" I asked.

"All the souls of the decayed," Corrine said, "are being held in prison. They can't move on to heaven until they're released."

"Any idea where this prison is?" I asked.

Corrine pointed at the ground. "It's below us. I'm sure you heard them crying earlier."

All those piercing wails hadn't been memories like I assumed. They were trapped souls.

"How do we get down there?" I asked.

"Follow me." Corrine took Livvy by the hand, and they headed toward the door.

"Hey, Nash." I rubbed his back. "How about a piggyback ride?"

He pulled back and rolled his eyes. "I can't carry you, silly."

I smiled, happy he still had his sense of humor. Maybe one day, he'd forget this whole nightmare. I glanced over at Reed, who still held Chloe. She was old enough to remember, though. She and Livvy were going to need some serious therapy after all this.

"You climb on my back." I set him down, and he quickly scrambled around me, jumping up and clinging to my neck. I scooped his little legs into my arms and followed Corrine out of the chamber with Nirah at my side.

Corrine led us down a rickety set of stairs at the end of

the hall. The Gray still trembled, making it difficult to maneuver, but we somehow made it to the dungeon below.

Shrieks and clattering teeth welcomed us. The decayed stood guard, trapping us from getting to the souls.

Corrine looked over her shoulder at me. "Any ideas?"

I set Nash down. "Everyone, scoot behind me."

I waited until they were several feet away, then summoned fireballs from my palms.

Nash gasped. "Whoa! That's so cool!"

Chloe sniffed, wiping her nose. "She did it before."

"I had my eyes closed!" Nash whined.

I looked over my shoulder and winked at him. "You kids might want to close your eyes now, too. This could get gross."

All three of them quickly slapped their hands over their eyes.

Turning my focus back to the decayed, I hurled fireball after fireball, sending them flying to the sides, their bodies catching fire.

"Gross!" I wasn't sure if it was Livvy or Chloe, but it was definitely one of them.

"She told you not to watch!" Corrine muttered something in Spanish. "Close your eyes. All of you!"

My energy began to deplete. Using the powers was taking a toll on me. My body wasn't used to it. Nirah joined in, projecting balls of fire from her mouth.

I stared at her in shock. "You never told me you could do that."

You never asked.

Once the last decayed had fallen, I held a ball of fire above my hand and moved toward a large metal door at the end of the hall, letting the fire light the way. The Gray seemed to calm the closer I got to the door.

Nirah zoomed in front and shot fire from her mouth,

melting the metal lock on the door. When I pushed the door open, I stumbled back in shock.

Thousands of souls were trapped in a huge ball of red light taking up most of the room. A few banged against the sides in a last-ditch effort to get out. Everyone else had their shoulders hunched, their head hung. They had completely given up hope.

I'll circle around. Nirah slithered off to the right.

"Thoughts, oh wise one?" Reed asked.

I turned to find him next to me, his tilted head taking in the trapped souls. He had his hands stuffed in his pockets, rocking back and forth on his feet, humming "Rock With You" by Michael Jackson.

"Where are the others?"

He absentmindedly pointed his head toward the door. "Corrine kept the kids out there. Didn't think it best to add to the trauma."

"Good." The less they saw, the better.

Suddenly, one of the souls pounded on the glowing red ball. "Help us!"

Other souls turned to see what the ruckus was all about. When they saw Reed and me standing there, so many fists hammered away, pleading for help.

I walked to the ball, running my fingers along it, and then quickly yanked my hand away. The vileness it radiated took me by surprise.

The ball had been crafted with dark magic so wretched and awful my stomach could hardly stand it. It needed to be destroyed, but I knew it would take all the energy I had left in me.

I turned to Reed. "I'm going to shatter this, and hopefully, when I do, a portal will open. I have no idea if I'll still be conscious, but can you make sure everyone gets through the portal before it closes?"

Reed clapped a hand on my shoulder, the fortitude in his eyes reminding me once again this was a changed man. "You have my word, Tessa."

Taking some deep breaths, I faced the ball and held out my hands, my skin just inches from the glass. Red lines zipped toward my hands, and I could feel the evil greedily wanting me. My stomach churned. I hadn't even touched it yet, and I could barely stand being so close.

"You can do this, doll," Reed said from beside me. "Remember who you are doing it for." He pointed inside the ball at a terrified soul. I locked eyes with them.

Greg. Graham's brother. He didn't know me, but I knew him.

Then I scanned more of the crowd. Trenton and his family were there, all huddled together.

An elderly lady walked toward me, a knowing twinkle in her eyes. I gasped. "Tessa?"

She nodded. My great-great-grandmother. My namesake.

"I knew you'd come," she said, so calm compared to all the worried souls around her. "I wasn't ready all those years ago." She tapped the glass. "But you are, my dear. You can do what I couldn't. Be brave, young Tessa." She smiled. "Be bold."

I thought back to the séance I'd had with Mrs. Morales. "Was that you speaking to us when we reached out?" I knew it wasn't my mom at the time.

Older Tessa held her hands close to her chest, her smile so comforting. "Yes."

Nirah came back around from the left, slid up my body, and settled around my shoulders. *I can be of assistance.*

Returning Older Tessa's smile, I pressed my palms against the ball of magic and held firm. The wretched, vile content swarmed me, trying to work its way through my body. Nirah combated it as best she could, but there was so much.

Layers upon layers of evil. All the bad things Thezanna had done flew through my mind. My hands so desperately wanted to retreat, but I rooted myself on the ground, forcing my soul to search for the beauty.

Thezanna may have done bad things, but she'd turned her life around. She'd sacrificed herself over and over as a penance for her sins. She'd done good. I needed to focus on those things.

The wickedness of the magic recoiled at my happy memories like it wanted nothing to do with them.

I thought of my family and friends. Dad, Amá, Felix, Graham, Leya, Jade. Their smiles and laughter. I let that warmth expand, pushing out all the negative thoughts and images attacking my mind.

The globe's glow grew brighter and brighter with each passing second, to the point it was almost blinding. My knees trembled, wanting to give way. Horrible wails and screeches sounded in the distance, getting closer and louder as I pressed on, pouring all the strength and love I could into the globe.

The ring that held Andras and Eribell heated to the point it burned my skin, but I clenched my teeth and pushed through the pain. They couldn't stop me. I wouldn't let them. There were too many souls at stake.

With one last effort, I surged all my energy into the globe. The blinding light caused me to close my eyes but not before I gazed upon my great-great-grandmother one more time. She smiled, so pure and sweet. Tears streamed down my cheeks. After all these years, she'd finally be set free.

The globe burst, a mirage of colors spiraling around the dungeon. So many relieved souls caught my eye before they faded, finally being sent on to heaven. Their period of torment had come to an end.

My knees gave way, and I fell to the ground. Nearby, a

portal opened, glowing blue. Fatigue gripped me tightly, latching onto my body, making it impossible to move.

Scrambled voices called my name, and blurry forms went in and out of my vision.

"...gotta go!" Corrine yelled.

"Well, as you can see, she's a little incapacitated." Reed's face came into view, the edges of his head throbbing as I clung to consciousness. "I'm going to pick you up, doll, so please don't try to sucker punch me."

I couldn't respond even if I wanted to.

Reed scooped me up in his arms and carried me through the portal.

CHAPTER 48

The second we stepped through the portal, Reed gasped and fell to the ground. I tumbled out of his arms, sprawling out on the sand. Voices and sounds bombarded me, all fighting to get my attention.

"What's happening to me?" Reed sounded a mix of scared and hurt.

Corrine screamed out in distress, the sound agonizing.

"Livvy!" Sheriff Hayes and Remi cried at the same time.

"Nash!" Jade yelled.

"What *is* that thing?" Blake's high-pitched tone made me smile on the inside. "It looked at me! It's coming near me!"

"Aww, I think she's kinda cute," Ace purred. "Aren't yo—" Incoherent mumbles followed. "Why, that snake bit me. Do you think I'll die?"

If only, Nirah said in a hiss.

I rolled onto my back and stared at the cloudless night sky. All the stars pulsated, their edges yellow. I blinked, trying to get my eyes to focus. My body felt like it had run about twenty marathons in a row.

"What did you do?" Nyx asked, unbelievably close to me.

"Tessa?" Dad's face appeared above me, relief in his eyes. "Can you hear me?"

I slowly nodded.

Graham and Leya kneeled on the other side of me, pushing a confused and slightly irritated Nyx away. Why was Nyx so mad?

"Can you speak?" Leya took my hand in hers. "Girl, you look terrible."

I swallowed, working moisture back into my mouth. "I feel terrible."

The three of them sighed in unison, happy to hear my voice.

"We need to get her to the hospital!" Jade screamed. "We need to put pressure on the wound to slow the bleeding!"

I tried to sit up, but my world swayed.

"Easy, there." Dad placed his hand behind my back and helped me into a sitting position before kissing the top of my head.

Nirah zoomed up my body and took residency on my shoulders, causing Dad, Graham, and Leya to step back in surprise.

"Who's bleeding?" I asked.

"Tessa, what *did you do?*" Nyx asked again.

"Is that red furry thing *Nirah?*" Leya asked.

"Uh, yes." I pressed a hand to my forehead as my vision continued to swirl. "Who's bleeding?"

"Corrine and Reed," Graham said, his rapidly blinking eyes on Nirah. "They came through the portal with you, but they both have the gunshot wounds they got before they died."

"Everyone, on the boat, now!" Sheriff Hayes' voice boomed over the little island we were on.

Graham quickly scooped me—with Nirah in tow—into his arms. My eyelids fluttered closed. No matter how hard I tried, I couldn't keep them open. I wanted to sleep for days. Weeks.

Just rest, Tessa, Nirah said. *There will be plenty of time for talking when you're all healed up.*

I suddenly jerked upright, making Graham set me down. "Nirah, can't you heal them?"

Do I have to? Nirah asked in a bored tone.

"Yes!" I shimmied my shoulders, trying to get her to move. "Now!"

Nirah growled, vibrating my shoulders. *I'll start with Corrine and then think about Reed.*

She slunk off my shoulders, taking her sweet, precious time before she slithered toward Corrine. A path cleared for her as everyone jumped back, still in awe at seeing a furry red super long snake with jumbo eyes and sharp fangs.

When Nirah got to Corrine, Mrs. Morales tried to run interference, so I spoke. "She's just trying to help. I promise."

Nirah flicked her long tongue at Mrs. Morales.

Not helping, Nirah, I sent to her.

Mrs. Morales reluctantly let Nirah wrap her body around Corrine's torso. Corrine was bleeding profusely, almost all the color gone from her face. She looked mere inches from death. We'd just got her back, so the thought of losing her all over again was too much.

I can heal flesh wounds. Nirah, with her body glowing, slowly went in circles around Corrine. *But there is nerve damage beyond my ability.*

What do you mean? I asked.

The bullet is lodged in her spine. I think there's a good chance she won't be able to walk.

"Look!" Mrs. Morales exclaimed. "Her color is coming back!" She switched to Spanish, going so quickly I couldn't understand all of it.

Corrine's eyes fluttered open. Mrs. Morales kissed her

forehead and cheeks repeatedly, mumbling softly in Spanish to her daughter.

Jade kneeled on the other side of Corrine. Tears fell like waterfalls down her cheeks, soaking the top of her tee. "I can't believe you're back." She hiccupped. "You're back."

Lars bent down next to me, his cloudy eyes holding something close to fury. "I believe it's Reed's turn."

Do I have to? Nirah asked, her glow leaving as she moved away from Corrine. *Honestly, aside from his brothers, who is going to miss the man?*

I would have once said the same thing, I sent to her. *But he did make sure I got through the portal before it closed. He may not be the best person, but you could at least try.*

"Whatever is happening?" Ace said in a wonderous tone, kneeling next to Reed, who lay on the ground, his body convulsing.

Lars and Ace watched in sheer amazement as their brother writhed, his body giving up on him. They bent close, mesmerized, and making me wonder if this was how they watched their prey die.

"He's dying," Sheriff Hayes said. "I don't think he's going to make it to the hospital before he does."

Nirah, please? I asked.

Fine, but know that Corrine took a lot of my healing energy. I promise nothing. Nirah slithered over to Reed, who still trembled on the ground next to the boat. She hissed at Lars and Ace, but neither moved back. Nirah coiled herself near Reed's heart above the bullet wound. She glowed softly at first like she wasn't really trying. But then she flickered like a light bulb on the verge of going out.

The wound is as stubborn as he is. Nirah's voice sounded strained like it was taking a lot of effort.

Nyx grabbed my arm and yanked me away from everyone. When we stopped, she took my hand, looking at the red and black pulsing ring on my left hand. "Tessa, what happened in The Gray? This ring, it's—" She suddenly dropped my hand as if it had seared her.

"Andras and Eribell were there." I watched the red and black throb on the ring.

"Are they both in the ring?" Nyx, who was always so calm and poised, almost sounded worried.

"Uh, I think so? Eribell went first, and then I kind of half-cremated half-trapped Andras."

Nyx pressed a hand to her lips and closed her eyes. We stood for what seemed like forever before she slowly lowered her hand and then spoke. "The ring, it was only meant for one."

"You said whoever was touching Andras would go in as well, so I figured the more, the merrier, no?"

Nyx took a few deep breaths. "Humans, sure. They would turn to ash upon entry."

I frowned. "You didn't mention that part—"

"But two demons?" Nyx continued like I hadn't cut in. "I'm not sure how long the ring will hold them."

"It was more like one and a half-demon—"

"Tessa, you could be in grave danger." Nyx came close, her desperate voice low. "We'll have to find another vessel for one of them to dwell in." She pursed her lips. "Better yet, we need to destroy the ring, Andras, and Eribell for good."

I folded my arms. "What were you planning on doing with having just one demon in there?"

"I thought I'd have time to find the correct way to dispose of it." She shook her head. "But this just pushed the timeline way up." She cupped her hands over my shoulders. "I have no idea what this ring will do to you, Tessa. With just one demon, you'd get their stray thoughts and feelings, but two? That would be quite powerful to overcome."

"Wait, having someone trapped in there will affect me?

How come you're just *now* telling me this?" I could help the tremble in my voice.

Would it be like how Nirah and Delilah sometimes took control of me? That was bad enough. If Andras or Eribell could take hold of me, who knew what they'd—I'd—be capable of?

Nyx lowered her hands. "We didn't have time before. I was just handling one step at a time." She motioned for Sheba and Allegra to join us. Once they were by our sides, she continued. "We have some serious work ahead of us. There are two entities trapped in that ring."

Sheba clasped her hands on top of her bald head, muttering things I couldn't understand. But by the look on her face, they weren't good.

"Oh, dear." Allegra pushed up on her toes. "This is very, very bad."

"Indeed." Nyx took my non-demon-infested hand and clutched it close to her. "Until we can research more into this, I urge you to be careful. Keep your family and friends at a distance. Seclude yourself when possible. Dark times are upon you, Tessa Isaacson, and it's going to take everything in you to conquer them."

"That's comforting...." I started.

Dad walked over to us, concern in his eyes. "What's going on? Is everything okay?"

Nyx dropped my hand. "No. It's far from okay, I'm afraid. So very far." She pressed a hand to my cheek. "You can overcome this, but it will not be easy. Stay strong, Tessa."

With that, she stepped away, leaving a horrible feeling growing inside me.

CHAPTER 49

Corrine ended up being paralyzed from the waist down. She took it like a champion, though. Being alive without the function of her legs still beat the alternative of being dead. There were moments when I'd see her lively face and couldn't believe she was back with us. It was all so surreal.

Fortunately, or unfortunately, depending on who you asked, Reed survived. It took quite a toll on Nirah, which she reminded me of daily.

Nyx tried her best to explain it, but it was complicated. It had something to do with the fact that the barrier between Willow Marsh and The Gray was so thin, and that Reed and Corrine weren't fully dead when they were sucked down in. Andras had kept their souls and bodies together in hopes of luring me down there, knowing they'd reach out to me for help.

Since their bodies and souls were intact, they hadn't decayed, either, so when they came back through the portal, it was like they had picked up where they left off. Dying from gunshot wounds. Thanks to Nirah, they both survived this time around.

Sheriff Hayes called a town meeting not long after the whole thing. He did his best to explain what happened, but it was a lot for people to take in. We would have kept it to ourselves, but we couldn't cover up the fact that Corrine and Reed were back from the dead. Paramedics had seen me floating and glowing during the incident near the lake. Willow Marsh Inn had been sucked into the earth, leaving a gaping hole. These were things you couldn't just hide from people, no matter how hard you tried.

Some people fled town. Just packed up everything and left.

Nirah was now in our realm, red fuzzy skin and all. We did our best to keep her hidden from people in town. Not only was it difficult to process seeing such a strange creature, but Nirah also wasn't the kind and cuddly type. She was a snake that loved to toss venomous actions about when someone made her mad. And it was super easy to make her mad.

Livvy, Nash, and Chloe were all reunited with their families. They'd all been seeing Rita weekly, trying to process everything that they went through. Just like I'd assumed, Nash took it the easiest. He thought the whole thing was a scary adventure, and I was the superhero.

If only it had been that simple.

❧

Reed sauntered up and wrapped an arm around my shoulder. He still had faint scars on his cheeks that he hadn't wanted Nirah to heal. He said it added character. "Lovely evening, no?"

I shrunk away from him, straightening the top of my baby

blue smocked chiffon dress. "You know, this whole thing we went through, it really doesn't make us friends."

He chuckled. "Oh, come on, doll. We are enemies turned allies. How about we let bygones be bygones?"

Reed had changed, but not completely. Thezanna proved to me you can't just rid yourself of all the evil when it's been part of you for so long. Deep in my heart, I knew Reed just wanted to keep me close. I was powerful, and he loved power. But still, death had definitely softened his heart and made him realize there were things worth caring for and protecting.

Ace and Lars moseyed up next to us, each holding a glass of champagne.

"I do love a good party." Ace winked at a lady in a tight, red dress. She just rolled her eyes and walked away, making Ace growl and me grin.

"Why are you guys here, again?" I asked.

Lars touched the tip of my nose with his glass. "You saved our brother. Reunited the Harrisons."

I swatted him away. "Not my greatest moment in my life, that's for sure."

All three chuckled in creepy unison.

"Besides, we want to support our new mayor." Reed snatched a glass of champagne from a waiter that passed us. "Speak of the devil." He winked at me and stuck out his hand when my dad approached. "Congratulations, Mr. Mayor."

Dad eyed Reed's hand but finally shook it. "Thank you, Reed. I wasn't expecting your vote."

"Well, of course!" Reed clapped Dad on the shoulder. "We are allies now. We must stay together."

"Is that sushi?" Lars moved toward a waitress holding a tray of hors d'oeuvres.

"Oh, I do love sushi." Ace followed after him.

Reed winked at me once again and sauntered away, a tilt in his steps.

Dad sighed and ran a hand down his baby blue tie. "Is there any way we can go back to being enemies with them?"

I wrapped my arm around him and squeezed. "Having them against us was never a good thing. Might as well keep them pacified instead of wanting to kill us." I watched the three brothers asking the waitress questions she most definitely did not have the answer to. "Although, I know they're just trying to get on our good side."

Dad kissed the top of my head. "True. We better keep a close eye on them."

My ring pulsed with anger, so I quickly dropped my arm from around my dad.

He frowned at me. "Is the ring acting up again?"

I rubbed my hand. "Yeah. I really hope Nyx finds some answers soon."

Dad pinched the bridge of his nose. "I just have a feeling when she does, we aren't going to like them."

"Probably not."

Barbie waltzed into the room with Fluffsies in the crook of her arm. They were both wearing bright pink dresses, and Barbie had her blonde curls so fluffed out you'd think it was an eighties-themed event. She'd finally healed of all the wounds Lars had inflicted upon her.

She strutted over to Dad and threw an arm around him. "Congratulations, Alec! You're going to be amazing."

Fluffsies reached out for me as Barbie and Dad awkwardly hugged.

I took her in my arms, and she licked my face. "This is still so weird, Fluffs. You're supposed to hate me." She barked and licked my cheek. "But I do prefer this."

Graham suddenly appeared behind me, wrapping his arms around my waist. He now had a deep, permanent indentation above his right eye from Lars, a constant reminder of what happened to him. "She just finally realized what I have known since the day I met you."

"And what's that?"

He kissed my ear. "That you're amazing. Also, you look hot in this dress."

I scratched under Fluffsies chin. "Is that true, Fluffs? You think I look hot?" She barked and licked my nose. "Okay, this licking has to stop, though. It's getting out of hand."

"That's life with a dog," Barbie said, petting Fluffsies on the head.

Barbie clung to Dad like they were a couple. His smile stayed polite, but I could see the struggle in his eyes.

Dad held up a hand and waved at someone. "Hal and Rita Hastings are here. I'm going to go say hi." He quickly walked away.

Barbie took Fluffsies back into her arm and smiled softly at me. "I don't know if I said thank you enough for helping us get out of the Harrison's basement."

Graham came to my side and interlocked our fingers.

"I still don't know what you two were thinking," I said. "Graham, you broke into their house. That's insane."

He quickly pointed at his mom. "It was all her."

Barbie frowned, glancing over at the Harrison brothers. "I still can't believe they're just free men. They killed my boy."

"Sheriff Hayes is gathering evidence," I said. "He wants everything locked tight so they can't walk away. Last I talked to him, he said the list of charges keeps getting longer and longer. Just be patient."

Barbie's eyes welled up with tears, and she stroked my cheek. "But you, dear, you released my Greg from that awful prison. You set his soul free."

Graham squeezed my hand. "Not to mention Trenton and hundreds of others."

I shrugged uncomfortably. The praise I kept getting was overwhelming. "I did what anyone would have done."

"Tessa!" Nash's curly blond self bounded into view. "Super Tessa!"

I reached down and scooped him up. He wrapped his arms around my neck and legs around my waist.

I kissed his cheek. "Kid, you gotta stop calling me that."

He pulled back and shook his head. "No way. You're a real-life superhero. I saw you!" He climbed down and held out his hand with his palm up. "You were throwing fireballs at zombies! It was so cool!"

I hadn't conjured up another ball of fire since being down in The Gray, but I hadn't really tried. I didn't want to. The whole thing terrified me in a way I couldn't explain.

Jade, Lola, and Mr. Jenson joined us, smiling down at Nash.

Jade ruffled the curls on his head. She had changed her hair to pink. "He won't stop talking about it. It's getting annoying."

Nash threw out his hands, making explosion sounds. "Die, zombie, die!"

Lola grabbed him and pushed his back into her. She bent down and kissed his head. "Not here, Nash. You can kill zombies when we get home."

"Or, go to bed?" Mr. Jenson offered.

Nash slumped in his mom's arms. "Aw, man! Why do I have to go to bed every night?"

I smiled at him. "Because superheroes need their sleep. We can't be saving the world running on empty."

Nash's eyes lit up. "Oh, yeah!"

Lola mouthed, *thank you,* and their cute family walked away.

Barbie had moved on to talking with other guests, leaving Graham and me alone.

Graham kissed my temple. "How are you feeling today?"

I held my hand close to my chest and rubbed it. "Today hasn't been too bad. I get little surges of anger, but they pass by so quickly."

"Good." He motioned to Jade, who had found Topher. They were holding hands. "When did that happen?"

I clasped my hands together. "Wait, I know something before you do? Finally. They went on a date the other night, and, by the looks of it, it went well."

"Has Leya finally admitted that she and Marcel are together?" Graham asked with a smirk.

I shook my head. "She claims they're just friends. They don't want to do the whole long-distance thing."

Graham rolled his eyes. "They can't stay in denial forever."

"Where is he, anyway?" I scanned the crowd until I spotted him and Corrine near Dad.

Marcel had been such a huge help with Dad's campaign. I had a feeling he had a bright future in politics. He wore a navy-blue suit with a baby blue tie. A lot of people had picked up on the fact that Dad loved baby blue, so the room was practically painted in it.

Corrine caught us staring and waved. Then she tugged on Marcel's arm and pointed over at us. With a wide grin, Marcel wheeled her over to where we were standing.

Corrine wore a sharp red pantsuit with a white dahlia pinned to her blazer. Her short hair was back to its natural black. She took my hand as soon as she was close enough. "So, I heard a rumor that you were going to do a 5k in my honor?" Her painted-on black eyebrow shot up.

I squeezed her hand. "Well, yeah, I wanted a memorial for you at school."

"That's so sweet!" Corrine grinned. "When are we doing it?"

I narrowed my eyes at her. "You lived, Corrine. No need for a 5k."

She patted her legs. "My legs died, though. So, you can honor them by running really fast, and I can watch on while eating donuts."

Marcel chuckled. "I'll keep Corrine company and eat donuts, too."

Graham's face turned serious. "We should still do one. In honor of all those souls that were trapped in The Gray."

I smiled at him. "I love that idea. Free the Souls 5k. I'll run it by the sheriff."

I'd still been interning for him, soaking up as much information as possible. The idea of a job in law enforcement was definitely growing on me. Somewhere in a small town, where I could make a difference.

Like Willow Marsh.

A throat cleared behind me. I spun around to find Blake Hayes in a black suit and skinny baby blue tie. His normal cockiness was gone, an extreme unease radiating from him.

Graham tensed next to me.

"Uh, Tessa, can we talk?" Blake asked, keeping his eyes trained on mine.

"No." I moved to step away, but Blake held out a hand.

"Please." Blake swallowed. "It will only take a minute, I promise."

With a sigh, I left the others and walked off to the side near the refreshment table. I scooped up an éclair.

"Make it quick, Hayes." I took a large bite of the éclair, the sweet cream exploding in my mouth and calming my nerves. A little.

Blake rubbed the back of his neck. "Listen, I." He sighed and shoved his hands into his pockets. "What I did, with Delilah, I'm sorry."

I chewed my food, trying to focus on the chocolate,

cream, and pastry melting together and not the anger throbbing in my ring. I didn't want to punch Blake Hayes at my dad's party. Not a good way to start his term, having the mayor's daughter beat up the sheriff's son.

"I ... we ..." He glanced at the ceiling like he was trying to gather his thoughts. He finally blew out a long breath. "I'm an idiot. What I did was totally wrong. I was just so wrapped up in thinking I could have Delilah back, and in my head, I thought you liked me, so I didn't think you'd mind." When I didn't say anything, he continued. "I made a huge mistake, and for that, I apologize. That's not who I am. That's not who I want to be. I want to make my mom proud, and I can't do that while pulling terrible stunts like that. I'm just, I'm sorry, Tessa."

At the mention of his mom, my heart softened. I knew how hard it was to lose a parent at a young age. It did things to your mind and body that were difficult to explain to the outside world. It made you irrational.

"Thank you for apologizing." I brushed off my hands, my éclair now finished. "I'm not sure I forgive you yet, but I'm working on it. It will take time."

Blake nodded. "I understand. I just wanted to let you know that I do regret it."

My demon ring pulsed, and I found myself stepping close to Blake and poking my finger into his chest. "Never try something like that again on anyone. When a girl says no, she means no. Understand?"

He swiftly nodded. "Got it."

I turned to walk away, but he gently put a hand on my arm, quickly dropping it when he saw the scowl on my face.

"I also wanted to thank you for saving Livvy. Our family is in your debt." Blake offered the smallest of smiles and then left, going to join his family, who was currently talking with my dad.

Livvy smiled and waved at me, which I happily returned. Seeing her reunited with her family confirmed why going into The Gray had been so important.

The ring heated, the throbbing intensifying with each passing second. I clutched my hand to my chest, hoping I wouldn't have to deal with this much longer.

But somewhere deep down inside, I knew this was only the beginning. Of what? Only time would tell.

CHAPTER 50

Settling into bed, I grabbed the ukulele Marcel had made for me and played some reggae in honor of Felix. Maybe one day, I'd branch out and learn new songs, but I liked having this one connection to him, something that was just ours.

Nirah slept at the foot of my bed, coiled in on herself, purring lightly. We were still adjusting to each other. She hated that she couldn't go wherever she wanted, whenever she wanted.

The automated voice from the smart screen on my nightstand rang out. *Incoming call from Leya Tourreau.*

"Answer." I shifted on my bed so I could see the screen better.

Leya's face appeared on the screen, covered in green cream. "How was the party? So bummed I couldn't be there."

"What's on your face?" I continued to strum the song on my ukulele.

"It's supposed to help with acne, but we'll see." She was lying on her stomach on her bed, facing the screen, a bag of

Cool Ranch Doritos next to her. "I'm not getting my hopes up. So, party?"

"There was a good turnout. Lots of people came to support Dad." I smirked. "According to the polls, it was a total blow-out. Dad won by a landslide."

Leya grinned. "Not surprised. Miller Morgan is totally sketch. His name alone just screams it."

"He definitely gives off the creepy vibe, that's for sure."

Leya took a chip from the bag and pointed it at me. "I'm telling you, something's not right with the man." She popped the chip into her mouth, the crunch loud.

My fingers moved across the strings of the ukulele. "Blake was there."

Leya stuck out her tongue, showing off her mashed-up chip.

"Gross!"

She nodded, finishing off her bite. "Exactly."

"Leya, he apologized for what happened."

Her jaw dropped. She had a new chip in her hand, holding it in the air. She stared at me in total shock.

"I couldn't believe it, either. It actually sounded sincere."

Her head cocked to the side. "Come on. His dad totally made him do it. No way he did it on his own accord."

I shrugged. "Either way, I think he meant it. Doesn't mean I'll forgive him any time soon. Maybe one day, but I need more time."

She scoffed. "Well, yeah, what he did was completely unacceptable." She frowned. "What song is that?"

It wasn't until she asked that I realized I'd changed melodies. I didn't recognize the tune, but it sounded utterly tragic.

I slapped my hand against the strings, stopping the song.

Leya sighed. "Let me guess. The ring made you do it? Seriously, Tessa, maybe you shouldn't play the ukulele until we know there's nothing dark haunting you. This isn't the first time this has happened."

It had happened when I first moved to Willow Marsh, and everything with Ellington and Delilah began.

I set the ukulele next to me on the bed. "I have this feeling that's never going to happen."

"Don't say that!" Leya scrambled to sit on the edge of her bed to get closer to the screen. "This will end. And soon! You'll be back to your boring, non-haunting life. Promise."

I stared at the ring pulsing red, black, and orange on my finger. "I think it's going to be a while until then. For now, I just need to stay sane." I looked at her. "You'll help keep my head on straight, right? Let me know when I'm being stupid?"

She waved a hand. "I do that already. Just a day in the life, you know?"

I chuckled. "True."

The doorbell rang, the chime echoing up the stairs. I checked the time on my phone. It was well after midnight.

I'll get it, Nirah said, slinking off the bed.

"Uh, who's that?" Leya's eyes went wide. "If you invited Graham over, that's the worst way to sneak into the house! He just announced his presence to your dad!"

I rolled my eyes. "It's not Graham. And Dad had to run over to his office to grab some things."

"Maybe it's him. Could have left his keys at home."

"Maybe." I stood and bent toward the screen. "Call you tomorrow. Love you."

She blew me a kiss. "Love you more, sugar."

With a wink, I ended the call.

The doorbell rang again.

I trekked down the stairs, pulling up the app on my phone that would show me the front porch camera. I made Dad install it after Blake randomly showed up at our house and brought me the sword that held Reed.

When the view came up, I leaned in closer. No one was there. But there appeared to be something sitting on the porch.

Who is it? Nirah slithered up my legs, over my back, and onto my neck.

"No one."

After tucking my phone in my back pocket, I opened the door. The porch lights flickered, making a weird buzzing noise. Seconds later, they went out, cloaking the porch in darkness.

I don't like this, Nirah hissed.

I went to pull my phone back out of my pocket so I could use the flashlight, but the object on the porch lit up, giving me all the light I needed.

I stumbled back, grabbing onto the door frame for support. It was the book *Lucifer's Reign.*

Nirah vibrated in a low growl. *Someone is nearby. Want me to check the perimeter?*

Not yet, I sent.

With a shaky breath, I scanned the area but didn't see anyone in the shadows. I bent down, my hand extended, not sure if I wanted to touch the book or not. Who had left it on the porch? And why?

And why on earth was it glowing?

The wind picked up, flipping the book open. The pages rapidly turned until they settled on a page near the middle.

Oh, what's this? Nirah slunk down my body and onto the porch.

I swallowed, staring at the book radiating yellow light. I knew I had to look, but I so didn't want to.

With a quick prayer, I slowly lowered myself to my knees. I tried to keep my hand steady as I reached forward. Both the glow of my demon ring and the glow of the book intensified as I drew closer.

Nirah coiled in front of me, almost in a protective way. *Someone's watching us.*

Stay put, Nirah.

She hissed but didn't move.

I finally got a good look at the page. A cloaked figure stood tall, their eyes glowing red. They held a warped wooden staff, and their long bony fingers draped over the handle.

Nirah suddenly raised her body, flicking out her tongue.

The porch steps creaked under someone's weight. A shadow came toward us, climbing up the stairs.

"Easy there," a deep voice said. "I mean you no harm, Nirah."

Oh, well, this just got interesting. Nirah lowered herself, slithering over to the man and circling him.

"Who are you?" I asked, surprised at the calm in my voice.

The porch lights flickered until they came to life, letting me get a good look at the man. He bent down, picking up the book that had stopped glowing, before tucking it under his arm.

He looked maybe nineteen or twenty, younger than I was expecting. His voice sounded older. Wiser. His thick brown hair had a slight wave to it. He wore a nice button-down shirt tucked into his jeans. The bottom of his jeans were rolled up like we were in the nineteen-fifties.

He leaned against the column, a sly smile on his face. "My friends call me Cromwell."

ACKNOWLEDGMENTS

First and foremost, thanks to Douglas for pushing me through this and brainstorming with me. I know I probably drove you crazy with all the questions, doubt, and procrastination. I'm about one hundred and ten percent certain you're the only reason I finish any of my books. Thanks for being my constant champion and the love of my life.

Thanks to Monster Ivy Publishing and everyone involved with this book. Your belief in me keeps me going. Michelle, Cammie, and Mary, you've all made me grow as an author. I could see a change in the writing process as I drafted this one over my initial draft of the first Willow Marsh. Thankfully, it led to less editing in the end!

To my niece Kaleya, my cousin Paul, and Grandma Gae: I miss you more than words can say. Having you gone has left a void in my heart, but knowing we'll be reunited again one day gives me all the hope in the world. See you on the flip side.

To my Father in Heaven, thank you for providing a light in all the darkness the world has to offer.

And to all my readers that kept asking for book two, here you go. Finally! Sorry it took so freaking long. Life happened. *shrug emoji*

ABOUT THE AUTHOR

 Jo Cassidy (aka Sara Jo Cluff) grew up in Yorba Linda, California right next to the happiest place on earth: Disneyland. She now resides in Utah with her husband and misses Disneyland so very much.

Along with being a two-time Whitney finalist, her spy thriller Harper took the gold in YA thrillers and her YA rom-com Daphne's Questionable Bet (under Sara Jo Cluff) was a finalist in the YA social issues category of the Reader's Favorite Awards.

She's a Dr Pepper addict, jigsaw puzzle enthusiast, and lover of all the creepy shows. You can find her on social media under @sarajocluff.

CHAPTER 1

I ran my fingers along the white eyelet canopy surrounding my bed. Daddy said it would protect me at night while I slept but still allow me to breathe. Sometimes I liked to sit on the bed with the canopy closed, soaking in the comfort and safety it provided.

I'd already finished my homework for the day. It was always the first thing I did when I came home from school so I'd have the evening free to spend with Daddy.

My leg bounced, my fingers drumming along with the motion. I glanced at the twin bell alarm clock on my nightstand. Only twenty more minutes until Daddy came home and unlocked my bedroom door. I could hold my bladder that long. I'd done it before. I needed to distract myself so I wouldn't think about it.

I leaned over the side of my bed, the canopy draping over my hair, and retrieved the journal tucked under my mattress.

Noah, my stuffed elephant, cleared his throat, which did nothing for the rasp in his tone. "Oh, Cora dear. You know not to write in that during the day. *He* may come home and see it."

I glared at the elephant sitting on my bed, his bright, blue eyes staring back at me. "I know that, *Noah dear*. I was just seeing how much room I had left." I thumbed through the empty pages in the back. "I'll have to steal another journal soon."

Noah guffawed. "So you can write more thrilling stories about me?"

Whoever manufactured the stuffed animal didn't bother with getting the facts straight. I'd never seen an elephant with blue eyes that sparkled. It certainly didn't match with Noah's sometimes rough and sarcastic demeanor.

Daddy had bought him for me when I was eight. He'd said the elephant's eyes matched mine. Little did he know, he'd brought me home an elephant with a soul that came alive when we were alone.

"Or is this about brushing up on your shoplifting skills?" Noah asked.

I put my hand on my hip. "Please don't judge me. There are extenuating circumstances."

"Keep telling yourself that." He laughed louder, though his stuffed body remained completely still on the bed.

I was about to flick his trunk when I heard footfalls in the hallway. Daddy was home early. Shoving the journal back under my bed, I surveyed the room to make sure nothing had been left out that I didn't want Daddy to see. I fumbled to refasten the top button on my shirt so only half of my neck was exposed. Then I rolled down my sleeves and buttoned the cuffs. Daddy liked his little girl to look a certain way.

"Are you going to start hiding me?" Noah asked.

Daddy didn't know about my relationship with Noah, and I wanted it to remain that way. Luckily, I was the only one who could hear Noah. It was the main reason our relationship was special and why I confided in him so much.

Right as the lock unlatched on the outside of my door, I

settled into place on my bed holding a regency book I'd brought home from the school library. At the last second, I moved my braid so it rested on my right shoulder. The door opened, and Daddy stepped inside the room. He still wore his blue work coveralls, and I immediately took in the scent of grease and sweat. I noticed his pomade had held his perfectly brushed hair in place all day.

Even though his presence caused unease to swirl inside, I plastered on the smile he loved so I wouldn't have to deal with his explosive anger. It was why I referred to him as Daddy in my head. I never wanted to accidentally call him something else to his face.

"Hi Daddy!" I set the book on my nightstand and went to him. I put my arms out to hug him, but he took a step back.

"I need a shower." He rubbed at his tired eyes. "My last appointment was a bit of a mess."

"Why don't I cook dinner while you wash up and then you can tell me all about your day over our meal?"

Daddy leaned forward and kissed my forehead, his dry lips causing my stomach to roll. "What would I do without you, Cora?"

"Not be such a creepy old man?" Noah offered in a haughty tone.

It took everything in me to not turn around and scold Noah. He shouldn't talk about Daddy like that. Thank goodness Daddy couldn't hear him, or we'd both be locked in the basement for the night.

"I could really use a decent BLT," Daddy said.

"Consider it done." My tone was as sweet as honey, but my insides were heavy like molasses.

He turned to leave, but then faced me and raised his eyebrows. "Make sure the bacon is crispy, but not over-cooked." He placed his hand on my arm and squeezed as a small storm brewed in his eyes. "Last time it was practically burnt."

I clasped my hands tightly in front of me so I wouldn't flinch from the pain. "Of course, Daddy."

The storm in his eyes retreated, and Daddy left the room. I wanted to yell at Noah, but I really needed to use the bathroom. It had been hours. As soon as I finished, though, I headed back into my room.

"Don't say things like that about him," I hissed. When it came to Daddy, Noah and I didn't see eye to eye. He didn't like the way Daddy treated me.

"The truth?" Noah whistled. "Fine. I'll feed myself lies like you do."

Going to the bed, I put my face in front of his. "Being nice to him makes him happy. He's done so much for us, Noah." I poked his trunk. "Remember that."

"That's right. All the things he does out of *love*. Well, if you want him happy, then you should start dinner and stop lecturing me."

I gave him one last glaring look before I went into the kitchen to prepare dinner. I put on an apron so the grease wouldn't splatter my shirt. That would make Daddy real mad. I kept a close eye on the bacon, making sure every inch turned brown but had no hint of black. Once it was perfectly cooked, I took the plate of bacon and gently placed it on the table. I used a towel to wipe away a drop of grease on the edge of the plate.

After smoothing out a wrinkle in the tablecloth, I used my hand to measure the length of the material hanging over the edge, double checking it was even all the way around, just how Daddy liked it. We had a round table so the chairs could be spaced perfectly apart; far enough so Daddy could look at me, but not too far so he could reach out and touch me if he needed to. It had been almost a year since I'd stepped out of line at the dinner table and he'd sent me to timeout. I planned on keeping it that way.

The white ceramic plates and bowls were on their placemats, with a fork on the left, fork above for the salad – even though we weren't having salad, it always had to be there – and a spoon and knife to the right. The glasses were up and to the right, with the cloth napkins flawlessly folded in a standing triangle on the center of our plates. It was perfect.

"Smells delicious, angel," Daddy said, joining me in the kitchen. He'd switched to his usual button-down shirt tucked tightly into his casual slacks. His shirt was buttoned all the way to the top like mine. My chest tightened at the sight of his leather belt.

He wrapped his arm around my shoulder and kissed the side of my head, my hair creating a barrier between his lips and my skin. His sweat and grease stench had been replaced by soap and Selsun Blue shampoo and his brown hair hung down, still wet from the shower. I preferred that look to his perfectly sculpted hair. It made him appear carefree.

"So, tell me about this last client of yours," I said, hanging up my apron in the pantry and softly closing the door.

Daddy grabbed a bottled beer from the fridge. "Not much to tell. A guy inherited everything in his dad's garage, which included some tools that hadn't been used in a very long time."

Keeping my hands steady, I pulled out his chair for him. He sat down, his thin lips turning into a smile as he did. I returned the smile, though my stomach fluttered. I hoped I cooked the bacon just right.

"Did you get them working again?" I sat down and tucked my napkin into the top of my shirt, just like Daddy had done. Then I made sure my braid hung over my right shoulder.

He winked. "Always do."

I grabbed two pieces of bread and spread mayo on them.

"Never leave a client unsatisfied."

He laughed. "So you *do* listen to me."

I tilted my head to the side and winked at him. "Always do."

The laughter reached all the way to his eyes and some of the tension released inside me. His eyes were much kinder when they weren't housing a storm.

I loaded up his sandwich with bacon, lettuce, and fresh tomatoes I had picked from the backyard the day before. I tried to keep my hands stable as I placed the BLT in the center of his plate.

Clasping my hands in my lap, I waited patiently for Daddy to take a bite of his sandwich.

"It's perfect, angel." He wiped his mouth with the napkin and nodded at the bread. "Go ahead and make yourself a sandwich now."

My heart calmed. "Thanks, Daddy."

"You deserve it," he said. "Having you gives me a reason to wake up every morning."

Tears welled up behind my eyelids. I was lucky to have a father who loved me so much.

After dinner and cleaning up under Daddy's watchful eye, I grabbed the playing cards from the closet in the hall. It was tradition to play every night. I let him win all the time because he hated to lose. The last time I won, he didn't let me out of the basement for two whole days.

Once Daddy locked me in my room for the night, I switched to my long sleeve crew neck shirt and cotton pants. It was what Daddy liked me to wear to bed.

They were comfortable, so I didn't mind. I waited for him to go to bed before I pulled out my journal. I sat down on the floor next to the large dollhouse and used the flower-shaped nightlight as my guide.

I wrote in my journal every night. I recounted everything

that happened to me during the day, not leaving a single detail out. At the end of the entry, I'd sketch a drawing of my favorite event from the day, whether it was something that happened or someone I saw that I thought looked interesting. Sometimes I wrote poems or song lyrics imagining myself in a happier life.

"Don't forget to mention my charming personality," Noah said from the bed.

"Hush!" I whispered.

"Why?" he asked. "It's not like someone else can hear me." He raised his volume. "I could shout all night long, and nothing would happen. Maybe I'll sing you a few songs. Except I'd have to make up the words since you can't listen to music."

I reached for my backpack, fished out an eraser, and threw it at Noah. "You're distracting me. Now please be quiet."

He grunted. "Was that necessary? Hitting me? Please don't turn into your precious *Daddy*."

His words punched me right in the gut. I was trying to be playful with him, not intentionally harm him. I never wanted to resort to violence to get my way. Noah had just proved that words could be more powerful than actions.

Suddenly the latch on the outside of my door lifted. Daddy. I wasn't close enough to the bed, so I stuffed the journal inside my backpack and pulled out my math book as the door opened.

Daddy flicked on the light and stared at my empty bed. He was still in his regular clothes. He never liked me to see him in anything less.

"I'm here, Daddy," I said.

He turned his attention to me on the floor, his voice coming out low and rough. "Were you just talking to someone?"

I held up my math book, holding tight so my hands wouldn't tremble. "I have a test tomorrow, and I wanted to review the material one more time. It helps me to repeat it out loud."

His eyes scanned the room, looking for anything out of place. He folded his arms. "Why are you doing it in the dark?"

I thumbed the pages of my math book. "I didn't want to wake you, Daddy. You work so hard for our family, and I wanted you to be able to have a good night's sleep for work tomorrow."

The strain in his face relaxed. "That's very thoughtful of you. But it's late. You also need your sleep."

I stood, hoping my legs didn't look as shaky as they felt. "Of course, Daddy."

He waited until I climbed back into bed. He tucked in the sides of my sheets, snuggling me in. "You're smart, angel. You'll do fine on your test." Grabbing my braid, he pulled it forward to its proper place. He kissed my forehead, but dark clouds flew into the back of his eyes as he squeezed my shoulder. "I never want to catch you outside of bed at night again, do you hear me?"

A painful lump landed in my throat, and it took me a second before I could speak. "Yes, Daddy."

"Sleep tight, my angel girl." His low, breathy voice caused me to shiver.

Once Daddy was out of the room, I took Noah and held him in my arms. His soft fur was soothing to the touch. My heart thudded in my chest from how close I'd been to being caught. Daddy would be furious if he knew I had journals that held our family secret.

He could never know I had them.

www.ingramcontent.com/pod-product-compliance
Lightning Source LLC
Chambersburg PA
CBHW060856210726
48293CB00006B/1832